# Fractured Narratives and Pandemic Identities

The book considers how identities have become more fractured since COVID-19, by thinking of COVID-19 in relation to other crises (economic, social, digital, and ecological) and by drawing parallels to literature, cinema, and visual art.

COVID-19 was a type of apocalypse, a catastrophic destructive event that produced dystopian measures in its wake and drew uncanny parallels to dystopic works of literature and speculative fiction. Yet the pandemic was apocalyptic in another sense too. The word apocalypse derives from *apokalupsis*, which means disclosure or uncovering. In this way, COVID-19 also revealed the dystopian processes already at work in the world, including digital forms of surveillance as well as the asymmetries within populations and divides in health outcomes between the Global North and Global South. Indeed, societies that have experienced the horrors of settler colonialism have already survived apocalypses. COVID-19 serves then as a premonition for our climate emergency as well as an echo of other apocalyptic situations, both real and imagined. The globe may have survived an apocalypse but it has yet to fully undergo a reckoning. This book consists of essays from acclaimed theorists and scholars writing amid the pandemic and exposes the asymmetries of our divided world. The volume will be indispensable for scholars and researchers of literature, postcolonial studies, cultural studies, and comparative literature including post-apocalyptic and speculative fiction.

The chapters in this book were originally published as a special issue of *Journal of Postcolonial Writing* and are accompanied by a new afterword.

**Om Prakash Dwivedi** is Associate Professor of English literature at Bennett University, India. He is the author of *Representations of Precarity in South Asian Literature in English* (2022); *Re-Orientalism and Indian Writing in English* (2014) and *Tracing the New Indian Diaspora* (2014). His latest publication includes a special issue of *The Journal of Commonwealth Literature* on "Partition: 75 Years On", and a special issue of *Metacritic Journal* on "Hope and Utopia in Global South Literature". He is the Vice Chair of the international research group, Challenging Precarity (UK).

**Aleks Wansbrough** is a writer and cultural theorist. The author of *Capitalism and the Enchanted Screen: Myths and Allegories in the Digital Age* (2021), his current research concerns ideological analyses of digital media and film. He is an editor of the *Journal of Asia-Pacific Pop Culture* published by Penn State University Press.

# Fractured Narratives and Pandemic Identities

COVID-19, the (Post)Apocalyptic, the Dystopic, and the Postcolonial

**Edited by
Om Prakash Dwivedi and Aleks Wansbrough**

LONDON AND NEW YORK

First published 2025
by Routledge
4 Park Square, Milton Park, Abingdon, Oxon OX14 4RN

and by Routledge
605 Third Avenue, New York, NY 10158

*Routledge is an imprint of the Taylor & Francis Group, an informa business*



*British Library Cataloguing in Publication Data*
A catalogue record for this book is available from the British Library

ISBN13: 978-1-032-72813-1 (hbk)
ISBN13: 978-1-032-72814-8 (pbk)
ISBN13: 978-1-003-42272-3 (ebk)

DOI: 10.4324/9781003422723

Typeset in Minion Pro
by Newgen Publishing UK

**Publisher's Note**
The publisher accepts responsibility for any inconsistencies that may have arisen during the conversion of this book from journal articles to book chapters, namely the inclusion of journal terminology.

**Disclaimer**
Every effort has been made to contact copyright holders for their permission to reprint material in this book. The publishers would be grateful to hear from any copyright holder who is not here acknowledged and will undertake to rectify any errors or omissions in future editions of this book.

# Contents

# Citation Information

The chapters in this book were originally published in the *Journal of Postcolonial Writing*, volume 58, issue 2 (2022). When citing this material, please use the original page numbering for each article, as follows:

**Introduction**
*Living in dystopia: Fractured identities and COVID-19*
Om Prakash Dwivedi and Aleks Wansbrough
*Journal of Postcolonial Writing*, volume 58, issue 2 (2022), pp. 147–155

**Chapter 1**
*Pandemic: Invisibility and silence*
Seán Cubitt
*Journal of Postcolonial Writing*, volume 58, issue 2 (2022), pp. 156–166

**Chapter 2**
*Thinking the delirious pandemic governance by numbers with Samit Basu's* Chosen Spirits *and Prayaag Akbar's* Leila
Tereza Østbø Kuldova
*Journal of Postcolonial Writing*, volume 58, issue 2 (2022), pp. 167–182

**Chapter 3**
*Infection rebellion in Bina Shah's* Before She Sleeps
Claire Chambers and Freya Lowden
*Journal of Postcolonial Writing*, volume 58, issue 2 (2022), pp. 183–198

**Chapter 4**
*The Adivasi and the undead: From (post)colonial carnage to Necrocene apocalypse in* Betaal *(2020)*
Johan Höglund
*Journal of Postcolonial Writing*, volume 58, issue 2 (2022), pp. 199–211

**Chapter 5**
*Septopia and the wastialized Other: Allegorizing neo-liberalism in the age of COVID-19*
Aleks Wansbrough
*Journal of Postcolonial Writing*, volume 58, issue 2 (2022), pp. 212–225

**Chapter 6**

*Fragmentations, phantom limbs, re-memberings: Negotiating bodies, representation, and subjectivity in Caribbean British writing*
Silvia Gerlsbeck
*Journal of Postcolonial Writing*, volume 58, issue 2 (2022), pp. 226–239

**Chapter 7**

*Flattening the curse: Cooling down with Zadie Smith's* Intimations
Pallavi Rastogi
*Journal of Postcolonial Writing*, volume 58, issue 2 (2022), pp. 240–252

**Chapter 8**

*The art of COVID-19*
Pramod K. Nayar
*Journal of Postcolonial Writing*, volume 58, issue 2 (2022), pp. 253–264

For any permission-related enquiries please visit:
www.tandfonline.com/page/help/permissions

# Notes on Contributors

**Claire Chambers** is a professor of global literature at the University of York, UK, where she teaches literature from South Asia, the Arab world, and their diasporas. She is author of *Britain Through Muslim Eyes* (2015), *Rivers of Ink: Selected Essays* (2017), and *Making Sense of Contemporary British Muslim Novels* (2019). Recently, she edited *Dastarkhwan: Food Writing from Muslim South Asia* (2021), co-edited *A Match Made in Heaven: British Muslim Women Write About Love and Desire* (2020), and co-authored *Storying Relationships* (2021). Claire was editor-in-chief for over a decade of the *Journal of Commonwealth Literature* and is a Fellow of the Royal Society of Arts.

**Seán Cubitt** is professor of screen studies at the University of Melbourne, Australia. His publications include *The Cinema Effect* (2004), *EcoMedia* (2005), *The Practice of Light* (2014), *Finite Media: Environmental Implications of Digital Technologies* (2017), and *Anecdotal Evidence: Ecocritique from Hollywood to the Mass Image* (2020). He is co-editor of *The Ecocinema Reader: Theory and Practice* (2012) and *Ecomedia: Key Issues* (2015) and is series editor for Leonardo Books at MIT Press. His research focuses on the history and philosophy of media, ecopolitical aesthetics, media technologies, and media art history.

**Om Prakash Dwivedi** is Associate Professor of English literature at Bennett University, India. His research interests lie in the field of postcolonial theory, Indian writing in English, and environmental humanities. He is co-author with Lisa Lau of *Re-Orientalism and Indian Writing in English* (2014), and co-editor of the journal *Alterity Studies and World Literature*.

**Silvia Gerlsbeck** is a research associate and PhD candidate in English literature and culture at Friedrich-Alexander-Universität Erlangen-Nürnberg, Germany. Her thesis examines intersections of authorship, masculinity, and ethnicity in Anglo-Caribbean artist novels and focuses on generic refractions and authorial self-fashionings in selected works of *Windrush*-generation novelists. She is co-editor of *The Male Body in Representation: Returning to Matter* (Palgrave, 2022), which unites multidisciplinary takes on the male body and gender performances. Her research interests and teaching activities include postcolonial and black British literature, masculinity studies, theories and representations of authorship, cultural and literary theory, speculative fiction, and posthumanism.

**Johan Höglund** is professor of English at Linnaeus University, Sweden, and former director of the Linnaeus University Centre for Concurrences in Colonial and Postcolonial Studies, 2017–2020. He has published extensively on how popular culture narrates colonialism, neocolonialism, and extractive capitalism. He is the author of *The American Imperial Gothic: Popular Culture, Empire, Violence* (2014), and the co-editor of scholarly collections and journal issues, including *Dark Scenes from Damaged Earth: Gothic and the Anthropocene* (2022), *Nordic Gothic* (2020), "Nordic Colonialisms" for *Scandinavian Studies* (2019), *B-Movie Gothic* (2018), *Animal Horror Cinema: Genre, History and Criticism* (2015), and *Transnational and Postcolonial Vampires* (2012).

**Tereza Østbø Kuldova** is a research professor at the Work Research Institute, Oslo Metropolitan University, Norway. She is a social anthropologist and author of *How Outlaws Win Friends and Influence People* (2019), *Luxury Indian Fashion: A Social Critique* (2016), co-editor of *Crime, Harm and Consumerism* (2020), *Outlaw Motorcycle Clubs and Street Gangs* (2018), and *Urban Utopias: Excess and Expulsion in Neoliberal South Asia* (2017), in addition to numerous articles. She currently works on algorithmic governance, surveillance, corruption, and artificial intelligence in policing.

**Freya Lowden** is a third-year PhD student at the University of York, UK, writing on 21st-century dystopian fiction from the Middle East and Muslim South Asia. After completing an undergraduate degree in English and German literature at the University of Warwick, she spent a year in China, studying Mandarin on a British Council Chinese Language Scholarship and working at the British Embassy in Beijing. She continues to teach part-time and to coordinate an online Model United Nations course. She has received funding from bodies such as the Sir Richard Stapley Educational Trust and the Sidney Perry Foundation Trust.

**Pramod K. Nayar** teaches at the Department of English, University of Hyderabad, India. His most recent books include *Alzheimer's Disease Memoirs: Poetics of the Forgetting Self* (2021), *The Human Rights Graphic Novel: Drawing it Just Right* (2021), *Indian Travel Writing in the Age of Empire, 1830–1940* (2020), *Ecoprecarity: Vulnerable Lives in Literature and Culture* (2019), *Bhopal's Ecological Gothic: Disaster, Precarity and the Ecological Uncanny* (2017), and *Human Rights and Literature: Writing Right* (2016).

**Pallavi Rastogi** is a professor of English at Louisiana State University, USA. She is the author of *Postcolonial Disaster: Narrating Catastrophe in the Twenty-First Century* (2020) and *Afrindian Fictions: Diaspora, Race, and National Desire in South Africa* (2008). She has edited *Vulnerable South Asias: Precarities, Resistance, and Care Communities in South Asia* (2020) and co-edited *Before Windrush: Recovering a Black and Asian Literary Heritage within Britain* (2008).

**Aleks Wansbrough** is a Sydney-based writer and cultural theorist, who lectures at Sydney College of the Arts, University of Sydney and at Bennett University, India, where he is an adjunct professor. The author of *Capitalism and the Enchanted Screen: Myths and Allegories in the Digital Age* (2021), Wansbrough's current research concerns the ideology of digital media and film. He is an editor of the *Journal of Asia-Pacific Pop Culture* published by Penn State University Press and co-editor of the journal *Alterity Studies and World Literature*.

# Introduction – Living in dystopia: Fractured identities and COVID-19

Om Prakash Dwivedi and Aleks Wansbrough

In literary terms, we seem to be inhabiting a post-apocalyptic dystopia. A virus has run rampant across the world. Millions have died. Breathing has become difficult. People often have to wear masks to venture outside. Social gatherings are tightly policed. Our movements are tracked by the state. Meanwhile on social media people share selfies that promote state edicts, and reveal that far from being individualistic, social media exhibit "the group character of online culture" (Wansbrough 2021, 43). But misinformation and anti-vaccination lies also continue to proliferate online. Poorer nations tend to suffer the most as social fractures have become more visible than ever, thus pointing to a continuing neglect of health infrastructure in the Global South. Travel between nations has become nearly impossible, as nation states increasingly adopt fortress mentalities. Reactionary mobs clash with police. What can literature tell us about how this might resonate within postcolonial and decolonial contexts? How might we understand COVID-19 textually? While linking the pandemic crisis to the precarious Global South, Wilson, Prakash Dwivedi, and Gámez-Fernández (2020) point to the therapeutic role of literature, and the "interventions" it can offer in "the forms of healing, resilience, and resistance represented through literature and art, which can imagine new futures and utopian worlds" (442).

Although the COVID-19 pandemic has been framed through apocalyptic cinema, television (Nulman 2021; O'Mahony, Merchant, and Order 2021), and literature (Kaminski 2021; Herrero and Royo-Grasa 2021), its significance to postcolonialism is still being considered. The COVID-19 pandemic's impact and relationship to postcolonialism has been examined from a number of angles. Kwok (2020), for example, notes the way that colonial prejudices come to the fore, with former President Donald Trump's characterization of COVID-19 as the "China virus". Kwok is also keen to accentuate the legacies of colonialism with respect to other pandemic responses, including how immigration is handled amid the crisis. Likewise, Dwivedi (2020) argues that "to see this pandemic through a racial lens alone would be naïve, as it obfuscates the larger issues that have unfolded from the present crisis" (n.p.). Other analyses have focused on healthcare in relation to social media (Roy, Das, and Deshbandhu 2021) in a postcolonial context, while still others have sought to accentuate the role of postcolonial histories in responses to COVID-19 (Anderson et al. 2021), and vaccine distribution. The very term "vaccine imperialism" helps designate the continued legacies of imperialism in relation to the COVID-19 pandemic.

This special issue of the *Journal of Postcolonial Writing* takes a broadly textual approach in considering the new realities of what seemed the unreality of COVID-19. The eight articles examine art, film, television, and literature, and emphasize the different textual registers of COVID. What does COVID-19 mean for literature? What are the cinematic and artistic antecedents to what online is often labelled as a "boring dystopia"?

Whole Facebook pages and memes are dedicated to charting this "boring dystopia", which indicates a sort of dreary, depressing but still threatening world, where the possibility of radical political change is repressed, but without the overt spectacular displays of force associated with totalitarian regimes. Mark Fisher (2018), who coined the term, in part meant it to function adjacently to the idea of capitalist realism, which he defined in terms of there being no viable alternative to capitalism (620; see also Hatherley 2021). The causes of capitalist realism include acceptance of neo-liberal measures by both sides of the political divide, Fukuyama's (1989, 1992) "end of history", and the union-busting measures that aimed to eliminate collective action. While this end-of-history narrative has been challenged and many now think that capitalist realism is over, the term "boring dystopia" also captures the idea that there are everyday indignities in daily life under the capitalist order. One might, for instance, think of the slogans found on the walls of Amazon warehouses, allegedly meant to inspire the workers who are told that they should "Think Big" while packaging goods (Burin 2019). Although Fisher coined "boring dystopia" to describe neo-liberal Britain, the frequent quiet desolation of the COVID-era years renders the term ever more poignant (Hatherley 2021). After all, people have adapted to the isolation, to rules preventing public and private gatherings. Many of us have become accustomed to QR (Quick Response) codes designed to facilitate tracking the virus and the surveillance considered necessary to containing the virus through contact tracing. Many of us have become even more reliant on the exploitation of the gig economy as food and supplies are delivered on demand. Of course, we were surveilled long before the virus – our data harvested for profit as part of surveillance capitalism (Zuboff 2019) – and the gig economy was nearly synonymous with precarity and contemporary exploitation. But COVID-19 heightens dependence on the gig economy and brings the state into fuller view.

There is, then, a myriad of potential after-effects of COVID-19: economic, political, and psychological, not to mention the consequences for individuals' health. Indeed, the term "long COVID" denotes COVID's lingering effects. The term "long COVID" originated as a hashtag on Twitter by user Elisa Perego (Callard and Parego 2021, 2) but soon found currency among medical professionals, governments, and health organizations. Although it refers to ongoing symptoms and health consequences of the coronavirus for individuals, the term could easily be deployed to capture a collective mood of fatigue and anxiety. After all, increasingly we are told to "learn to live with the virus". As Slavoj Žižek (2020) writes in the second volume of *Pandemic!*:

> We should change our imaginary here and stop expecting one big clear peak after which things will gradually return to normal. What makes the pandemic so unbearable is that even if the full Catastrophe fails to appear, things just drag on – we are informed that we have reached the plateau, then things improve a little bit, but the crisis continues. As Alenka Zupančič put it, the problem with the idea of the end of the world is the same as with Fukuyama's end of history: the end itself doesn't end, we just get stuck in a weird

> immobility. The secret wish of us all, what we think about all the time, is only one thing: when will it end? But it will not end: it is reasonable to see the ongoing pandemic as announcing a new era of ecological troubles. (12)

We are beset by an existential drag, a sense of fatigue whereby initial hopes that the pandemic might be permanently eradicated through social distancing or vaccination have been defeated with COVID-19's mutations. While relieving for many, new COVID-19 safety measures often increase a sense of despair – that the pandemic will never end, and that things won't go back to normal. Communities are fragmented. Individuals are grappling with policies of social distancing, and self-isolation. The very terminology here gestures to riven, fractured identities. While there is a rhetoric of "we're all in this together", the reality tells multiple different tales, with clear differences in the vaccination rates between the Global South and Global North. Surveillance is part of everyday life, and while these measures are relaxed in some countries, civil liberties groups have voiced concerns (Gregoire 2021). Lockdowns often meant that marginalized members of the community (the poor, the disabled, people of colour) became ever more marginalized. And of course, they are even more marginalized with disparate health outcomes mapping along race and class contours with higher COVID-19 fatality rates for black and marginalized people across the world.

Yet despite the purgatorial "never ending" outlook engendered by the pandemic, we must not lose sight of its incredible acceleration. The global coronavirus pandemic sent shock waves across the world, affecting every nation. After its arrival in late 2019, and spread in 2020, massive transformations occurred. Suddenly the world seemed to reinforce what Byung-Chul Han called a "burnout society" (2015), driven and governed by terms such as "social distancing, quarantine" and "isolation". Ever more accounts of technological fatigue circulated. Pramod Nayar views this social condition as a mode of "hyperincarceration exclusion" (2020, 2), because it results in the "invisible practices of isolation and exclusion", as exemplified in the exodus of migrant labourers in India with the declaration of a lockdown. Such images are too easily forgotten.

At first the virus perversely signalled the possibility of a transformation of the economy and changes to production. The state was encouraged to take action. It seemed clear to many that the neo-liberal mantra of "small government" would not suffice. Britain, Sweden, and the US seemed to be punished for their leaders' "market first" attitudes, with high COVID-19 mortality rates. And it was also clear that if there was any hope for COVID zero, vaccinations would need to circulate among the Global South as well as the Global North, and that geopolitical coordination would be needed to avoid regressive border policies. The hope that the virus would accelerate a political turn towards socialism, or a more benevolent, emancipatory postcapitalism, or even a more caring form of capitalism, almost seems laughable as the wealth of tech giants continues to grow. Sean Cubitt in his article in this issue eloquently makes this case, noting the compatibility between neo-liberal capitalism and the virus. Cubitt writes that "the virus is not its enemy but a savage contingency, precisely the kind of emergency that disaster capitalism wallows in".

The current pandemic exacerbates precarious global conditions. If there is ever a post-coronavirus period, it will likely spell precarious times ahead for such groups as workers, labourers, and the precariat (Standing 2011). Indeed, there are already job cuts, diminished funding for education, weakening of the economy and the global supply chains, and concomitant individual and social health (mental and physical) disorders. This is a moment of global crisis, and hence it demands deeper attention and careful intervention. Transformation, disruption, and uncertainty are conditions that the world must confront, but they are also the issues explored in postcolonial and apocalyptic literature. One function of art and literature is to offer cultural, political, and literary theory, images of the world, and of possible worlds, namely, how might the world be different. Given the strange temporalities of COVID, being able to textually examine and picture the situation becomes ever more vital, especially within postcolonial situations.

Science fiction (SF) and (post-)apocalyptic horror have emphasized key notions of marginality, and otherness, since Mary Shelley's ([1818] 2007) *Frankenstein* – a story about a proto-subaltern figure learning to speak, after being reassembled from identities torn asunder. As Halberstam (1995) notes: "The monster itself is an economic form in that it condenses various racial and sexual threats to nation, capitalism, and the bourgeoisie in one body" (3). The possible racial dimension is accentuated by Shelley when her main character, Victor Frankenstein, contemplates creating a mate:

> Even if they were to leave Europe, and inhabit the deserts of the new world, yet one of the first results of those sympathies for which the dæmon thirsted would be children, and a race of devils would be propagated upon the earth, who might make the very existence of the species of man a condition precarious and full of terror. Had I right, for my own benefit, to inflict this curse upon everlasting generations? ([1818] 2007, 139)

It is curious and possibly telling that the threat is posited as coming from populations amid the so-called New World. There is a clear subtext of "miscegenation" and a sense of being "overrun". But of course, the monster of Frankenstein is in fact Frankenstein, the man. (The pedantic objection that Frankenstein is the scientist and not the creature is not really right – the creature may be a monster but he was made a monster; and his maker was the greater monster.) There is something Malthusian about Frankenstein's concern and something neo-Malthusian about our present moment, with heavy policing of borders, and "natural immunity" becoming a sort of default for many nations in the Global South deprived of vaccines. It would seem that some populations are regarded as important while others are not, and some populations are regarded as threats by the Global North, thus heightening a situation where "certain populations suffer from failing social and economic networks of support more than others, and become differentially exposed to injury, violence, and death" (Butler 2015, 33).

Another Frankensteinian connotation is present, though. The narrative that the virus may have escaped from the Wuhan laboratories itself recalls a common reading of Frankenstein, namely the dangers of "playing God". After all, Frankenstein wished to find a cure for death, but the undead creature signified a horrifying immortality, and the possibility that the dead might replace the living. Something of this theme is also present in Shelley's (1826) *The Last Man*, which concerns a disease emerging in the 21st century that leaves only one survivor. It is a much-revisited text amid the pandemic, alongside Camus's ([1948] 1991) *The Plague* (itself potentially read from a postcolonial vantage, set in the city of Oran).

While it is no secret that speculative fiction explores potential dangers, often focusing on apocalyptic and post-apocalyptic settings, it can be overlooked how often speculative fiction critiques colonialism.After all, it was the colonial evisceration of the Aboriginal peoples of Australia in Tasmania that in part motivated H.G. Wells to write *The War of the Worlds*. One particularly striking passage draws attention to the genocide of First Nations People in Tasmania

> [B]efore we judge of them [the Martians] too harshly we must remember what ruthless and utter destruction our own species has wrought, not only upon animals, such as the vanished bison and the dodo, but upon its inferior races. The Tasmanians, in spite of their human likeness, were entirely swept out of existence in a war of extermination waged by European immigrants, in the space of fifty years. Are we such apostles of mercy as to complain if the Martians warred in the same spirit? (Wells [1897] 2011, 7)

Curiously, then, there is an almost literal self-*alienation* (if one excuses the pun), a self-identification with the alien invaders. While the *other* is usually deemed alien – a tendency still present in SF – here the alien is somewhat atypically a stand-in for the European settler-colonialist. As importantly, the apocalypse is induced by colonization.

There is then the very real issues of the post-apocalyptic setting that postcolonial writing addresses. Colonization created various apocalyptic conditions in the continents of Africa, America, and Asia, with famines, genocide, exploitation, enslavement, and the imposition of foreign hierarchies. While the colonial exhibited in much of speculative fiction/science fiction is itself worthy of deconstruction, so too are the explorations of destitution, impoverishment, and fractured identities, recurring themes in postcolonial literature. Postcolonial literature, from this vantage point, already explores pockets of post-apocalyptic survival.

But there is also postcolonial speculative fiction. In fact, Tereza Kuldova's contribution to the issue explores postcolonial speculative fiction: Samit Basu's *Chosen Spirits* (2020) and Prayaag Akbar's dystopian novel *Leila* (2017). Similarly, Freya Lowden's and Claire Chambers's article looks at dystopian fiction from a postcolonial lens, focusing on Bina Shah's novel *Before She Sleeps*. Other articles in this issue encounter cinematic works exploring postcolonial settings through speculative fiction: Sean Cubitt's analysis of *A Girl Walks Home Alone at Night*, Aleks Wansbrough's reading of *District 9*, and Johan Höglund's exploration of the Netflix streaming television series *Betaal*. But there are also other navigations of textual form ranging from Pramod Nayar's examination and close textual analysis of Banksy to Pallavi Rastogi's meditation on the essays of Zadie Smith.

The problems this issue addresses (ecological, economic, and artistic) are at once textual and existential. All identities are in some sense textual – we are all defined by how we relate to one another and our environments. As such, articles in this issue tackle subjects that are interrelated, whether with ecology, economy, or race and gender (recall that "text" means woven). Each contributor explores the theme of "fractured identities" in a different way, although with significant overlays, intersections, and parallels. A crisis forces us to realize a break within social identity. Given that the self is mediated through a network of relations, ruptures within the social fabric must inevitably engender ruptures within the self. It is from very real social wounds caused by economic disparities, legacies of colonialism, and forms of social alienation that ruptured identities emerge.

In this vein, the issue opens with Sean Cubitt's evocative and provocative contribution, the hauntingly titled "Pandemic: Invisibility and Silence", which sets the stage in its exploration of life after the apocalypse. In his article, Cubitt poses the question whether COVID-19 can be understood in decolonial and ecocritical terms. He intimates that there is no other credible way to grapple with COVID-19. The article provides a wide-ranging exploration of ecological thinking, Xi's China, the aesthetics and materiality of noise, and an analysis of Ana Lily Amipour's film *A Girl Walks Home at Night*. Contending that the film captures a type of hybridity between nature and un-nature, and exploring the silence which is inflicted upon the colonized, Cubitt interprets the film as affirming a sort of decolonial aesthetics, with special attention not just on the vampire, but also on the character of the cat.

Tereza Østbø Kuldova draws on the concept of governmentality in her article "*Thinking the delirious pandemic governance by numbers with Samit Basu's Chosen Spirits and Prayaag Akbar's Leila*". The article accentuates the way that the pandemic heightens a sort of metric politics of manipulation and social engineering amid tech neo-feudalism. Controversially, Kuldova positions neo-liberal governmentality as exceeding Soviet measures of control that were exhibited in dystopian classics such as Zamyatin's *We*. Instead, Kuldova turns to India and Indian speculative fiction to explore the end-point of technocratic neo-liberalism.

Freya Lowden and Claire Chambers also draw on dystopian fiction, namely that of Pakistani writer, Bina Shah. In their analysis, "Infection Rebellion in Bina Shah's *Before She Sleeps*", they accentuate forms of gendered control. Transposing themes familiar to readers of *The Handmaid's Tale*, and indeed viewers of the televisual adaptation, the authors underscore the importance of the theme of rebellion to *Before She Sleeps*, noting that we are living through the predictions of the speculative fiction genre with increased modes of social repression and rises in domestic violence amid the pandemic.

Extending post-apocalyptic themes, Johan Höglund explores the violence of capital-ism and colonialism in the Netflix zombie series *Betaal*. In "The Adivasi and the Undead: From (Post)colonial Carnage to Necrocene Apocalypse in *Betaal* (2020)", Höglund skilfully develops Justin McBrien's concept of the necrocene through *Betaal*. The necro-cene refers to the destruction of land by capitalist practices and in Höglund's reading is fused with Jason W. Moore's concept of the capitalocene, whereby capitalism is the chief engineer of anthropogenetic climate catastrophe. Citing McBrien's claim that capitalism "necrotizes" the earth itself, Höglund turns to extractive capitalism. Like Cubitt, he focuses on the ecological dimension in his analysis of colonial violence and ecocidal violence.

Aleks Wansbrough also explores the topic of zombies in his article "Septopia and the wastialized Other: Allegorizing neo-liberalism in the age of COVID-19". Wansbrough draws on Fredric Jameson's analysis of allegory to make sense of neo-liberalism, class, race, and cinematic texts. Using the concept of septopia, Wansbrough contends that fictive representations of neo-liberalism in Hollywood cinema gesture to current concerns regarding sanitization amid COVID. He notes the way that COVID-lockdown protestors and anti-vaxxers even draw on tropes from Hollywood movies, arguing that both Hollywood and the protestors redirect attention away from the underlying tensions within neo-liberal capitalism even as they see-mingly decry them.

While Wansbrough alludes to racializing abjection, Silvia Gerlsbeck goes further in exploring corporeality in her article, "Fragmentations, Phantom Limbs, Re-memberings: Negotiating Bodies, Representation, and Subjectivity in Caribbean British Writing". Drawing on a rich variety of philosophic and literary traditions in her analysis of Caribbean British literature, Gerlsbeck underscores the traumatic qualities inscribed upon the racialized and othered body, particularly highlighting the diasporic traumas of the Windrush generation. Yet despite noting the fractures of diasporic identity, she nevertheless complicates the picture of identity and the body by concluding that "Caribbean British literature post-*Windrush* [ ... ] negotiat[es] issues of oppression and inferiorization, but also of cultural participation, questions of representation, and theorizations of subjectivity."

Issues of affect re-emerge in Pallavi Rastogi's exploration of the underlying causes of what she refers to as "a disorderly world" (indeed, a post-apocalyptic one) in her sensitive analysis of Zadie Smith's *Intimations*. In "Flattening the Curse: Cooling Down with Zadie Smith's *Intimations*", Rastogi underscores the significance of reflection, of slowing down or rather cooling down, and highlights the need for empathy. For instance, Smith is able to examine issues from both sides, registering the appeal of Trump as a sort of prophet while also being able to frame him as the treacherous serpent, straight out of Genesis. She argues the necessity for Smith's endeavour by accentuating form, affect, and politics, challenging us to think about our emotional response to our post-apocalyptic situation.

The issue concludes with a textual analysis of visual art in relation to the pandemic. Pramod Nayar's contribution, "The Art of COVID-19", explores the role of parody in the work of the street artist Banksy. Nayar focuses particularly on Banksy's responses to COVID-19, such as his exploration of the masked nurse. In the work, a child is depicted playing with a nurse figurine, replete with a cape and a mask to prevent COVID. While the more traditionally masculine heroes Spiderman and Batman are shown in the bin, the (literal) elevation of the nurse suggests a change in how heroism is imagined: from saving the world to treating the sick. Nayar, in his exploration of rats in Banksy's art, notes their ambiguous associations, being historically linked to plague, but also to medical experimentation. As an anagram for arts, rats combine varied connotations. Nayar provides a unique exploration of the fracturing of identity: not in the sense of broken subjectivities or fragmented selves, but in the sense of split identities and meanings in the times of COVID-19.

Taken as a totality the issue maps identity in post-apocalyptic and postcolonial settings. The eight articles help us consider how identities are becoming ever more fractured amid COVID-19, providing an important critical function that connects COVID to other crises whether economic, social, or ecological. The editors owe a great debt to the authors who contributed to this issue, but also the co-editors of the *Journal of Postcolonial Writing*, Janet Wilson and Chris Ringrose, who provided invaluable guidance and insight throughout.

## Disclosure statement

No potential conflict of interest was reported by the authors.

## ORCID

*Om Prakash Dwivedi* http://orcid.org/0000-0001-5914-9086

## References

Anderson, Clare, David Arnold, Juanita De Barros, Luka Bair, and Robert Peckham. 2021. "Epidemics in the Past and Now: A Roundtable on Colonial and Postcolonial History." *Journal of Colonialism and Colonial History* 22 (1): n.p. doi:10.1353/cch.2021.0003.

Burin, Margaret. 2019. "They Resent the Fact that I'm Not a Robot." https://www.abc.net.au/news/2019-02-27/amazon-australia-warehouse-working-conditions/10807308?nw=0&r=HtmlFragment

Butler, Judith. 2015. *Notes toward a Performative Theory of Assembly*. Cambridge, MA: Harvard University Press.

Callard, Felicity, and Elisa Parego. 2021. "How and Why Patients Made Long Covid." *Social Science & Medicine* 286: 1–5. January. https://www.sciencedirect.com/science/article/pii/S0277953620306456?via%3Dihub

Camus, Albert. [1948] 1991. *The Plague*. Translated by Stuart Gilbert. New York: A.A. Knopf.

Dwivedi, Om Prakash. 2020. "Coronavirus and the Animal within Us." *The Massachusetts Review Blog*, March 28. https://www.massreview.org/node/8743

Fisher, Mark. 2018. *K-Punk: The Collected and Unpublished Writings of Mark Fisher*. London: Repeater Books.

Fukuyama, Francis. 1989. "The End of History?" *The National Interest* 16: 3–18. Summer. https://www.jstor.org/stable/24027184

Fukuyama, Francis. 1992. *The End of History and the Last Man*. New York: New Press.

Gregoire, Paul. 2021. "COVID-19 Restrictions and the Civil Liberties: Human Rights Quagmire." *Sydney Criminal Lawyers Blog*, October. 2. https://www.sydneycriminallawyers.com.au/blog/covid-19-restrictions-and-the-civil-liberties-human-rights-quagmire/

Halberstam, Judith. 1995. *Skin Shows: Gothic Horror and the Technology of Monsters*. Durham, NC: Duke University Press.

Han, Byung-Chul. 2015. *The Burnout Society*. Translated by Erik Butler. Stanford, CA: Stanford University Press.

Hatherley, Owen. 2021. *Clean Living under Difficult Circumstances*. London: Verso.

Herrero, Dolores, and Pilar Royo-Grasa. 2021. "Introduction: Special Issue 'Dystopian Scenarios in Contemporary Australian Narrative'." *Humanities* 10 (3): 90. doi:10.3390/h10030090.

Kaminski, Johannes. 2021. "Necropolitics in a Post-Apocalyptic Zombie Diaspora: The Case of AMC's *the Walking Dead*." *Journal of American Studies* 55 (4): 910–938. doi:10.1017/S0021875820000687.

Kwok, Henry. 2020. "Beyond the Anti-Racist Reason: A Postcolonial Perspective on Pandemic Politics." *Health Sociology Review* 29 (2): 122–130. doi:10.1080/14461242.2020.1785320.

Nayar, Pramod K. 2020. "The Long Walk: Migrant Workers and Extreme Mobility in the Age of Corona." *Journal of Extreme Anthropology* 4 (1): 1–6. doi:10.5617/jea.7856.

Nulman, Eugene. 2021. *Coronavirus Capitalism Goes to the Cinema*. London: Routledge.

O'Mahony, Lauren, Melissa Merchant, and Simon Order. 2021. "Necropolitics in a Post-Apocalyptic Zombie Diaspora: The Case of AMC's *The Walking Dead*." *Journal of Postcolonial Writing* 57 (1): 89–103. doi:10.1080/17449855.2020.1866265.

Roy, Dibyadyuti, Madhurima Das, and Aditya Deshbandhu. 2021. "Postcolonial Pandemic Publics: Examining Social Media Health Promotion in India during the COVID-19 Crisis." *Health Promotion International*. July 19. doi:10.1093/heapro/daab076.

Shelley, Mary. [1818] 2007. *Frankenstein, Or, the Modern Prometheus*. edited by David H. Guston, Ed. Finn, and Jason Scott Robert. Cambridge, MA: MIT Press.

Shelley, Mary. 1826. *The Last Man*. London: Henry Colburn. Accessed 18 January 2022. https://www.gutenberg.org/files/18247/18247-h/18247-h.htm

Standing, Guy. 2011. *The Precariat: The New Dangerous Class*. New York: Bloomsbury.

Wansbrough, Aleks. 2021. *Capitalism and the Enchanted Screen: Myths and Allegories in the Digital Age*. New York: Bloomsbury.

Wells, H.G. [1897] 2011. "The War of the Worlds." *Reproduced by Planet PDF*. https://www.planetpublish.com/wp-content/uploads/2011/11/The_War_of_the_Worlds_NT.pdf

Wilson, Janet M., Om Prakash Dwivedi, and Cristina M. Gámez-Fernández. 2020. "Planetary Precarity and the Pandemic." *Journal of Postcolonial Writing* 56 (4): 439–446. Special Issue: "Planetary Precarity and the Pandemic", edited by Janet M. Wilson, Om Prakash Dwivedi, and Cristina M. Gámez-Fernández. doi:10.1080/17449855.2020.1786904.

Žižek, Slavoj. 2020. *Pandemic! 2. Chronicles of a Time Lost*. New York: OR Books.

Zuboff, Shoshana. 2019. *The Age of Surveillance Capitalism*. New York: Public Affairs.

# Pandemic: Invisibility and silence

Seán Cubitt ⓘ

**ABSTRACT**
Can the COVID pandemic be understood in any other than ecocritical and decolonial terms? It has brought nothing new except perhaps a certain fatalism in politics, borrowed from eco-catastrophism. Apocalyptic visions of migration, the Anthropocene, pestilence, and neo-populism exacerbate longer-term trends. Religious fanatics with machine guns take whips to outsiders whose gender or skin colour they despise at the behest of billionaire warlords from the Texas border to Kabul. But COVID-19 coincides with some intriguing cultural novelties, most of all a plague of visibility traced here through Ana Lily Amirpour's film *A Girl Walks Home Alone at Night*, paired with a simultaneous mode of disappearance associated with the video image. Hegemonic transitions, the rise of financialization, and extractive postcolonization tie pandemic to fading (and therefore vengeful) American individualism and the rising (and therefore aggressive) Chinese command economy. The virus is occasion for profit: only a new and ecologically scaled cosmopolitanism can save us.

Can the COVID pandemic be understood in ecocritical and decolonial terms? Can it be understood in any other?

## Four versions of apocalypse

St John's Apocalypse calls them famine, pestilence, war, and death. The horses of the contemporary apocalypse carry plague, eco-catastrophe, migration, and neo-populism on their backs. We have historically specific names for them. We don't like to call neo-populism "fascist" for historiographically correct reasons: there are no Boy Scout uniforms associated with the macho individualism of Proud Boy vigilante fashion. Plague is technically something apart from "virus". The focus on climate, admirable as it is, elides the other devastating assaults of the Great Extinction underway in the 21st century (Otto 2018). Migration is an impolite but politic term that avoids the legal repercussions of using the word "refugee", but it fails to grasp the most significant migration of our times: the migration of power.

All four contemporary apocalypses could be renamed. Many of the global economic and political crises of the late 20th and early 21st centuries will one day be placed clearly and simply as symptoms of the westward movement of hegemony, from the imperial moment of the British Isles in the 19th century to the republican moment of US hegemony in the 20th towards the command economy of China in the 21st and, waiting in the wings if *Hindutva* does not derail it, India preparing patiently for its ascent. The real crisis of migration is this drift of power and wealth. It is typical of hegemonies to blame the victims. As Jimmie Durham (1993) wrote, it wasn't First Nation Americans who scalped: it was white bounty hunters. The European Union's refusal to accept arrivals by boat (while grudgingly accepting arrivals by plane) is victim-blaming that ignores (and declines to mitigate) the causes of migration. Fascistic neo-populism is a refusal of the cosmopolitan ideals that have for so long provided the ethical basis for global resistance and for metropolitan solidarity with decolonial struggles. The cost is withdrawal from the previous US hegemony of neo-liberal globalization. The current collapse of global trade – laid at the door of the pandemic and of greed and trickery in the finance markets (as if that were unprece-dented) – is a retreat towards an imagined past entrenched inside the boundaries of an ethnically defined community. It mobilizes infantile fantasies of security, expressed in a resurgent patriarchy with its flags, four-wheel drives and AK47s from Arizona to Teheran, a newly unifying orthodoxy that links the outlaw chic of US "patriots" with the machismo of the Taliban, under the guise of rebellion and liberation under the sway of billionaire warlords.

The ethnically monolithic policy priorities of Xi's faction in the Chinese Communist Party (CPP) are only another symptom of the same rejection of cosmopolis. Philosophically, Xi's CCP is in the vanguard of a postmodern, even postcolonial rejection of universalism, the ideological wing of the European Enlightenment that drove colonial expansion and the emergence of capital as a global system (Mignolo 2003). As if Germany in the 18th century poses the greatest threat to the contemporary world. Still, it is true that universalism is in crisis. As I write, the Biden administration is securing preliminary agreements from the major powers to a joint effort to rein in global warming. Planetary problems demand planetary solutions, despite the intrusive truth that not everyone has contributed to or benefitted from global warming in the same degree, while "everyone" is expected to bear their part in the effort to ameliorate its effects (Chakrabarty 2012). Ecological calamity requires common, collective, collaborative responses, but still requires us to consider difference, not the universalist claims of ethnicity and patriarchy, as the roots of cosmopolitanism (Papastergiadis 2012). The saddest assessment of ecopolitics is that, as with colonization, the worst has already happened; what was dreamed of as an event has become an ongoing catastrophe, and we already live in the end times after the apocalypse. Migration of wealth, like the migrations of the poor, is always hopeful, always looking for the next thing and the next. In the opposite temporal direction, retrenchment into ethnic enclaves, even if they are con-tinental in scale as here in Australia, sees the past as redemptive, although its nostalgia is always tinged with the doubt that the worst has already occurred, that miscegenation has already infected Islamic, Aryan, or Han purity. The true enemy of ethno-fascist neo-nationalism is not the Outsider but the traitor within, the deceit curled up in the heart of the purest of the pure, the self-doubt that at the last they might discover sympathy in their inmost gizzards. This is the ground of those deathly if risible displays of unrestrained, foaming anger that gun fanatics of all religious persuasions allow themselves, and that their political and economic masters foster at every turn.

Where ethno-fascism is locked in the past, and hegemonic migration in an imaginary future, eco-catastrophe thinking is trapped in a present it can't get out of. Its vice is fatalism. Mortality used to be the condition of individuals. Now we face it as a social, even planetary event. The temptation to a fatalist descent into melancholy contemplation has rarely seemed so tempting, not since "midnight in the century" (Serge 2014) that preceded this one. Ironically, that very fatalism is what makes ecopolitics the only genuinely political agent in the modern apocalypse. However deeply they seek renewal and movement, however much they mine the future for profit in the form of debt, modern hegemonies have no goal beyond maintaining the current state of the world. Taking a greater share for a different polity, a different kleptocracy, does not change the pile of suffering and exploitation to be shared out: that remains always the ground hegemonies stand on. But they can mobilize desire for change, the hope that springs eternal, the unanswerable human desire which is always for what we do not (yet) possess and is therefore endless. Shaping that desire to the requirements of the hegemony is crucial. The British Empire did it with jingoism; the US hegemony with consumerism; from a distance it seems as if Xi's CCP is offering security as the goal. Taming desire, deflecting and disciplining needs, as Foucault (2007) might have said and Arendt (1958) did, modern politics has turned away from the public debate over what constitutes the good life in common and reduced it to the management of biological needs. The future is the illusion that makes the present administrable. For catastrophe environmentalism the opposite is the case: the absence of any future removes all obligation to be concerned with even the biological survival of the species. It is not uncommon to hear broadly Green people say that the pandemic is a good thing when it reduces atmospheric and sonic pollution, and to whisper, if only to ourselves, that it would not be so ill if Corona reduces the human population.

The pandemic must be understood in these terms. The wet markets of Wuhan can stand as emblems, and as sacrificial or ideological pictures of everything we fear most. The virus speaks of the contagion of autonomous humans by a repressed and savage nature through the unnatural assertion of biology (foodstuffs) over prohibition (the marker of humanity). It lies at a frontier between ethnicities and religions where the certainties of identity are most at risk, and enters through the kitchen, women's domain, where the prized heterosexuality of the patriarch is most at risk of pollution by the very women it has trained itself to desire, despise, sanctify, and oppress. And as the very idea of pandemic belongs to the movements of people, so we have learned to dread festivals and holidays, not for concentrating crowds but for allowing them to scatter across states and climate zones, a nomadic cosmopolis of contagion.

## Anti-cosmopolis and the neo-consensus

Private health is an oxymoron, a contradiction in terms, a categorial error. I cannot be healthy if my neighbours and my environment are unhealthy. But neither neo-liberal globalizers nor neo-nationalist border-builders – effectively consensual antagonists who only disagree on the levels at which goods, services, or people have the power to move – can confront the obvious contradiction in "private health". They cannot criticize it because to do so they would have to contradict the profit motive as such, and the principle of individualism it depends upon. The neo-consensus is therefore prepared to contemplate a global and even colour-blind, even class-blind pandemic as a price worth paying to maintain the profit motive. Of course, it can export risk: to ex-colonial UberEats delivery riders, hospital cleaners, and the even more invisible workers of "Internet" shopping whose logistical labour in warehouses and postal delivery the rhetoric disguises as imaginary robotic systems. In effect this is all too accurate a description of their situation seen from the point of view of the deracinated consumers who nonetheless, in all bad faith, know perfectly well that there is an oppressed and exploited manikin inside the Mechanical Turk.

The casualties – exceeding five-and-a-half million at time of writing – are an acceptable price for the cyborg corporations that buy and sell governments. We know these corporations are cyborgs, not because no human would ever make decisions like this, but because any living creature displays an instinct for survival, while these corporations, vast aggregations of computers with human bio-implants, are obviously prepared to destroy not only humans, not only the planet, but the future sources of their wealth in order to secure present profits. More than any living thing, most of whom know how to nest in order to procreate, the cyborg corporation is capable of acting out an inbuilt performance imperative to make profit regardless of any other motive, including its own survival. The perversion of the neo-consensus is to place itself in service to this Moloch. Thus the neo-consensus opens borders to goods and finance but pretends to close them to people, while in the event filtering people according to the amount of profit that can be derived from them, in cash or as data. The *Evergreen* Suez Canal blockage only revealed that live animal exports travel more freely than people, including the sailors now trapped aboard the ship. Matteo Salvini, Italian Minister of the Interior, is arraigned for refusing to allow boat-borne migrants to land: he has never been accused of stopping cattle coming into harbour.

Private health makes pandemic the responsibility of individuals. We are counselled to contact-trace, wear masks, get vaccinated, and socially distance (another powerful oxymoron). Not surprisingly, the success of the individualist ideology among neo-nationalists leads them to refuse these responsibilities. The rest of us look on aghast at their irresponsibility and the irresponsibility of their spokesmen (and they are almost exclusively men: Putin, Bolsonaro, Trump . . .). The parallel with "sustainable" capitalism is striking in its dependence on "responsible consumers". This is not responsibility in the sense of reciprocity of the kind observed in Indigenous cultures where everything taken from the land or sea must be respected, and in some way returned. Individualized consumer responsibility is instead a matter of filing, a filing of matter, sorting the integral waste that capital cannot persist without, in ways that make further exploitation possible, that offers a kind of gratification through the imitation of work and a depiction of connection (rather than its reality); and that furthers the real subsumption of consumer discipline into the profit-making obsession of cyborg capital. "Responsible consumerism" imitates liberalism's strategy of apologizing after the event for its worst excesses, its genocides and ecocides, with the excuse that ecocide and genocide, like waste, are exceptions and accidents, whereas in fact the exception is the very core of liberal (and we should add illiberal, command-led) capital (Povinelli 2018).

Responsibility is a matter of response, which in our time has been reduced to a measure of feedback, the guarantee of the efficiency of a communication system. Consuming has been wholly subsumed ("real subsumption" in Marx's terminology) into such a communicative loop, where purchase is incomplete without the return of data to the corporations involved in the sourcing, manufacture, and logistics feeding the once-terminal moment of purchase. Now recycling proves to us the incompletion of that moment, and the extension of discipline from the demographic probability that you will purchase according to your age, gender, income, and ethnicity towards the new individualist demographics collected by data harvesting in social media, loyalty cards, credit cards … The mass societies of Fordism gave way to household consumption, then in the postmodern moment to individual consumption. Now we enter a moment when the most advanced economies track not individuals but behaviours – swipes, clicks, likes. In this movement, we have passed from the age of probabilities to the age of contingency. Data capture no longer seeks pattern and prediction: it seeks randomness. Humans are the last source of such profitable instability. Our last work, as fully integrated consumers, is to be lucky.

The scales of luck are far smaller than the mass consumerism of Model T Fords. They are far smaller than the vast movements of capital and hegemony, but like the molecules that make up the great ocean currents, at their own scale of operation they make a difference. And difference is the only possible motor for a direction out of the dystopian present.

## A Girl Walks Home Alone at Night

Ana Lily Amirpour's 2015 film *A Girl Walks Home Alone at Night* predates the pandemic by five years but offers some ways of thinking it. Like all vampire movies it evokes blood as a medium, unsettles the connotations of menstruation and thus of femininity as lunar and reproductive, thus proximal to nature. The gender-switch – Amirpour's vampire is female – already breaks the code: the Girl (unnamed throughout the film) is un-natural. Beyond the obvious allegories – perfect in their ambiguity – there lies the challenge of the film's ending and of the role of one of its principal characters. The plot is a love story and ends as the young male character Arash and the Girl drive away from Bad City, the petroleum-powerhouse town they inhabit and that inhabits them, shot in chiaroscuro black and white in another petrol-economy town in Southern California, a diasporan doppelgänger that displaces the Farsi dialogue with evocations of American youth culture (US rock among the Farsi songs on the soundtrack, Arash in James Dean clothes and poses, his US classic convertible, and in a marvellous sequence the Girl skateboarding in a chador). After driving for a while, they park up. Arash gets out. He seems to be making some kind of decision. He gets back into the car and drives. The final shot shows tail lights receding. But which way are they going – escaping the city or returning to it?

The love story involves a boy and the Girl, but elsewhere the film plays with all the roles. With flamboyant make-up, Arash dances with the Girl at a costume party dressed as Dracula; earlier she has been treated to a would-be erotic dance by a pimp whom she bites and kills. In another unexplained insert sequence, a trans character we have been introduced to briefly as a streetwalker controlled by the now-dead pimp dances alone on a rooftop with a helium balloon for partner. This mirror of the pimp's attempted, assertive, almost bullying seduction routine is far more joyous, celebratory, and asexual, as the core love story also appears to be. The play of roles, genders, sexes, and asexualities elevates the movie from realist narrative towards some kind of symbolism. But of what?

Perhaps the question is best asked of the rooftop trans dance, and another sequence of the Girl dancing alone: who is watching? In many films the answer, as André Gaudreault (2009) descries it in early cinema, would be "the cinema", what he calls "*le grand monstrateur*", the great showman, the One that shows us the events on screen. But *A Girl Walks Home* presents an alternative.

In the opening scene, Arash collects a feral cat from the outskirts of town. The cat accompanies him through the story, often caught in close-up, watching events unfold. At moments it enters into the plot, first being sexed by the pimp (who calls it Mr Cat), later threatened by Arash's junkie father who accuses it of "having your mother's eyes" – another gender uncertainty. The cat is a cat, as real as any of the actors. In sequences in the car, where it perches between Arash and the Girl, it seems to follow the alternating lines of dialogue, turning its head towards each speaker, perhaps a trained animal, an actor, but no less a cat than Arash is less a man for being an actor. At the same time, obscurely, and in ways I have yet to find a satisfying resolution to, it seems to have some other function, specifically to watch, to witness, to see. It is a principle of Merleau-Ponty's (1968) late phenomenology that in order to see, we make some kind of compact with the world that admits that we must also be seen, inscribed in the field of the visible. The cat then operates in the film as the world's view of the action, an inhuman gaze beyond the suturing of male desire into the order of continuity editing (Mulvey 1975), even as the turns of its head suggest a classical shot-reverse-shot structure that, however, replaces the implicit masculinity of the *grand monstrateur* with a feline look, dispassionate, almost objective except that it is too an object of the camera's gaze and therefore not free to be the impartial frame that actions and objects take their places in.

The grounding ambiguity, the non-identity of the cat (simultaneously cat, symbol, observer, actor, function of the film, emblem of the world that sees rooftop dances and automobile romances, impartial but at risk at least twice in the narrative . . .) undermines any ordinary reading of *A Girl Walks Home*. Rippling between the anthropomorphisms (Mr Cat, mother) and animal embodiment, between feral and domesticated, between subject and object of the film's partition of looking, the cat is an unsettled and unsettling presence of un-nature, an absence of either nature (dispelled from Bad City) or reason (or why would it matter if a cat sees anything?). The cat that persists throughout the movie is, rather precisely, nothing. A mote in the eye, a patch of invisibility in the omnivoyant world of cinema.

The film was shot – and most frequently shown, in the age of digital content package (DCP) projection, optical discs, and streaming media – digitally. A line in Godard's (1963) *Le petit soldat* echoes through the history of analogue cinema: "Photography is truth. Film is truth twenty-four times a second." Almost certainly he wanted to say something about the presence of the image, either as witness to what it observes, or in the sense of a truth-statement a form of language capable of proving that some state of affairs is or was indeed the case. But there is another way to read this: "twenty-four times a second" the shutter comes down, in the camera and the projector, to hide the film transport mechanism. Nothing appears on screen. And what is nothing? For Frege ([1884] 1953), as for Aristotle, everything that exists is identical to itself: this cup is this cup, not that cup or that tree. What then is zero, which by definition does not exist? It is the name of the non-identical. The darkness we plunge into, and during which we are, again in the full technical senses of the word, unconscious, is this zero: the integral non-identity of successive frames that their presence as images emerges from. The multiple non-identities of the cat may as well serve as on-screen personification (animation) of this precisely invisible generation.

Except that this is not film in the sense Godard spoke of in 1963, long before he moved to video. This is video, where there is no shutter. Instead, each frame is scanned, from top left to bottom right, the screen illuminating as the program instructs it to, and fading just slowly enough to maintain the optical illusion of a whole image, but swiftly enough to clear the way for the next image to emerge. In video, unlike film, there is never a whole image. But equally there is never a complete darkness, only this pulse of emerging and fading. This rhythmic infrastructure, which only operates on the condition of being invisible to human eyes (but which cats can see, hence their general lack of interest in screens), tells us something odd about the digital image (equally true of stills, which are also scanned repeatedly): there is neither presence nor absence, no zero and no one, in digital media. We piously tell ourselves that the truth of video is not what it pictures but the code running beneath it, the really real code. In this way, digital video seems both an even more truthful medium – it rigidly portrays itself as medium, in the modernist sense (Greenberg 1960) – speaking of an even more fundamental ontology of flux and difference, but only by recusing itself from being anything more than a statement about statements, by withdrawing from the world into an aesthetic autonomy. Yet we know this is impossible: we know that it depends on code from somewhere, administered by global standards for image transport, running on some kind of device, made from materials fabricated in some plant, of metals and plastics transported, refined, and managed, derived from some mineral resource ... And we recognize the activities involved: actors human and non-human, locations, lights, microphones, production crew, props ... The ontologically subjunctive form of video, never wholly present or absent, echoes the untruth, the subjunctive "might", the quantum uncertainty of electrical charge, which can never decline to zero, and never achieve completion. The language of zeroes and ones is a fiction. The cat in *A Girl Walks Home* looks less like a Persian cat and more like Schrödinger's.

This is the scale of difference: between one image and the next, between one form of unconsciousness and the next. For the viewer, watching *Casablanca* on film or video makes no difference *because we are unconscious* for a suspiciously large proportion of the movie's running time. But we are no longer unconscious in the same way: not plunged in non-identity, but swept into the rhythm of an electronic pulse. Losing analogue cinema's absences, its non-identity, we enter another space where image and darkness are no longer fundamentally separate states. Appearing and disappearing are our ontology. We are no longer inscribed into the visible: we are constantly being marked as visible and equally constantly being erased. Video is colonizing the unconscious.

## Virus

These changing states affect the apparatus and its spectators equally, so that they are increasingly indistinguishable (whence the neologism "produser" that acknowledges that we are increasingly makers as well as viewers, and that the two activities are decreasingly distinguishable). The "we" that emerges is no longer the common identity of a mass audience. It is increasingly the cloud of micro-behaviours clustering around an Internet meme, or a way of recycling. Lyle Vincent's noir cinematography invites us to watch the film as a cloud of pixels, as records of light – and all light is ultimately solar, whether daylight, fossil-fuel powered, or hydroelectric – and as retinal effects. The collaborative nature of film – capture, processing, storage, transmission, viewing, responding – restores response to a contingency to which otherwise economies of micro-behaviour condemn us.

The pandemic, like hegemonic power's nomadic geography, like global warming and pollution, like the increasingly logistical logic of the neo-consensus (Mezzadra and Neilson 2013; Rossiter 2016; Tsing 2009), like coloniality, and like capital, is unevenly shared. We are not all in this together: we are in it apart, from the macro-scale of polity and poverty to the granular intricacies of behaviours and unconsciousness. These scales are not only spatial. They involve the engineering of new temporealities – new operations from the geological time of the Anthropocene to the microHerz frequencies of computer clocks. Equally they deploy new political administrations, temporamentalities (by ana-logy with *mentalités* and Foucault's governmentality) that manage the specific difference of becoming human in the displacement of circadian rhythms by vaster and smaller timescapes of risk, hope, desire, security, and fatalism.

Pandemic management employs both temporealities and temporamentalities. The statistical figures we scan so anxiously, tables and graphs of infection rates and the geographic information systems articulating organized panic with migration and muta-tion, are all devices honed in the heyday of empires when ecology and climate science were invented (Coen 2018) alongside anthropology and the ethno-sciences that mined Indigenous knowledge for the metropolitan centres. Temporeal technologies and their temporamental deployment (for example, the delay applied to financial data, absurdly high-priced in what passes for real time, freely disseminated at the end of the trading day) introduce another dialectic of scalar inequalities. On one side the temptation was for the new planetary sciences to be fully assimilated into the maw of capital as intellectual property, in exactly the same way as physical materials. On the other was Science, the imagined community of scholars and the equally imaginary body of knowledge, far greater and more detailed than any one mind might cram into a lifetime. The oscillation between these poles, between commodification and commons, plays out still in the government of COVID-19. Vaccine as saviour is the current trope at time of writing, but already some of the leading tropes of 2020 sound like historical relics ("the new normal", "flattening the curve"). It has the classic form: the communal will to understand that no one is safe until everyone is safe versus the right of inventors to make a profit from their knowledge. The enclosures that began with the commons in Europe and became a planetary policy in the wake of Columbus (Milun 2011) have bled into the assumed right to extract knowledge of the illness from its unpaid victims in order to manufacture products that can be sold to them. Colonialism no longer stops at the epidermis, and the colonization of the unconscious is only one step from the extraction of language, and one step before the extraction of viral RNA.

As Nabhan (1997, 21) has it, "whatever we can read about biodiversity will be written in less than 5 percent of the languages that have existed since Gutenberg's print revolu-tion", a truth that extends to knowledge about the coronavirus and its technical and commercial applications. It is not a question of discovering a counter-knowledge: that too would only be captured and deployed by omnivorous colonial capitalism. It is a question of creating conditions for an Other way of knowing, and we have models. The master's tools will never dismantle the master's house, but, once it is dismantled, there is little reason to throw them out. Instead we – a "we" that on the model of cinema now includes humans, technologies, and ecologies – will seek out new affordances of the old tools, new hybridities, Creole epistemologies.

This "we" has never existed before, and only exists now as potential: in the ideal of science, however often betrayed; in the ideal of cinema, however often monetized; in the dream of cosmopolis that now outgrows the limits of a single species, but equally learns from the dialectic of time/space scales to think and act not just globally and locally but cosmically and microscopically. The noisy, neo-romantic soundtrack to Amirpour's *A Girl Walks Home* gives way from time to time to the surface noise of a needle running over the vinyl groove towards the music. It carries with it John Cage's experiments, inspired by the *I Ching*, in the anechoic chamber, where in pursuit of silence he discovered his body as involuntary sound-source, and subsequently, in *4'33"*, made the world's sounding the simultaneous object and subject of a listening as omnipresent and undefined as A *Girl Walks Home's cat*. The colonial experience is that silence is an enforced condition; carnival its appropriate force of resistance. The data visualizations, animations, and diagrams that picture and communicate the virus are also silent. Silence, in Amirpour's film, in the postcolony (Mbembe 2001), and in pandemic crisis management, is never complete, nor is it coherent. Like digital video, it fails the tests of absence and presence, not least through the familiar repression of the natural body's capabilities for making and hearing sound (soles of the feet, long bones, and chest cavity as receptors; intestines, lungs, and nervous system as generators). The virus is as silent as regimes of pandemic management make it. The silence of catastrophe has too often been the silencing of its occurrence (only to be alluded to as exception to the harmony of the invisible hand sweeping the strings of the human exception).

The actuality of silence, as Amirpour deciphers it in the record player's surface noise, is noise, the unwanted exterior of organized sound, the ejected waste of efficient communication. Admittedly neo-populism has embraced anarchist libertarianism (Malcolm McLaren's punk slogan "Cash from chaos") from Amazonia to Kashmir as much as it has ramped up even as it occludes its totalitarian extension into dreams and cellular metabolism. The Cage analogy is illuminating once more: Cage (1968) offered 4 minutes and 33 seconds of silence, in 3 movements, thus organizing the contingent clatter of the world for the system of music. Capital's assimilation of contingency is as source of profit parallels the political espousal of anarchy as the extreme form of liberalism. It organizes noise into a tool for communication: the efficient extraction of data from the flux. Virus is not its enemy but a savage contingency, precisely the kind of emergency that disaster capitalism wallows in. Humans are vulnerable to the extent that we have silenced the nature that we defined by leaving it, that we despised, gendered, ethnicized, and ultimately wrecked and abandoned. Nature's revenge is that human populations are the environment the virus inhabits, economic and political externalities to be exploited without end or consequence. Yet as we become environments, we have the opportunity to overcome our alienation from the world. Our one hope is to learn to observe ourselves, hear our world in ourselves in all the alienated ruin of our historical rifts, from elsewhere: a view from the feline camera, a ruffling of silence from the rumble of a record deck. We must not and in all probability cannot steal cosmopolis back from Indigenous peoples who alone seem to possess its secrets today. We can, however, learn from them the skills of enduring after the end of the world.

## Disclosure statement

No potential conflict of interest was reported by the author.

## ORCID

Seán Cubitt http://orcid.org/0000-0002-7633-6809

## References

Arendt, Hannah. 1958. *The Human Condition*. 2nd ed. Chicago, IL: University of Chicago Press.
Cage, John. 1968. *Silence: Lectures and Writings*. London: Calder and Boyars.
Chakrabarty, Dipesh. 2012. "Postcolonial Studies and the Challenge of Climate Change." *New Literary History* 43 (1): 1–18. doi:10.1353/nlh.2012.0007.
Coen, Deborah R. 2018. *Climate in Motion: Science, Empire, and the Problem of Scale*. Chicago, IL: University of Chicago Press.
Durham, Jimmie. 1993. *A Certain Lack of Coherence: Writings on Art and Cultural Politics*. London: Kala Press.
Foucault, Michel. 2007. *Security, Population, Territory: Lectures at the Collège de France 1977–1978*. Translated and edited by Graham Burchell and Michel Senellart. Basingstoke: Palgrave Macmillan.
Frege, Gottlob. [1884] 1953. *The Foundations of Arithmetic*. Translated by J.L. Austin. 2nd rev ed. New York: Harper
Gaudreault, André. 2009. *From Plato to Lumière: Narration and Monstration in Literature and Cinema*. Translated by Timothy Barnard. Toronto: University of Toronto Press
Godard, Jean-Luc. 1963. *Le petit soldat*. Les Productions Georges de Beauregard / Société Nouvelle de Cinématographie (SNC). 88 mins.
Godard, Jean-Luc, dir. 1963. *Le petit soldat* [The Little Soldier]. Paris: Georges de Beauregard, Producer.
Greenberg, Clemen. 1992 [1960]. Modernist Painting. *Art in Modern Culture: An Anthology of Critical Texts*. Edited by Francis Frascina, and Jonathan Harris. Phaidon, London. 308-314.[first [originally given as a radio lecture in Forum Lectures (Washington, D.C.: Voice of America), 1960].
Mbembe, Achille. 2001. *On the Postcolony*. Berkeley, CA: University of California Press.
Merleau-Ponty, Maurice. 1968. *The Visible and the Invisible*. Translated by Alphonso Lingis. Evanston, IL: Northwestern University Press
Mezzadra, Sandro, and Brett Neilson. 2013. *Border as Method, Or, the Multiplication of Labor*. Durham, NC: Duke University Press.

Mignolo, Walter D. 2003. *The Darker Side of the Renaissance: Literacy, Territoriality, & Colonization*. Ann Arbor, MI: University of Michigan Press.

Milun, Kathryn. 2011. *The Political Uncommons: The Cross-Cultural Logic of the Global Commons*. Farnham: Ashgate.

Mulvey, Laura. 1975. "Visual Pleasure and Narrative Cinema." *Screen* 16 (3): 6–18. doi:10.1093/screen/16.3.6.

Nabhan, Gary. 1997. *Cultures of Habitat: On Nature, Culture and Story*. Berkeley, CA: Counterpoint.

Otto, Sarah P. 2018. "Adaptation, Speciation and Extinction in the Anthropocene." *Proceedings of the Royal Society B* 285 (1891): 20182047. doi:10.1098/rspb.2018.2047.

Papastergiadis, Nikos. 2012. *Cosmopolitanism and Culture*. Cambridge: Polity.

Povinelli, Elizabeth A. 2018. "Horizons and Frontiers, Late Liberal Territoriality, and Toxic Habitats." *E-flux Journal* 90 (April) https://www.e-flux.com/journal/90/191186/horizons-and-frontiers-late-liberal-territoriality-and-toxic-habitats/.

Rossiter, Ned. 2016. *Software, Infrastructure, Labour: A Media Theory of Logistical Nightmares*. London: Routledge.

Serge, Victor. 2014. *Midnight in the Century*. Translated by Richard Greeman. New York: New York Review Books

Tsing, Anna. 2009. "Supply Chains and the Human Condition." *Rethinking Marxism* 21 (2): 148–176. doi:10.1080/08935690902743088.

# Thinking the delirious pandemic governance by numbers with Samit Basu's *Chosen Spirits* and Prayaag Akbar's *Leila*

Tereza Østbø Kuldova ⓘ

**ABSTRACT**
Globally, the COVID-19 pandemic has accelerated the adoption of technocratic near-real-time data-driven governance, in that new rules, measures, and prohibitions have been introduced and revoked in response to predictive statistical and epidemiological models, graphs, charts, and aesthetically powerful data visualizations. Pandemic governance has enforced an extreme governance by numbers. The real has come to mirror the structure of dystopian fiction. In his analysis of governance by numbers, Alain Supiot shows how this form of governance ushers in a return of ties of allegiance and the re-emergence of feudalism in new guises. While the rise of technocratic autocracy and security regimes has been remarked upon, the simultaneous return of bonds of allegiance has been to a large degree overlooked. And yet it appears in recent postcolonial dystopian literature from India, Samit Basu's *Chosen Spirits* and Prayaag Akbar's *Leila*, which this article reads as illuminating the extreme endpoint of this delirious governance.

Dystopia is pornographic, Olamina. You see it and shiver but it's also kind of fun because it's happening somewhere else, to someone else, you know? It requires distance. Some of us are actually sitting in the fucking middle of it and we may never learn to care in time. This isn't dystopia. This is reality. (Basu 2020, 141)

In response to the COVID-19 pandemic, governments across the globe rapidly developed new intelligent surveillance technologies and embraced near-real-time data-driven governance – in close collaboration with private tech companies – relying on lockdowns, behavioural engineering, vaccine and immunity passports, building on pre-existing digital surveillance infrastructures. New rules, prohibitions, regulation, laws, measures, and penalties have been introduced, eased, and reintroduced in response to predictive statistical and epidemiological models, graphs, charts, indicators, and aesthetically powerful data visualizations – seductive for their simplicity, elegantly removing context and ambiguity. Our health and behaviours have become the target of "regulatory capitalism" (Levi-Faur 2017) reliant on technocratic expert systems. As with 9/11, COVID-19 has led to the intensification of data-sharing across governmental and private–public infrastructures, now in the name of the war on the virus. The enforcement of governance by numbers (Supiot

2017) has been accelerated, accompanied by the utopian faith in smart technology and data analytics to solve our problems, predict the future, and optimize ourselves out of the crisis.

Numbers have informed governance decisions and made media headlines, fuelled by a renewed naive faith in neopositivism and in the power of "objective", "neutral", and "hard" data and bits of information to optimize social outcomes (Spoelstra, Butler, and Delaney 2020) – an epistemology that disregards decades of critiques of positivism. After all, more information can result in less understanding and, paradoxically, a lesser ability to govern rationally (Postman 1993; Tsoukas 1997). Contact tracing and quarantine apps have been introduced, as in South Korea, under the banner of "smart governance" and "smart justice" (Choi, Lee, and Jamal 2021), often backed by the expanded powers of law enforcement, as in Poland (Bartoszko 2020). Many citizens subject to this expanded neo-liberal surveillance and datafied security regime in western liberal democracies have felt for the first time the state's technocratic governance and monopoly on violence, as well as the extended powers of corporate actors, on their own bodies – an experience otherwise common among those excluded and marginalized, or else, those subject to what Catherine L. Besteman (2020) terms the "militarized global apartheid". In India, 45 out of 100 smart cities "renamed their Integrated Command and Control Centres into 'COVID-19 war rooms' to monitor and track the spread of infected bodies and their encounters" (Datta 2020, 234). While inequalities increase, as many have been pushed into unemployment and poverty because of lockdowns and restrictions, and tech cor-porations have accumulated even more wealth and power, sealing their "digital dom-inance" (Moore and Tambini 2018; Tiku and Greene 2021), the pandemic crisis has created an opportunity to re-imagine governance. Or rather, it has accelerated the global expansion and reach of technocratic data-driven governance underpinned by a "cybernetic imaginary" (Supiot 2017) into new domains – a vision backed by powerful transnational organizations, international development actors, and corporations.

Alain Supiot (2017) has argued that this cybernetic imaginary "enacts the dream of an arithmetically attainable social harmony", producing an "idea of normativity not as legislation but as programming", where "people are no longer expected to act freely within the limits laid down by the law, but to react in real time to the multiple signals they receive" (10). In other words, producing a utopia of techno-social engineering where humans are imagined as programmable and optimizable through real-time governance, behavioural "nudging" (Thaler and Sunstein 2009), and smart choice architectures devised by experts, and legitimized by reference to science, data, and numbers. This article contends that we need to pay far closer attention to the normalization of this form of governance by numbers and its potentially totalitarian endpoint. Further, this article argues that dystopian literature, particularly from postcolonial settings, can help us think about this endpoint.

By and large, questions of technology and science in governance have been posed from a technical perspective, or, at best, in terms of legal and ethical issues – rather than being discussed as matters of principled political debate. But some researchers are asking critical questions; it is my goal here to build on these insights, while using the power of literature to expand our critical imaginary of governance by numbers. Critical algorithm studies scholars highlight many concrete instances of algorithmic injustice (O'Neil 2016; Noble 2018; Amoore and Piotukh 2016), legal scholars offer their views on the consequences of code-ification of law (Susskind 2018), and science and technology researchers reveal the complexities of human–machine interactions, unsettling notions of data neutrality (Egbert and Leese 2020). But few have thought about the consequences of the transformation of the legal order through governance by numbers.

Supiot is a notable exception. In his legal anthropological analysis of governance by numbers, Supiot shows how the decline of the figure of equality before the law and of the social state has resulted in the "return of ties of allegiance" and re-emergence of feudalism and servitude in new guises. Hence, there is also no contradiction between authoritarian leaders and technocratic governance; these modes of governance are perfectly compatible. The key paradox of the quest for impersonal forms of power (whether legitimized in the name of protecting lives from terrorism or a virus) is that it has made personal dependence and bonds of allegiance reappear (Supiot 2017). Recent anthropological, criminological, and legal works support this line of argument, showing that where the social state has been hollowed out and replaced by the security state and technocratic governance, organized crime groups, gangs, and other non-state actors tend to insert themselves into governance, offering protection and social security to those who submit to them, while intimidating others (Kuldova 2019; Winlow, Hall, and Treadwell 2017; Lea and Stenson 2007). Alas, when confronted by impersonal governance backed by the concentrated power of experts, few dare challenge the reigning "scientism", especially the idea that science can answer moral and political questions (Postman 1993).

## "This isn't dystopia. This is reality" (Basu 2020, 141)

Postcolonial dystopian literature, characterized so well by Mrinalini Chakravorty (2015) as "delirious", captures the very surreal contradictions and "irrevocable destructions wrought by globalized modernity" (268) and the power of capital. It does so while unsettling the "developmental narrative of how dystopia is usually conceived" (269) by, among others, its presentist character, playing out as a rule in the (near) "now". It is not only "surreally tragic in its indictment of present conditions" (278), but also in its capacity to ponder the links between capital, technology, and governance in a "delirious" manner, so to speak. In Chakravorty's words, it challenges "the idea that modernity is reasonable and that its rational terms are beneficial" (277), revealing the moments when reason flips into unreason, when what could be deemed a rational concern with security becomes fanatical and irrational, even totalitarian. And when our obsession with decontextualized information, data points, and indicators undermines our ability to create meaning and symbolic order and thus to meaningfully govern ourselves (Postman 1993; Tsoukas 1997), an ontological insecurity emerges, limiting the possibilities for resistance.

The two postcolonial dystopic novels discussed here – Samit Basu's (2020) *Chosen Spirits* and Prayaag Akbar's (2017) *Leila* – capture the convergence of governance by numbers and the simultaneous emergence of new bonds of allegiance which Supiot identifies, making us feel the resulting social injustices and dehumanization in a way that social theory cannot. Additionally, they reveal how this "rational" governance by numbers tends to flip into its opposite, a delirious form of governance. I offer an analytical and original reading of the foregrounded *background* from which both novels draw their power. COVID-19 has made this convergence acutely visible: we read simultaneously of the emergence of "autocratic technocracy" (Windholz 2020) and of how "the pandemic is putting gangsters in power" (Kennedy and Southerm 2021). These two processes are often considered separately, but it is imperative toconsider them together; in this sense, these postcolonial dystopias have already revealed their anticipatory potential in troubling the distinction between the real and the imaginary.

Dystopias can be read as tales of warning – but in the case of a postcolonial dystopia, they speak to an all too real "present" (Chakravorty 2015). Basu's *Chosen Spirits* oscillates between allusions to real events and a near-future dystopia of New Delhi in the 2030s, but, as the author remarks, "the truth is that the real world will probably be much harsher: this book is set not in a dystopia, but in a best-case scenario" (2020, 197). Put differently, the novel reveals the dystopian in the present; that is, that which many would like to push into the future, but which is already here. Speaking of his dystopian novel, *Leila*, set in near-future India, which is divided by walls into residential sectors based on religion, caste, and community, animated by the fundamentalist ideology of purity, and integrated into biometric technologies, Akbar (2017) remarks that it points to the "uncomfortable truth about 'our already-dystopian cities'" (quoted in Chatak 2017). Both novels disrupt the linear or developmental narrative in favour of what could be deemed a postcolonial realist dystopia marked by a temporal "delirium" (Chakravorty 2015), which in Basu's case adds to its already delirious narrative form. While Basu's novel is a wild ride through a world of extreme inequality, invasive surveillance, social media distortions, climate change, right-wing fundamentalism, and technocratic governance, Akbar's portrays fundamentalism and inequality through the utopian promises of security, purity, and luxury in gated communities.

Both novels speak in their own way to the same phenomena. Both exaggerate features of technocratic governance, security and surveillance regimes, and neo-feudal bonds of allegiance to create their fictional worlds of extreme inequality and dehumanizing governance, where truth is systematically overlaid – be it by media, commercial messaging, or ideology. Both feature upper-middle-class heroines forced to confront their complicity in the reproduction of structures of oppression, while the most dramatic horrors play out in the background. Mark Fisher's (2009) remarks about *Children of Men* (2006) can be echoed here: these dystopias read "more like an extrapolation or exacerbation of our" world rather "than an alternative to it", where

> ultra-authoritarianism and Capital are by no means incompatible: internment camps and franchise coffee bars co-exist [ ... ] public space is abandoned, given over to uncollected garbage and stalking animals [ ... ] there is no withering away of the state [ ... ], only a stripping back of the state to its core military and police functions (2).

Dystopias identify and exaggerate features of existing realities, bringing them to extreme conclusions, thus laying out possible bleak future scenarios (Bhattacharyya 2014). They force us to consider the "extreme case" by being in a sense "radical realizations of particular ideals and potential" (Mikkelsen 2020, 2). First and foremost, dystopias bring the systemic (governance, injustice, and power relations) into the foreground. As Tom Moylan (2000) observes,

> dystopia's foremost truth lies in its ability to reflect upon the causes of social and ecological evil as systemic. [ ... ] In its purview, no single policy or practice can be isolated as the root problem, no single aberration can be privileged as the one to be fixed so that life in the enclosed status quo can easily resume. (xii)

Dystopias refuse technocratic solutions, cost-benefit analysis, cosmetic solutions, precisely because they explore the dehumanizing consequences of technocratic governance, economic reductionism, and techno-social engineering. They foreground injustices and violations of human rights and dignity, asking fundamental political and moral questions, and positioning dilemmas as a matter of principle, thus striking at the core of what it means to be human vis-à-vis a world of machines or/and dehumanizing governance. The conflict is often between an oppressive, *omniscient*, and *omnipotent* government and an individual character or a group that faces, or witnesses, injustice at its hands and aims to resist it. Dystopias foretell the dangers of taking principles of governance to the extreme, in the form of technocratic governance by experts and/or machines. They warn of the ways in which expert rationality can flip into its opposite – irrationality – and of hyper-focus on singular issues that are impossible to argue against, whether health, security, or prosperity. Considering the autocratic technocracy of pandemic governance, these warnings could not be more acute.

The language of literature, art, interpretation, and humanities often stands in opposition to the mechanistic, instrumental, pragmatic, and seemingly rational language of science and technology, namely that of governance and power. Problems arise when the latter is not balanced by the former. Today, we are witnessing the assault of scientism on the arts and humanities. "In extreme forms", Jason Blakely (2020) writes, "scientism even tries to actively ban or eliminate other ways of knowing and experiencing as prescientific and illegitimate. The humanities, history, literature, the arts, philosophy, and religion are all disparaged as a kind of soft or even magical thinking" (xxviii). Dystopias such as Yevgeny Zamyatin's (1972) *We* and Aldous Huxley's (2000) *Brave New World*, inspired by *We*, confront us with the consequences of scientism's drive towards the elimination of the language of humanities and art. Simultaneously, they reveal technocratic governance itself to be an instance of magical thinking – with its aesthetics and ritual practice, such as the worship of mathematical simplicity. In doing so, dystopias reveal how fundamental questions are erased, impossible to be asked and answered through the concepts of technocratic language and how the "technopoly", or "totalitarian technocracy", to use Neil Postman's (1993) notion, becomes a Faustian bargain for humanity. But these questions force themselves through, driving the narratives of these works as they reveal the violence and injustice resulting from the only permissible abstract expert language through which one can see oneself, the Other and the world. Techno-social engineering by experts, conducted in the name of one ideal or the other – security, health, happiness – is brought to its logical conclusion where the ideal turns into its opposite as the language of the humanities is displaced.

There is little doubt that we are increasingly being governed by anticipatory, techno-social engineering reliant on real-time data flows that such dystopias warn us about, and that are becoming ever more delirious. Governance by numbers integrates the ideology of free market capitalism, predictive economic modelling, behavioural economics, and the utopian "techno-solutionist" visions pushed by Silicon Valley (Morozov 2013); its magical language is spoken not only by states, accelerated by the pandemic state of exception, but also in workplaces, on digital platforms, and in private life. Or as Frischmann and Selinger (2018) put it in *Re-engineering Humanity*, "instrumental reason is valorized to such a degree that it has become fetishized" (11). In her iconic article "Sex and Death Among Defense Intellectuals", Carol Cohn (1987) analyses an instance of "technostrategic language", which, in her case, is embraced by nuclear deterrence theorists. What fascinates Cohn, and no doubt dystopian writers as well, is "the extraordinary abstraction and removal from what I knew as reality" (688) of this techno-strategic language, "the elaborate use of abstraction and euphemism, of words so bland that they never forced the speaker or enabled the listener to touch the realities of nuclear holocaust that lay behind the words" (690). The language of power, of "clean bombs" and "surgically clean strikes" that "'take out' – i.e. accurately destroy" (692), Cohn observes, "can only be used to articulate the perspective of the users of nuclear weapons, not that of the victims" (706).

Simultaneously, techno-strategic language prevents its speakers from asking certain questions; words such as "peace" are excluded and to utter them is "to brand oneself as a soft-headed activist instead of an expert, a professional to be taken seriously" (Cohn 1987, 709). Techno-strategic language can be likened to the algorithmic choice architectures, or else a mode of "design-based regulation" built into algorithmic structures which nudges us and our decisions, while limiting the scope of our possibilities and political imagination with "troubling implications for democracy and human flourishing" (Yeung 2017, 118). For techno-strategic language to work, reality must be abandoned in favour of abstraction; techno-strategic (and technocratic) language, according to Cohn, was "invented largely by mathematicians, economists, and a few political scientists. It was invented to hold together abstractly, its validity judged by its internal logic. Questions of the correspondence to observable reality were not the issue" (1987, 709).

When abstractions detached from reality inform governance, humanity and human creativity are eliminated, resulting in societal and civilizational mismeasure (Hummel 2006). Zamyatin's *We* confronts us with a dystopian society where Taylorist principles of scientific management underpin One State's totalitarian governance seeking to engineer and mathematically optimize happiness, reducing its citizens to numbers – such as the main character called D-503 – who must submit to this mathematical order. Even things that cannot be calculated become calculable: One State simply assigns + and –, positive and negative designations, to all possible experiences, people, and events, eliminating any confusion and presenting the result as an objective, neutral, mathematical judgment. This is, indeed, reminiscent of how today's automated filtering of harmful online content, based on binary classification, functions – removing context, cause, and intent, relying on correlations and probabilistic judgement. The process, like most algorithmic decision-making, is similarly "black boxed" (Pasquale 2015). The human labour and exploitation that goes into training machine learning algorithms is rendered invisible (Altenried 2020) along with the biases that are coded into algorithmic systems, while the results are presented as neutral and objective. In *We*, mathematics is worshipped, but the Utopia of scientifically engineered happiness fast becomes dystopian.

Technologies, too, are subject to the "'double hermeneutic effect', in which an interpretation of the world shapes the very interpretations that comprise it" (Blakely 2020, xxvi). As Supiot explains, governance by numbers intensifies the fantasy of the governing machine and "ensnares managers and workers alike in feedback loops governed by numerical representations of the world increasingly disconnected from experience"; it replaces "territory with the map, and action with reaction" (169), leading to intellectual and institutional breakdown. Zamyatin's *We* addresses this effect of governance by numbers, anticipating the extremes of Soviet planning and the ideology of instrumental scientific calculation. Neo-liberal governance by numbers goes one step further than Soviet planning:

> [A]s in economic planning, calculation replaces law as the basis of the norm's legitimacy. But the norm is now akin to a biological norm or a computer programme, it results from the interaction of individual calculations and it results *from within*. This interiorisation, or eradication of heteronomy, is precisely what governance means: whereas *government* implies a commanding position above those governed, and the obligation for individual freedoms to observe certain limits, *governance* starts out from individual freedoms, not to limit but rather to programme them. (Supiot 2017, 115–116; original italics)

*We* is in this sense a dystopia of "government" by numbers. Basu's and Akbar's near-future postcolonial dystopias, instead, speak to "governance" by numbers, where legislation becomes "replaced by programming and rules by technical regulation" (Supiot 2017, 284). Distinctions between states, corporations, the private and the public are erased, and, with them, the notion of public interest and of commons disappears. Supiot's prediction is that "the establishment of calculations of individual utility as the sole norm – flying in the face of democratic principles – will generate new forms of violence". A world where new bonds of dependence and networks of allegiance will emerge, both legal and illegal, where "people will inevitably pledge allegiance to any group claiming to provide" physical and economic security, "be it clans, religious factions, ethnic identities or mafia networks" (284–285).

Basu's novel is driven by this double movement between the ever-proliferating technological "hypernudging" as a form of regulation and governance by design (Yeung 2017) that promises technologically optimized security and happiness alongside the dissolution of public interest and a shared horizon. Joey, the main character, tries to navigate a world of information glut, nudged by algorithms, while working as a "Reality Controller", staging "real" lives of Flowstars (a kind of real-time Instagram) for the consumption of the hyper-segmented audiences and thus in the business of nudging and capturing the attention of others. In this world, private and conflicting interests rule, and violence and exploitation are omnipresent – it is a world where surveillant technologies promise to deliver happiness and security, but the reality is one of new bonds and allegiance or "a loyalty-based economy" (Basu 2020, 8). Gang leaders, oligarchs, corporations, political unions, residence associations, and more – demanding loyalty, allegiance, or ransom for protection – all make an appearance in *Chosen Spirits*. The novel captures a world spinning out of control the more we try to control it, one of intellectual and institutional breakdown: the accelerating informational glut intertwined with different forms of algorithmic governance is mirrored in the dizzying range of particular interests, loyalties, groups – most of them either above or outside the law – all of which compete to subject others.

This world without a shared unifying narrative and purpose is reflected in the novel's delirious form, which similarly bombards the reader with snippets of information, glimpses into the world, but with something always lacking. As such, the novel perfectly captures the hollowing-out of meaning and morality through its very form. We follow Joey and her friend Rudra who tries to escape from his elite privilege, superficiality, and corruption. But through their passivity and shallowness, their complicity in society's disorientation and weak attempts at resistance, we encounter the ways of this world – the novel being more intriguing for its setting than its plot. The same can be said about Akbar's *Leila*, where the middle-class heroine Shalini searches for her daughter, from whom she has been separated by an increasingly totalitarian regime. Our concern is not with the plot or characters of these novels, but rather the foregrounded background from which they draw their power. Both Basu and Akbar point to the convergence of governance by numbers and the new ties of allegiance, the representation of a future that is "no longer one of revolution but of catastrophe" (Supiot 2017, 285).

## Techno-solutionism, surveillance capitalism, and "Reality Controllers"

Let us now approach Basu's delirious dystopia through a digression into the present pandemic governance and utopian technosolutionist promises of control. In the 1960s, Robert C. Elliott (1963) analysed the rising fear of utopia being actually realized and turning into dystopian nightmares: "in anti-utopia it is the life of the future, created in response to man's longing for happiness on earth, that is the evil [ ... ] utopia itself has become the enemy" (241). This is reflected in the dystopian and apocalyptic narratives that dominate the literary marketplace (Gidley 2017). While little is left of utopian literature, we *are* surrounded by utopian texts: namely, commercials – in particular those selling technologies that promise to predict, shape, and optimize futures, creating a seamless and harmonious world without friction; technologies that embody the utopian promise of automated control of reality. In the world of "surveillance capitalism", there are few problems – manufactured or real – that cannot be solved by data extraction and big data analysis; every minute detail can be captured, controlled, predicted, optimized, tweaked – in the name of profit (Zuboff 2019). The war on the virus has in many ways taken precisely this form of "technological solutionism" (Morozov 2013), often of new intelligent surveillance products (Bedi 2020): selfie-demanding quarantine apps (Datta 2020; Bartoszko 2020); smart wristbands, as in Hong Kong, Israel, or the Cayman Islands (Connolly 2020); biometric surveillance in the form of thermal facial recognition technology and "smart wearables" (Norris 2021); digital immunity and vaccine passports (Phelan 2020); digital IDs collating GPS tracking with health status data and digital footprints, such as the Chinese "health code" (Shi et al. 2021); intrusive workplace surveillance such as IBM's Watson Works; remote employee monitoring products; or inventions pushed by the World Economic Forum, such as smart masks that display your speech on the phone as text and translate it into different languages (WEF 2020b), or measure your breathing rate.

The National Health Service (NHS), using Palantir – Peter Thiel's secretive data-mining company backed by the Central Intelligence Agency (CIA) – to deliver COVID-19 data analysis, remarked on its blog that the software will enable "disparate data to be integrated, cleaned, and harmonised in order to develop the single source of truth that will support decision-making" (Gould, Joshi, and Tang 2020). Single source of truth (SSOT) may be a concept from information systems theory, but it is ideologically revealing, speaking to the imaginary of both "truth" and control in data-driven governance. During the COVID-19 "infodemic", new algorithmic modes of combatting fake news, misinformation, and untruth have proliferated, challenging legal protections on freedom of expression; some governments have even resorted to "criminalizing expression about Covid-19 or government's response to it" (Pomeranz and Schwid 2021). The same technologies that created deepfakes and fake social bots now promise to automate truth arbitration. But deception is a "constitutive element of these technologies" that "provide an *illusion* of intelligence" (Natale 2021, 2–3; emphasis in original), hence, rather than delivering on these promises, they are bound to fuel confusion. And yet both reality and what can be uttered about it are to be governed and controlled by them. What is the endpoint of such pandemic governance? Do these technosolutionist utopian promises result in a delirious dystopian form of governance?

Basu's *Chosen Spirits* might help us here; it confronts us with "New" New Delhi, where surveillance capitalism, real-time governance by numbers, and new bonds of allegiance march hand in hand, and where "Reality Controllers" like Joey curate real-time "Flows" of the perfectly shallow Flowstars to conceal oppressive realities on the ground: blasphemy laws, fights over limited resources such as water, mass de-citizenings, re-education camps, mafia and gang rule, curfews, data-driven home invasions, post-human upgrades, gene-testing prison camps, organ-growth sweatshops, voter-list erasures, lynchings, police violence, perfect child breeding projects, and more. The task of the Reality Controllers is to keep the Real at bay. Joey's father "often complains that his life has turned into some kind of totalitarian reality show: she's fairly sure he still doesn't understand that managing one is his daughter's job" (Basu 2020, 14).

Despite these efforts to conceal, "everyone knows", but the vast majority look the other way. The novel channels the disavowal of the "entitled young upper-caste upper class corporate-job safety-first liberal(s)" (Basu 2020, 182), betraying the structure of "cynical ideology" that sustains the oppressive relations (Žižek 1989). Basu generates a sense of permanent discomfort through his delirious writing, which stems from this cynical disavowal, and the cacophony of different forms of oppression, behavioural manipulation, technological optimization, reality manipulations, surveillance, exploitation, and violence, perpetrated by different actors with conflicting interests. Power rests on surveillance, monitoring, and prediction. Successfully navigating this reality demands tracking permissible utterances in real time, a micro-customization of the self, and accurate responses to the governance by a multitude of actors.

In a single paragraph, Basu captures the intertwined dynamic of "surveillance capitalism" (Zuboff 2019), real-time technocratic governance, and the emergence of new bonds of allegiance; all designed to control, demanding loyalty and compliance, while constantly changing the rules of the game:

> It's your house spying on you now [ ... ] it isn't just the government snooping any more, but a peak-traffic cluster of corporations, other governments, religious bodies, cults, gangs, terrorists, hackers, sometimes other algorithms, watching you, measuring you, learning you, marking you down for spam or death. [ ... ] in New New Delhi the only crime was non-conformity, and conformity was fast-shifting, ever-angry chimera that must be constantly fed. (Basu 2020, 12–13)

This cacophony of networked actors that insert themselves in multiple, often contra-dictory ways into "governance", which Basu captures so well here, creating new alle-giances, precisely reflects the logic of governance by numbers. The totalitarian in dystopian literature typically takes the shape of an oppressive state and centralized authority, with a unified ideology and agenda, allowing for both coherence and a degree of predictability. Orwell's *1984* has often been referenced when discussing today's China, where technocracy, propaganda, and fear are supported by new digital surveillance technologies, and where the Party is the "artistic director" of the China Dream, forcing all "to merge in the great utopia" (Strittmatter 2020, 25). Basu's novel draws us into a much more likely world of "post-Orwellian" totalitarian *governance* underpinned by a "regime of surveillance" (Giroux 2015), where the state is one among many actors that govern people. In such a world, the Chinese model of the Social Credit System progressively gains traction, and totalitarian technologies become desirable. As attempts at a democratic implementation of similar social credit systems in "New" New Delhi have failed, the elites and thought leaders discuss that

> "[t]his time, the new idea is the old idea: we're just buying the Chinese systems wholesale" [ ... ] This time, [ ... ] it'll be wholly secret, wholly automated, based on every transaction, every observed adherence to or violation of every unwritten rule, every movement, every word spoken or messaged, every act of consumption, participation or expressed emotion, and then categorised and filtered, obviously, by [ ... ] family, his community, his friends, his biometrics and his overall performance relative to the ideal life he should be living as a Good Citizen. (Basu 2020, 49–50)

In the regime of surveillance, privacy becomes both impossible and obsolete – and with it also democracy. In his essay "The Obsolescence of Privacy", Günther Anders [1958] 2017 analyses precisely this function of surveillance technology:

> [E]very society that allows itself the use of such [listening/surveillance] devices inevitably acquires the habit of considering humans as fully exposable and as entities that are allowed to be exposed [ ... ] *where bugging devices are used as a matter of course, the main precondition of totalitarianism has been established and totalitarianism is achieved.* (24–27; emphasis in original)

These Indian postcolonial dystopias capture this totalitarian endpoint of surveillance capitalism as a mode of governance. While the Chinese Social Credit System (wherein citizens are reduced to a number based on an algorithmic analytic of trustworthiness, with rights assigned and revoked in real-time [Strittmatter 2020]) serves as inspiration, states like India, which consider themselves democracies, are headed closer towards hybrid models, where corporate and state power are mixed, and where different interest groups compete for; a model of "hybrid surveillance capitalism" (Østbø 2021).

In portraying the smooth alignment of authoritarian, technocratic forms of govern-ance with neo-liberalism, these novels reach the same conclusions, revealing neo-liberalism's and technopoly's contempt for democracy. They unpack the crisis of social institutions and return of tribalism and communalism – a world without limits, without solidarity, and without an "efficient Symbolic Order" (Hayward and Hall 2020), and so also a world of securitized walls and gates.

## Seamless security, social sorting, and "purity for all"

In such a world, one must have protection. Where the state is failing in providing basic needs and protection, organized crime groups, gangs, mafias, rogue politicians, clans, businessmen, and others tend to step in. New bonds of allegiance and dependence emerge. In *Chosen Spirits*, gated communities, and Residence Welfare Associations have become securitized and weaponized. Physical and digital walls dominate these dystopias. Surveillance and security regimes inevitably result in different forms of gating, enclosures, and expulsions (Sassen 2014). The logic of securitized gated communities, merging with the consumerist dreams of luxurious living – or else "guarded luxotopias" (Kuldova 2017) – is presented here as the extreme, flipping into a dystopia. Simultaneously, these novels capture the elites' fears of the masses rising – the multi-billionaire owner of Cartier, Johann Rupert, once remarked that this is what keeps him awake at night (Withnall 2018) – social warfare, mass unemployment, widespread misery, all wrapped in tech utopian narratives. The rich are already building secure, hidden, and luxury post-apocalyptic bunkers (Stamp 2019), while the middle class is securitizing their gated communities, keeping undesirables, suspect, and low class outside their walls. Basu captures intensely the sense of apocalyptic fear that fuels this gating and segregationist logic:

> The walls are going to crack, because a tide of people will try to break them, just billions of people who are useless, lost in the world, people who are angry and desperate to survive: they're going to try to take everything down with them, burn it all. Climate change will break walls. The robots will break walls. New diseases, tech disasters [ ... ]. They're coming, all at the same time, until one day there's only one wall, and the people inside it are gods, and the people outside it are monsters, or dead. It's going to get fucking mythological. I'm going to be inside the wall. (2020, 125)

COVID-19 stimulated further securitization of gated communities, helped by tech-solutions. Apps like MyGate, "India's No. 1 Security and Community Management App", have seen rapid expansion, embraced by gated communities and businesses across India (Mathur 2020).

These apps promise convenience; smart, secure living; and "seamless gates" – the utopian promise of integration, anticipation, and efficiency – gated communities where everyone, every detail, and every financial transaction are monitored, evaluated, and optimized. Closed-circuit television (CCTV) cameras; security guards trained in using the app; residents using the app to communicate with each other, pay their bills, manage community accounts, start opinion polls and track responses, raise complaints, order maintenance, book amenities, shop through e-commerce integrations within the app, organize events, remote-manage kids' checkout at the gate, approve, auto-approve, and pre-invite visitors – delivery persons, workers, maids, drivers, and others – but also rate, profile, and book them. These are some of the many features. Extra features have been added during COVID-19 – displays of a health metre of visitors, or the marking of flats with residents in quarantine.

The vision behind the app that performs more than 15 million validations at the gate per day, according to the chief executive officer (CEO), founder, and former air force pilot, Vijay Arisetty, is to "reduce friction at the gate", "enhance convenience", "seam-lessly connect the external and internal world", and "increase security and eliminate trust deficit" ("Up Close with Vijay Arisetty" 2019). Trust is reduced to a personal trustworthiness rating – thus becoming its opposite: control. By default, nobody can be trusted; everyone must be illuminated through self-exposure or surveillance technologies. The "transparency society" can flip into an inhumane society of control (Han 2015). Ratings, numbers, codes, graphs, charts, and more play a key role in both the management of gated communities, and local and global governance; these numbers legitimize intrusive surveillance and new forms of "social sorting" (Lyon 2003). The utopian promise of apps such as MyGate is a world where "our lives will be increasingly *rateable*, subject to scores, ratings and rankings that pit us against each other for access to social goods" (Susskind 2018, 127, emphasis in original), and where (predictive) algorithms will "determine the terms of access to social goods" (268). When equality before the law disappears and "social sorting" (Lyon 2003) is institutionalized, securitized walls breed the need for bonds of allegiance.

Akbar's *Laila* and its Netflix adaptation as a miniseries by Deepa Mehta (2019) confront us with the securitization and purification of gated communities brought to their logical endpoint: intrusive surveillance is utilized to reinforce social segregation and sorting. The vision is one of a society divided into sectors, protected by walls that keep those within "uncontaminated" and pure – a society permanently threatened by class warfare, identity politics, communitarianism, and violence. Elitism, in which the main character Shalini is complicit, has actively produced this tribalism, to which she herself, as many others, falls victim. The dystopian promise is one of "Purity for All", enforced violently by the all-powerful Council that insists on dividing people in its name. Behavioural conditioning and programming are prevalent: " 'We protect our people from what-all goes on outside', the second guard said. 'Filth in air. In character'. Two fingers of his right hand went across his chest. 'Purity for all' " (Akbar 2017, 36). Gating becomes a way of securitizing morality through discrimination and the inhumane expulsion of all deemed impure, but in *Leila* Akbar reveals this as a shallow form of staged morality, and a mere legitimation strategy for the brutalities of capitalist exploitation and the greed that drives the economy:

> Anyone who can afford it hides behind walls. They think they're doing it for security, for purity, but somewhere inside it's shame, shame at their own greed. How they've made the rest of us live. That's why they're always secluding themselves, going higher and higher. They don't want to see what's on the ground. They don't want to see who lives here. (159)

Even here, the most intriguing element of the novel lurks in the background, the protagonist being simultaneously complicit, impotent, and victimized, and yet still relatively privileged.


## Conclusion: Delirious pandemic governance?

The "war on the virus" has led to the rise of real-time data-driven governance by numbers underpinned by the promises of technosolutionism, while generating new and reinforcing old inequalities, expulsions, and conflict lines, and, with them, new bonds of allegiance. The daily "flows" of real-time data, disconnected news stories, social media outrages, and polarizing messages are increasingly taking on a delirious form. The more we try to control the virus, the more uncontrollable the outcomes and harm resulting from control measures become. Or as Hartmut Rosa (2021) puts it, modernity's "drive and desire toward controllability ultimately creates monstrous, frightening forms of uncontrollability" (ix).

Further expansion of the surveillance and security regime is presented by governments as a trade-off for gradually opening up. The demand is for more regulation, more control, more measures: either we submit ourselves and our data to a regime of intrusive surveillance, or we face endless self-isolation and other "expulsions" (Sassen 2014). The endpoint of this logic is surveillance, segregation, and demonization of those who refuse to comply with the latest rules and dictates which are increasingly built into technological and algorithmic architectures, and issued by a multitude of governmental, private, and hybrid actors. Those who comply secure a relative but likely only temporary freedom, possibly revoked – along with what used to be fundamental human rights – at any moment by a decision informed by the latest predictive model. The endpoint is a delirious form of governance disoriented by "flows" of data, where reason flips into unreason, security into insecurity, and common good into tribalism and expulsions. Basu and Akbar make us experience through the literary power of their novels precisely such a near-future dystopian world. Sensitivity to multiple forms of expulsions, foregrounding the background of these novels raises fundamental questions: are we not sacrificing our privacy, equality, fundamental rights, and liberties on the altar of techno-optimized purity, health, and security? Is the endpoint totalitarian? Do we wish to live in a world where a minority lives hermetically sealed lives in "guarded luxotopias", while the majority suffers injustices, exploitation, violence, and harms? Is this the best world we can imagine?

## Disclosure statement

No potential conflict of interest was reported by the author.

## Funding

This work was funded by the Research Council of Norway under project no. 313626 – *Algorithmic Governance and Cultures of Policing: Comparative Perspectives from Norway, India, Brazil, Russia, and South Africa* (AGOPOL).

## ORCID

Tereza Østbø Kuldova (iD) http://orcid.org/0000-0002-7810-7233

**References**

Akbar, Prayaag. 2017. *Leila.* London: Faber and Faber. (Kindle).

Altenried, Moritz. 2020. "The Platform as Factory: Crowdwork and the Hidden Labour behind Artificial Intelligence." *Capital & Class* 44 (2): 145–158. doi:10.1177/0309816819899410.

Amoore, Louise, and Volha Piotukh. 2016. *Algorithmic Life: Calculative Devices in the Age of Big Data.* London: Routledge.

Anders, Günther. [1958] 2017. "The Obsolescence of Privacy." *CounterText* 3 (1): 20–46. doi:10.3366/count.2017.0073.

Bartoszko, Aleksandra. 2020. "Accelerating Curve of Anxiousness: How a Governmental Quarantine-App Feeds Society with Bugs." *Journal of Extreme Anthropology* 4 (1): E7–E17. doi:10.5617/jea.7861.

Basu, Samit. 2020. *Chosen Spirits.* Faridabad: Simon and Schuster.

Bedi, Aneesha. 2020. "Geo-mapping, CCTV Cameras, AI – How Telangana Police Is Using Tech to Enforce Covis Safety." *The Print*, June 2. https://theprint.in/india/geo-mapping-cctv-cameras -ai-how-telangana-police-is-using-tech-to-enforce-covid-safety/433856/

Besteman, Catherine L. 2020. *Militarized Global Apartheid.* Durham, NC: Duke University Press.

Bhattacharyya, Saurabh. 2014. "The Theme of Dystopia in Indian Fiction in English: An Exploration." *UGC Funded Minor Research Project; Executive Summary of the Final Report.* Kolkata. http://www.cssmberachampa.org/UploadedFiles/156942AExecutive%20Summary% 20MRP%20Saurabh%20Bhattacharyya.pdf

Blakely, Jason. 2020. *We Built Reality: How Social Science Infiltrated Culture, Politics and Power.* Oxford: Oxford University Press.

Chakravorty, Mrinalini. 2015. "Of Dystopias and Deliriums: The Millenian Novel in India." In *A History of the Indian Novel in English*, edited by Ulka Anjaria, 267–281. Cambridge: Cambridge University Press.

Chatak, Lopamudra. 2017. "Urban Ghettos in Delhi and Mumbai are Creating Isolated, Insular Experiences: Prayaag Akbar, Author." *The Economic Times*, April 29. https://economictimes. indiatimes.com/magazines/panache/urban-ghettos-in-delhi-and-mumbai-are-creating-isolated -insular-experiences-prayaag-akbar-author/articleshow/58430844.cms

Choi, Jiyoung, Seunghoon Lee, and Tazim Jamal. 2021. "Smart Korea: Governance for Smart Justice during a Global Pandemic." *Journal of Sustainable Tourism* 29 (2–3): 541–550. doi:10.1080/09669582.2020.1777143.

Cohn, Carol. 1987. "Sex and Death in the Rational World of Defense Intellectuals." *Signs* 12 (4): 687–718. doi:10.1086/494362.

Connolly, Norma. 2020. "COVID Wristbands: How They've Worked in Hong Kong." *Cayman Compass*, September 18. https://www.caymancompass.com/2020/09/18/covid-wristbands-how- theyve-worked-in-hong-kong

Datta, Ayona. 2020. "Self(ie)-governance: Technologies of Intimate Surveillance in India under COVID-19." *Dialogues in Human Geography* 10 (2): 234–237. doi:10.1177/2043820620929797.

Egbert, Simon, and Matthias Leese. 2020. *Criminal Futures: Predictive Policing and Everyday Police Work.* London: Routledge.

Elliott, Robert C. 1963. "The Fear of Utopia." *The Centennial Review* 7 (2): 237–251.

Fisher, Mark. 2009. *Capitalist Realism: Is There No Alternative?* Winchester: Zero Books.

Frischmann, Brett, and Evan Selinger. 2018. *Re-engineering Humanity.* Cambridge: Cambridge University Press.

Gidley, Jennifer M. 2017. *The Future: A Very Short Introduction.* Oxford: Oxford University Press.

Giroux, Henry A. 2015. "Totalitarian Paranoia in the Post-Orwellian Surveillance State." *Cultural Studies* 29 (2): 108–140. doi:10.1080/09502386.2014.917118.

Gould, Matthew, Indra Joshi, and Ming Tang. 2020. "The Power of Data in a Pandemic." *Technology in the NHS Blog, Gov UK*, March 28. https://healthtech.blog.gov.uk/2020/03/28/the- power-of-data-in-a-pandemic/

Han, Byung-Chul. 2015. *The Transparency Society.* Stanford, CA: Stanford University Press.

Hayward, Keith J., and Steve Hall. 2020. "Through Scandinavia, Darkly: A Criminological Critique of Nordic Noir." *The British Journal of Criminology* 61 (1): 1–21. doi:10.1093/bjc/azaa044.

Hummel, Ralph P. 2006. "The Triumph of Numbers: Knowledges and the Mismeasure of Management." *Administration & Society* 38 (1): 58–78. doi:10.1177/0095399705284202.

Huxley, Aldous. 2000. *Brave New World*. New York: RosettaBooks LLC.

Kennedy, Lindsey, and Nathan P. Southern. 2021. "The Pandemic Is Putting Gangsters in Power." *Foreign Policy.com*, February 15. https://foreignpolicy.com/2021/02/15/the-pandemic-is-putting-gangsters-in-power/

Kuldova, Tereza. 2019. *How Outlaws Win Friends and Influence People*. New York: Palgrave Macmillan.

Kuldova, Tereza. 2017. "Guarded Luxotopias and Expulsions in New Delhi: Aesthetics and Ideology of Outer and Inner Spaces of an Urban Utopia." In *Urban Utopias: Excess and Expulsion in Neoliberal South Asia*, edited by Tereza Kuldova and Mathew A. Varghese, 37–52. New York: Palgrave Macmillan.

Lea, John, and Kevin Stenson. 2007. "Security, Sovereignty, and Non-State Governance 'From Below'." *Canadian Journal of Law and Society* 22 (2): 9–27. doi:10.1017/S0829320100009339.

Levi-Faur, David. 2017. "Regulatory Capitalism." In *Regulatory Theory: Foundation and Applications*, edited by Peter Drahos, 289–302. Australia: ANU Press.

Lyon, David. 2003. *Surveillance as Social Sorting: Privacy, Risk and Digital Discrimination*. London: Routledge.

Mathur, Nandita. 2020. "Covid Triggers Spike in Demand for Security Apps for Gated Societies." *Mint*, September. 7. https://www.livemint.com/technology/tech-news/covid-triggers-spike-in-demand-for-security-apps-for-gated-enclaves-11599474698745.html

Mehta, Deepa, Pawan Kumar, and Shanker Raman. 2019. *Leila. Miniseries*. Mumbai and Los Gatos, CA: Open Air Films and Netflix.

Mikkelsen, Henrik Hvenegaard. 2020. "Out of the Ordinary: Monsters as Extreme Cases among Bugkalot and Beyond." *Journal of Extreme Anthropology* 4 (2): 1–19. doi:10.5617/jea.8107.

Moore, Martin, and Damian Tambini, eds. 2018. *Digital Dominance: The Power of Google, Amazon, Facebook, and Apple*. Oxford and New York: Oxford University Press.

Morozov, Evgeny. 2013. *To Save Everything, Click Here*. New York: Public Affairs.

Moylan, Tom. 2000. *Scraps of the Untainted Sky: Science Fiction, Utopia, Dystopia*. Boulder, CO: Westview Press.

Natale, Simone. 2021. *Deceitful Media: Artificial Intelligence and Social Life after the Turing Test*. Oxford: Oxford University Press.

Noble, Safiya Umoja. 2018. *Algorithms of Oppression: How Search Engines Reinforce Racism*. New York: New York University Press.

Norris, Michele L. 2021. "Thanks to COVID-19, the Age of Biometric Surveillance Is Here." *The Washington Post*, March 22. https://www.washingtonpost.com/opinions/thanks-to-covid-19-the-age-of-biometric-surveillance-is-here/2021/03/22/04b24f76-8b24-11eb-a6bd-0eb91c03305a_story.html

O'Neil, Cathy. 2016. *Weapons of Math Destruction: How Big Data Increases Inequality and Threatens Democracy*. New York: Crown.

Østbø, Jardar. 2021. "Hybrid Surveillance Capitalism: Sber's Model for Russia's Modernization." *Post-Soviet Affairs* 37 (5): 435–452. doi:10.1080/1060586X.2021.1966216.

Pasquale, Frank. 2015. *The Black Box Society: The Secret Algorithms that Control Money and Information*. Cambridge, MA: Harvard University Press.

Phelan, Alexandra. 2020. "COVID-19 Immunity Passports and Vaccination Certificates: Scientific, Equitable, and Legal Challenges." *The Lancet* 395 (10237): 1595–1598. doi:10.1016/S0140-6736(20)31034-5.

Pomeranz, Jennifer L., and Aaron R. Schwid. 2021. "Governmental Actions to Address COVID-19 Misinformation." *Journal of Public Health Policy* 42 (2): 201–210. doi:10.1057/s41271-020-00270-x.

Postman, Neil. 1993. *Technopoly: The Surrender of Culture to Technology*. New York: Vintage Books.

Rosa, Hartmut. 2021. *The Uncontrolability of the World*. Cambridge: Polity.

Sassen, Saskia. 2014. *Expulsions: Brutality and Complexity in the Global Economy*. Cambridge, MA: Harvard University Press.

Shi, Lei, Chen Shi, Xun Wu, and Liang Ma. 2021. "Accelerating the Development of Smart City Initiatives Amidst the COVID-19 Pandemic: The Case of Health Code in China". *Journal of Asian Public Policy* 29: 1–18. March. doi:10.1080/17516234.2021.1902078.

Spoelstra, Sverre, Nick Butler, and Helen Delaney. 2020. "Measures of Faith: Science and Belief in Leadership Studies." *Journal of Management Inquiry* 30 (3): 300–311. doi:10.1177/1056492620901793.

Stamp, Elizabeth. 2019. "Billionaire Bunkers: How the 1% are Preparing for the Apocalypse." *CNN Style*. August 7. https://edition.cnn.com/style/article/doomsday-luxury-bunkers/index.html

Strittmatter, Kai. 2020. *We Have Been Harmonised: Life in China's Surveillance State*. Exeter: Old Street Publishing.

Supiot, Alain. 2017. *Governance by Numbers: The Making of a Legal Model of Allegiance*. London: Bloomsbury.

Susskind, Jamie. 2018. *Future Politics: Living Together in a World Transformed by Tech*. Oxford: Oxford University Press.

Thaler, Richard H., and Cass R. Sunstein. 2009. *Nudge: Improving Decisions about Health, Wealth, and Happiness*. London: Penguin Books.

Tiku, Nitasha, and Jay Greene. 2021. "The Billionaire Boom." *The Washington Post*, March 12. https://www.washingtonpost.com/technology/2021/03/12/musk-bezos-zuckerberg-gates-pandemic-profits/

Tsoukas, Haridimos. 1997. "The Tyranny of Light: The Temptations and the Paradoxes of the Information Society." *Futures* 29 (9): 827–843. doi:10.1016/S0016-3287(97)00035-9.

"Up Close with Vijay Arisetty, Founder and CEO of MyGate, India's First Gated Security App." 2019. *Yourstory, YouTube*, November. 20. https://www.youtube.com/watch?v=BWRza0IW6fI&t=636s

Windholz, Eric L. 2020. "Governing in a Pandemic: From Parliamentary Sovereignty to Autocratic Technocracy." *The Theory and Practice of Legislation* 8 (1–2): 93–113. doi:10.1080/20508840.2020.1796047.

Winlow, Simon, Steve Hall, and James Treadwell. 2017. *The Rise of the Right: The English Defense League and the Transformation of Working Class Politics*. Bristol: Polity Press.

Withnall, Adam. 2018. "Cartier Boss with $7.5 Billion Fortune Says Prospect of the Poor Rising up 'Keeps Him Awake at Night'." *The Independent*, March 23. https://www.independent.co.uk/news/business/cartier-boss-7-5bn-fortune-says-prospect-poor-rising-keeps-him-awake-night-10307485.html

World Economic Forum (WEF). 2020b. "This Smart Phone Mask Displays Your Speech as Text on a Phone." October. 1. https://www.weforum.org/videos/19505-a-japanese-robotics-startup-has-invented-a-smart-mask-that-translates-into-eight-languages-uplink

Yeung, Karen. 2017. "'Hypernudge: Big Data as a Mode of Regulation by Design." *Information, Communication & Society* 20 (1): 118–136. doi:10.1080/1369118X.2016.1186713.

Zamyatin, Yevgeny. 1972. *We*. New York: Avon Books.

Žižek, Slavoj. 1989. *The Sublime Object of Ideology*. London: Verso.

Zuboff, Shoshana. 2019. *The Age of Surveillance Capitalism: The Fight for a Human Future at the New Frontier of Power*. London: Profile Books.

# Infection rebellion in Bina Shah's *Before She Sleeps*

Claire Chambers and Freya Lowden

**ABSTRACT**

In her 2018 novel *Before She Sleeps* Bina Shah depicts an oppressive, dystopian society. This has emerged as one consequence of an uncontrollable virus outbreak which resulted in a disproportionate ratio of men to women. In such a gender-imbalanced world intimacy is commodified, allowing women some means of revolt in a misogynistic and fertility-obsessed world. Shah explores the horrifying aftermath of pandemics, identifying opportunities for the emancipation of citizens living under discriminatory policies. As the COVID-19 pandemic causes economic and human devastation across the globe, its repercussions, aside from fatalities, are clear. Entrenched in complexities surrounding employment, political liability, and stretched healthcare systems, the pandemic has challenged society to respond adequately and ethically. Although it predates coronavirus's ravages, we argue that Shah's novel imagines apt spaces for rebellion. Both in her imaginative universe and the wider society, transformative action and liberation are identifiable in the aftermath of infection outbreaks.

## Introduction: Dystopian fiction

Well before the emergence of COVID-19, pandemics had spread through contemporary dystopian writing. Disease outbreaks and their aftermaths are proving an increasingly attractive area for dissection in fiction – a trend that seems set to accelerate. Over a similar time frame of the last 40 years, dystopian fiction itself has been growing rapidly in popularity. Typically, this fiction depicts nightmarish settings, offering up chilling distortions of current realities. We will argue that dystopian fiction, which often depicts devastating disease outbreaks, is instrumental in portraying women and their bodies as subject to cruel structural coercion. Although feminist dystopian fiction paints gender inequality as exacerbated by pandemics, it also envisions the ways in which women rebel against their oppression, finding opportunities for liberation. Through the lens of the COVID-19 pandemic, the issues facing women in dystopian fiction no longer seem premonitions of a distant future or a reflection of past inequality. Instead, COVID-19 has shed light on the idea that the dystopia, and its manifestation in forms of persistent misogyny, is already here.

---

## Women in dystopias

Dystopian fiction often provides the convenient mask of fictive settings and imagined events for authors to articulate their frustrations with current realities. Expressing her own exasperation with Pakistani politics and misogynistic attitudes, in her dystopian novel *Before She Sleeps* (Shah 2018), Bina Shah explores authoritarianism and incessant surveillance, which result in the violent oppression of women. Routinely compared by critics (such as Kirkus 2018; Maguire 2018) to *The Handmaid's Tale* (Atwood 1996) the novel reflects on the unjust limitations which 21st-century women face, just as Margaret Atwood did in 1985. That said, Shah writes about a more recognizable and intersectional world than Atwood's. As the Pakistani author notes (Shah 2017, n.p.), her imaginative universe reflects the everyday lived experience of women in orthodox religious (especially Muslim) communities around the globe.

A country decimated by a contagious, deadly disease is a common trope in much dystopian fiction. Plagues, incurable illnesses, and the fallout of nuclear explosions form the backdrops for many authors' explorations of communities struggling in post-apocalyptic landscapes. Dystopian novels commonly explore two forms of demographic change: overpopulation or population implosion (Domingo 2008, 732). These factors express intertwined fears: of a loss of identity among teeming crowds or of mass deaths. Such desolate and terrifying scene-setting is reminiscent of our present circumstances. Many people have experienced unprecedented precarity due to the COVID-19 pandemic, hit by bereavement, ill health, vast job losses, or shaky future prospects. In her article on reading fiction during the pandemic, Margaret McCartney (2020, 526) notes that dystopian novels harness a similar unpredictability in their depictions of disease. Recent dystopian fiction dramatizes today's confusing cacophony of misinformation and general anxiety, which has engendered a popular malaise and a worldwide sense of distrust in governments.

Written and published before COVID-19, Shah's text appears to prognosticate the current pandemic. The defiance to which women resort in Shah's novel results from the stark gender imbalance caused by the "Virus" she conjures up.[1] Within a foreboding, dark landscape, women are subjected to brutal, restrictive patriarchal control. Authoritarian governments implement unjust policies which subjugate women in the name of society's recovery or to maintain their own totalitarian leadership, rendering half of the population silent. Thanks to its televised adaptation, Atwood's *The Handmaid's Tale* has in recent years become an even better-known example of a feminist dystopian novel. Indeed, *The Handmaid's Tale* and its Netflix adaptation have been harnessed by pressure groups as a means for revolt against misogyny. Women activists in the US and beyond resorted to wearing the red cloaks and white bonnets of the novel's protagonists in their protests during Donald Trump's far-right presidency of 2016–20. *The Handmaid's Tale* provides a base on which feminist dystopian authors can build as they explore/deplore regulated reproduction mandates, which reduce women to objects in systems of capitalist exchange. Such exploitative systems place women's capacity to bear children at the centre of the economy. However, the rise of dystopian fiction should not be misconstrued as only responding to landmark cases in North America such as *Roe vs Wade* and, more recently, Trump's attempt to defund Planned Parenthood. As Nudrat Kamal (2018, n.p.) highlights, South Asia also has a long, well-established tradition of science fiction writing. This spans the oral realm of djinn narratives and *dastangoi* to a later concentration on short stories as a cheap and accessible method of textual storytelling.

Often theorized as the antithesis of utopia, dystopia nevertheless "opens up a space of contestation and opposition" for women and other marginalized groups, according to Raffaella Baccolini (2004, 520). Self-reflexive, resistant dystopian fiction is not intrinsically dismal, instead encouraging the reader to question the status quo. Writing before Baccolini, M. Keith Booker (1994) anticipated her thesis, arguing that dystopia fiction is popular with feminist authors as it is concerned with the fault lines between unorthodox lifestyles and conformism. Citing Aldous Huxley's *Brave New World* and George Orwell's *1984*, Booker shows that sexuality is often a tool of "social control" in dystopian texts (337). He later contends that feminists can appropriate and reclaim dystopia, a genre which as his examples illustrate was long dominated by male authors (348). Expanding on this, Elisabetta Di Minico (2019, 5) establishes a feminist theoretical framework for dystopia, asserting that dystopian governments organize, limit, and subjugate linguistic utterance, places, and people – especially women. She explains that feminist dystopian texts often depict cities created for the use and advantage of men, so that women find themselves on the receiving end of the male gaze, robbed of any autonomy. Of course, not all dystopian fiction concerns women. However, dystopian feminist writers including Naomi Alderman (2016), Ling Ma (2018), Larissa Lai (2018), and Thea Lim (2018) as well as Shah are creating a corpus of intersectional dystopian novels in which women articulate and counter gender inequalities amid crises caused by disease outbreaks.

Shah's (2017, n.p.). early interest in dystopian fiction, like Booker's, was sparked by reading Orwell's *Nineteen Eighty-Four*. However, the classic text's women characters are defined in terms of their passive sexuality (Patai 1984) and *Nineteen Eighty-Four's* focus is Eurocentric. Departing from Orwell's model, Shah recognizes totalitarian control in the "deep-rooted patriarchal traditions" of South Asia, which limit her movement and behaviour (2017, n.p.). Her writing is a form of resistance to pervasive social constraints, shown by the clandestine revolt of the women in her novel who refuse to marry or have children. While much dystopian criticism has drawn connections between dystopia and feminism, less research has focused on the role disease outbreaks play in this relationship. Triangulating the three factors, we argue that dystopian fiction, which regularly poses women's bodies as subject to violent social control, demonstrates how pandemics exacerbate gender inequality. Women become the victims of multiple "viruses", the most virulent of which are physical disease and an infectious social degradation.

This emphasis on gender is not intended to downplay (neo)colonialism, its fallout, or resistance to race and class-based discrimination. From the perspective of Euro-America, while it is true that women (as caregivers, mothers, and workers in service industries, etc.) have been significantly affected by COVID-19, there are more striking racial inequalities manifested by disproportionate death rates among Black, Asian, and Latinx populations. One of us is exploring public health crises and deeply unequal access to vaccines and medical care in forthcoming research (Chambers, forthcoming). However, as this novel is so focused on women's rights, our critical attention is particularly drawn to gender.

Reflecting on suffering in Pakistan, Shah published an essay in December 2020 about Pakistan's response to COVID-19. In the piece, entitled "Déjà Vu in Pakistan", she argued that danger and lockdowns were nothing new for Pakistanis, accustomed as they have been since the nation state's inception to regular army rule, and more recently to terrorist attacks and urban violence. This familiarity with crisis has been both a help and a hindrance for the South Asian country. Pakistanis struggle to contain the virus amid some laudable local community and voluntary initiatives but also show a tendency, "maddening and comforting all at once", to leave everything to God (Shah 2020, n.p.). In an email interview with the authors in March 2021, Shah provided this insightful suggestion:

> There are parallels between how casually Pakistan has treated the pandemic, and how casually and carelessly it treats misogyny and all its manifestations – the gender-based violence, the domestic violence, the rapes and assaults. We do and say all the right things – on paper, or in real life, for a little while. But then attention, money and motivation peter out and we revert back to the status quo: social gatherings, unmasked and undistanced in the case of the pandemic; ignoring or accepting the harm that is done to women in the name of patriarchy. Both are deadly, but while we expect Covid to disappear after a couple of years, the endemic violence against women in our society seems more of a permanent plague. (Shah 2021, n.p.)

This is instructive for our reading of Shah's novel as an exploration of misogyny as a disease. It should not escape our notice, though, that in *Before She Sleeps* men's treatment of both the Virus and women is not casual but rather defined by a deliberately coercive micromanagement.

Shah recognizes in her interviews and essay that the Virus is a figurative rendering of misogyny, which is the real societal sickness gripping nations and regions today. Shah told us that she had been especially influenced by the work of Kate Manne (Shah 2021, n. p.). In *Down Girl: The Logic of Misogyny*, Manne (2018) defines misogyny not as blanket hatred of women by individual men but the control system that has developed to keep women in their place. This system, as Manne explains, includes but is not limited to individual acts of violence:

> My approach to misogyny [ ... ] tries to avoid two extremes that I take to be mistaken here: the first being to think about misogyny as a blight spread by individual "bad apples", and the second being to think about it in terms that are *purely* structural and social, to the exclusion of the distinctively agentic and interpersonal. (Manne 2018, 74; emphasis in original)

The rules and prohibitions that come as a result of the Virus in Shah's novel, amid the near-total wiping out of women and the severe curbing of their reproductive rights, are effects of the control structure. In other words, these deleterious effects on women belong to the larger global system of misogyny which is at once personal and nightmarishly structural.

The synergies between COVID-19 and the novel notwithstanding, in *Before She Sleeps*, Shah is more concerned with what a post-pandemic world might look like, and what social, economic, and political legacies will be left for survivors. Shah explores ways that women can unite to challenge the unequal circumstances imposed upon them. The novel thus encapsulates covert but necessary collective rebellion. By examining Shah's key literary themes, such as sleep and intimacy, fertility and medicalization, and the suffering of women within patriarchal social structures, readers can perhaps better grasp the role of pandemics in a society already diseased by misogyny.

## A diseased society

A significant and recent postcolonial dystopian novel, Shah's *Before She Sleeps* is set in and around the semi-autonomous Green City. This city is located in a southwest Asian country that shares some of its topological and climactic features with Muscat in Oman, the United Arab Emirates (UAE), and rich cities of the Gulf such as Saudi Arabia's Riyadh. The so-called Green City is in fact desert territory, whose corniche (similar to that found in Abu Dhabi) is frequently buffeted by sandstorms. Originally called Mazun, meaning "permission", the fictional metropolis was built around a grid system. Here initiatives such as Plant Your Future, a tree cultivation programme which parallels the UAE's One Million Trees scheme, seek to reclaim verdure in a parched land. Explaining the conscious infusion of Green City and the wider fictional country with geographical elements from the Gulf region and social aspects from Pakistan, Shah (2021, n.p.) told us that over the last five decades Pakistani women began to be treated poorly in emulation of Gulf practices. The rights of women in Saudi Arabia, the UAE, Qatar, and Kuwait were severely restricted in the 1970s and 1980s. When Pakistani workers, both middle- and working-class labourers, went to work in the Gulf during that period's oil boom, they saw Arab women being segregated and made to wear veils. Many of these male migrants were impressed, and imported these values and ideals back to Pakistan (Waterman 2014). In an instance of the "invention of tradition" (Hobsbawm and Ranger 2014), this was the time when some Pakistani women began wearing black abayas, niqabs, and other garments associated with Gulf women.

In the 1980s, the Pakistani President Zia-ul-Haq was notorious for his edict "Chador aur char diwari", prescribing for women a veil and the four walls of the house. Zia's slogan derived from the teachings of the South Asian purist Abul A'la Mawdudi (1903–79), who himself had been influenced by these ways of thinking from frequent trips to Saudi Arabia. This importing of how women should be treated had not previously been characteristic of Sufistic Pakistan. Before that, such sequestration was unusual, reserved for Sayed families and other upper-class women of Muslim South Asia. Shah submits that such restrictions on women should be considered "a virus that jumped national borders, thanks to air travel and globalization, and came to infect the Pakistani psyche" (2021, n.p.). Once again, misogyny is positioned as an infection: unseen, contagious, mutable, and hard to recover from. Shah subverts the well-worn, damaging military tropes associating disease with war (Sontag 1977), twisting such imagery to expose women's unequal status.

The veil has long been contested in Muslim feminist debate (Ahmed 2012; Babar 2017, 42–75; Tarlo 2010). Yet just as chadors and niqabs can enable women to leave their houses under cover, so too the women in Shah's novel cloak themselves with the glittery veil-like substance of "gold silicon powder" to evade surveillance (2018, 7). This allows them to roam outside their refuge, secretly carrying out activities in a hostile cityscape. Veils are frequently referenced, with Lin, the leader of a women's rebel group, appearing "spectral and shapeless in her full black veil" (131). The veil of Sabine, the novel's most pivotal character, lies abandoned on the pavement when she is transported in an unconscious state to a hospital (137). Veiling not only adds to the women's secrecy but suggests the power they retain in choosing who can see them and when.

Gender inequality is inscribed into Shah's disease-ridden fiction world. For all its opulence and glittering skylines, Green City's gender politics are germane to the present-day Pakistani nation state. Shah's imaginary country is war-weakened, 50 years after a nuclear winter cast its chill across the region. In the wake of atomic detonation, a human papillomavirus has decimated the female population via a new strain of cervical cancer. The mutation Shah envisages has selectively killed off most women, leaving men untouched. Polyandric marriages are imposed to rebalance Green City's precariously lopsided gender ratio. To bolster the population count, the government has introduced legislation which assigns multiple "Husbands" to one woman. These "Wives" are pumped full of hormones and forced to have the maximum possible number of children, echoing the Nazis' Lebensborn programme, Ceausescu regime's pronatalist policies, and the violent enforcement of China's one-child policy, among other real-world examples.

Green City's men behave as if they are the ones suffering to protect women: "They had been noble enough to make the sacrifice of sharing wives" (Shah 2018, 167). Meanwhile, they wink at the terrible mistreatment of women as they control and enforce degrading reproductive policies. The polyandry system suppresses monogamy and sexual jealousy. Substituting intimate human relationships with clinical multiperson households, it ultimately encourages men's violent, degrading behaviour. As an example of this, Reuben Faro, the wealthy and powerful man Lin is intimate with and relies upon, is described as having some level of humanity: "Faro was no monster, he was a man trapped in a life that promised him absolute power but in return had stripped him of everything good and honourable" (234). Reuben has exchanged his softer side for a life of power and privilege, thus indicating the detrimental impact of Green City's regime on men as well as women. At the end of the novel, Sabine explains that Green City, and not the men within it, is the real monster (246). In *Down Girl*, Manne (2018, 211–212) debunks the idea that rapists are monstrous with reference to Hannah Arendt's (1958) notion of the banality of evil. Similarly, Shah portrays a hackneyed society that is nonetheless capable of causing great pain, corrupting men and leaving women passive and victimized.

Some of the novel's women and girls independently mutiny against the legislated system of childbirth, seeking shelter in a hidden sanctuary for defiant women. This subterranean society is called the Panah, a noun for "refuge" in Urdu (itself a loanword from Persian). It had been founded by Fairuza Dastani and her best friend the enigmatic Ilona Serfati, whose voice notes punctuate the narrative in an instance of e-epistolarity (Jolly 2011, 158). Following first Fairuza's and then Ilona's deaths, the Panah is led by Ilona's niece Lin. Lin helps those women who have escaped from enforced polyandry to live an underground life. They earn money by furnishing government officials like Faro with non-sexual intimacy, furtively spending whole nights simply holding them. They therefore survive off the grid by providing comfort without sex to men of power.

However, the women's secret emancipation in Shah's text hinges on their becoming products in yet another exploitative system. If they submitted to the authorities their lives would revolve around procreation, but in the Panah they are used by men to provide a lost intimacy. Clients sign contracts to affirm that they will only go to the Panah's women for help with sleep and not for sex. In parallel, the women are forbidden to indulge in alcohol or narcotics that might be a conduit to their seduction. Despite this business-like arrangement, they are often prey to the men's sexual advances. Indeed, Sabine is impregnated during her rape when in a drugged stupor. It therefore becomes clear that with its rigid system and secrets, the Panah is almost as repressive as the government of Green City. What is more, even women like Ilona and Lin who set out to create an escape from oppression eventually foment hierarchical oppression.

The novel dramatizes the unassailable spread of infection, which causes the outbreak of stringent misogynistic policies to render women victims both to the pandemic and a patriarchal government. Shah writes presciently of three waves in the collapse of global society, which pre-empt the devastating restrictions placed on her novel's female characters:

> The first wave came from the east. The middle of the twenty-first century saw devastating climate change in South Asia, bringing floods and unprecedented torrential rain for months on end.
>
> The shock waves juddered both eastward and west, claiming not just lives, but also millions of acres of arable land and drinkable water. The second wave destabilized the economies of all the countries in the region, shutting down major trade routes that stretched from China to Europe, as if a part of the world was simply amputated from existence.
>
> Every student knew what the third wave was, hearing about it straight from the mouths of their parents and grandparents, when the women [ ... ] began to die. (2018, 123–124)

This account is timely given the climate emergency, ongoing disruption to trade, and infection-related deaths around the world. Women have been adversely affected on all three fronts. First, they are vulnerable to climate change, being more likely than their male counterparts to live in poverty or reside in places badly affected by natural disasters (*ActionAid* 2021, n.p.). Second, they have a good chance of being impeded by trade disruption, as sectors in which women work have experienced worse effects from the pandemic (World Trade Organization [WTO] 2020, 1). Finally, restricted access to sexual and reproductive health services because of pressures on hospitals during the pandemic have left women lacking the necessary health services (United Nations [UN] Women 2020, 2). The ongoing challenges facing women as a result of COVID-19 are not about to dissipate, as new waves and strains continue. Shah's diction also intentionally evokes feminism's three waves. In the west these comprised the suffrage movement, followed by the so-called women's liberation and post-feminist movements. In Pakistan they were the immediate post-Partition women's movement; Zia-ul-Haq's dictatorship countered by the Women's Action Forum; and the present digital-activist wave.

The Virus in *Before She Sleeps* arrives in the wake of multiple wars. Noxious and life-threatening, this contagion damages people's respiratory systems and curtails the lifespan of unborn children (Shah 2018, 34). Shah's description of citizens "emerg[ing] like ants out of [ ... ] subterranean sanctuaries" (34) into their war-scarred homes is evocative today as populations surface from multiple lockdowns into a different world, facing crumbling economies, grieving families, and struggling education systems. Later, Shah describes the chaos wreaked by the Virus. Riots tear up the streets, and cases of murder and suicide are on the rise.

Shah shines a light on how an infection's killing spree can make human death a matter of practical nonchalance. In quarantine situations, the novel's dead bodies are disposed of by dousing them in liquid nitrogen. Despite his position as a junior doctor, the male protagonist Julien blanches at the thought of his own cadaver eventually being dissolved, since "the idea of being irreversibly turned into powder made [him] shudder" (Shah 2018, 189). This recalls Zygmunt Bauman's (2004) discussion of global capitalism's emphasis on surplus and disposability that gives rise to vast numbers of "wasted humans" (5). The bodies that litter the pages of *Before She Sleeps* are made abject – in Julia Kristeva's (1982) sense of a struggle with "a threat that seems to emanate from an exorbitant outside or inside, ejected beyond the scope of the [ ... ] tolerable" (1) – being thrown like rubbish onto heaps. The treatment of bodies during the pandemic was not dissimilar, and in April 2021 corpses were cremated, without the presence of mourners, on mass pyres in terrible scenes from Pakistan's neighbour India. Amid the terror caused by disease, memories, family ties, and personal dignity are all discarded.

Such fear and degradation also seem infectious, spreading like "tentacles" into Green City (Shah 2018, 35). The Gender Emergency, prompting the restrictive legislation which some of the novel's women try to escape, is greeted with urgency and panic. Women become an "endangered species" (35), this image associated with the animal kingdom fixing women as objects for scrutiny and safeguarding in Green City's regime. The Virus thus legitimates the Perpetuation Bureau's emphasis on marital fidelity. Because of women's vulnerability if infected, would-be husbands are tested for the Virus before being allowed to marry them. Men were originally complicit in passing on the Virus to their Wives, but are reluctant to recognize this history. Still, in a post-Virus society, adultery's potentially harmful consequences for their Wives is enough to make "ordinary men fearful enough to respect the boundaries of marriage" (186). This so-called respect leads the city's men to bestow on woman the responsibility "to bring an entire nation back to life" (35). What this apparent idealization really denotes is oppression and the cloistering of women within a harsh and constraining governmental regime.

## Pandemics and inequality

The devastating effects of COVID-19 have been seen on a global scale. However, the impact of the virus has been experienced very differently according to a country's geographical position, its government's preparedness, and the political conditions and existing healthcare. In *Ten Lessons for a Post-Pandemic World*, Fareed Zakaria (2020) calls for "investing more time, resources, and energy toward stopping" present and future pandemics (8). Akhtar Sherin (2020), in a study of Pakistan's response to the COVID-19 outbreak, stresses the Islamic Republic's proximity to countries that experienced high virus-related death rates in the early phase, namely China and Iran (79). Shah's Green City is similarly part of a network of countries which were previously ravaged by the fictional pandemic. However, Green City is "encircled by desert" (Shah 2018, 12), and is thus one of the few places in the novel that survived the climate emergency and consequent disease outbreak. As people emerge from protective bunkers, women enter a new kind of isolation imposed by the city's authorities. These leaders make Green City a cocoon of restrictive legislation which supposedly protects the people living there. Also looking inwards to protect itself, Pakistan closed its borders soon into the pandemic, with initial positive effects. Nevertheless, Sherin highlights how a lack of scientific awareness and an openness among ordinary Pakistanis to myth-spreading and conspiracy theories soon became detrimental to the country's handling of the outbreak. Furthermore, he suggests that a widespread and understandable lack of faith in the government has made it difficult to enforce social distancing or other necessary measures, culminating in a dramatic rise of COVID-19 cases across Pakistan in summer 2020 (Sherin 2020, 79). Green City is a harbinger of the turbulent response to the pandemic. At first the West Asian country's designated capital is celebrated as a natural, luscious ecosphere (Shah 2018, 13). However, wars give an excuse for turning the city into a "police state" (35). Despite the metropolis's initially positive rejuvenation (like Pakistan's initial suppression of the virus's spread through protective measures), the fictional city state descends into a fearful, oppressive, and corrupt dystopia.

Meanwhile, Shah's fictional society seems to function well, as it is "blessed" with the "great responsibility" of leading the newly founded region in which it sits (Shah 2018, 34). Motivational political slogans interpellate women as a "precious resource" (167). Female subjects are nonetheless most at risk in the power dynamic where they carry much more than their share of the burden to help society recover. Women are invited to sacrifice themselves for the cause of social revivification: "if you willingly give your bodies to us in trust, we are honor-bound to return your trust a thousandfold" (93). However, just as Imran Khan's seemingly progressive leadership functions as is a smokescreen for repression and misogyny in Pakistan (Singh 2018, n.p.), Green City's patriotic overtones are tinged with threat. Any women who dare to rebel against the new rules will be imprisoned or executed. Since high birth rates are seen as the key to Green City's recovery, rebellious women are painted as a "malignancy" (42), a cancerous growth in an otherwise orderly and healthy society.

As Green City is dysfunctional underneath its veneer of stability, so too Pakistan's government has long been accused of fostering dystopia. A semi-visible reliance on constrictive legislation and military machinations has lent the state authoritarian undercurrents since its inception. Pakistan is notoriously dangerous for its politicians and journalists. The murders of premiers including Liaquat Ali Khan (in 1951), Zulfikar Ali Bhutto (1979), and Benazir Bhutto (2007) are well known. Tending to oscillate between elected governments and army rule, whoever has taken power in the Islamic Republic over the last 40 years has sought to quash criticism. Successive leaders have thus helped to drag Pakistan into what Saad Hafiz (2012) calls "a dystopian era" (n.p.).

The dystopian censorship encouraged by recent political leaders is replicated in Shah's novel, within which women are "bowed down, shrunken and meek" (2018, 23). Fearing reprisals, they are too afraid to speak out against their oppression. For instance, early in the novel a dead woman is described animalistically, her "arms and legs splayed in grotesque angles, blood pooling around her body, trapping her like an insect in a circle of red amber" (11). While the authorities attribute her death to suicide, reporting of her violent death is intended by the Bureau to show what happens "when human nature isn't contained" (12). The victim is depicted as a criminal, her Husbands and children being compensated for experiencing such tragedy. They are given a new Wife to take the deceased one's place, women being replaceable like products bought, sold, and exchanged. The authorities thus send out the sinister message that without leadership and guidance, people fall astray, leading to violence and societal turmoil.

## Women and sleep

At the heart of Shah's text, sleep is a source of frustration, dissent, and even revolt for many of the female characters. Shah identifies slumber as a flashpoint issue when it comes to the infectious rebellion of her female protagonists. The Panah's women hire out "a type of contact and comfort", which had been prohibited ever since the Virus's spread, when they sleep alongside their Clients (Shah 2018, 158). Yet one of their most popular members, Sabine, suffers from debilitating insomnia and cannot sleep. Even so, she and her colleagues give wealthy men nocturnal but chaste company to fund the Panah's social reclusion. In a world where sex is supervised, Shah indicates, oneiric embraces and the possibility of love are hot properties. Their semi-innocent bed-sharing contrasts with the hormone-fuelled multiple marriages and procreation imposed by the controlling leadership.

Insomnia is a psychophysiological affliction, and thus as an insomniac Sabine might be seen as having a disability. Indeed, because of her chronic insomnia, Sabine calls herself "Morpheus" as if she were a dreamlike apparition (Shah 2018, 14). She often refers to her sleeplessness as a "lifetime's curse" which incessantly plagues her (5). The other Panah women wish to relieve Sabine from the insomnia which she wears "like penitence; guilt over her mother's suicide lingered like poison in her blood" (46). Sabine's damaged past, her mother's death, and her own escape from one repressive society into another make her life seem diseased. The stigmata of her suffering prevent her from surrendering to the refuge and renewal of sleep. And yet her insomnia also makes Sabine even more of a rebel. Under the cover of darkness, secretive and intimate activities take place. This allows the Panah's women in general and Sabine in particular to regain vestiges of an independence which has been stymied by their repressive society. Sabine transforms her sleep disorder into a "weapon of the weak" (Scott 1987), remaining wakeful and sometimes turning the tables on the usually watchful men in power.

Sleep has been a disruptive influence during COVID-19, which has impacted negatively upon many people's circadian rhythms. Women's sleep cycles have been worse affected than men's (Pérez-Carbonell et al. 2020, 172). Laura Pérez-Carbonell et al. suggest that sleep disorders during the pandemic have caused increased anxiety, stress, and depression. Their research participants, especially the women, attested to a change to waking times and sleeping rhythms, as they experienced worse sleep overall. Hence, the authors drew the conclusion that sleep disorders have increased throughout the pandemic, with insomnia and nightmares heightened as symptoms of a virus-incited trauma.

In the novel, too, via Julien the doctor's musings, Shah links Sabine's chronic insomnia to hypervigilance. Shah thereby portrays Sabine's fight against a restrictive and punitive society as causing her symptoms similar to soldiers experiencing post-traumatic stress disorder in war's aftermath. Sleep is, moreover, a site of stress and anxiety, with the novel often linking it to violence. For example, Sabine is raped while she is unconscious after unwittingly ingesting an anti-insomnia drug with the telling name of Sleep. Rape is a violation which she compares to a burglary committed under cover of darkness: "I may have fallen asleep long enough for one of them to steal his act of sex from my body. That makes him a thief, not just a rapist" (Shah 2018, 151). Sleep may be prohibited or stolen, and under a drug-induced sleep the worst crimes can occur. Yet rest is also something valuable, as a source of recovery, comfort, and escape. The description of sleep enabling a thief to steal from Sabine shows how Shah often treats sleep like a commodity. For example, Sabine says a deep, unbroken sleep feels "wrong, as if I've stolen it from someone, and now I'm probably going to pay" (84). Sleep is presented, therefore, as a valuable resource, just as the women themselves are products circulating in a capitalist service industry.

Although in relation to her rape Sabine might seem an unwitting victim, the women arguably retain some agency. They can control their own behaviour with a level of decision-making as to who they work for and when. Clients necessarily become vulnerable during their time together with the Panah's women, underscoring the inherent fragility associated with a person's lack of consciousness during sleep. Usually commanding men become temporarily dependent on the women, reversing the power dynamic that is in play for much of the narrative. As a source of rebellion, rest also connotes secrecy. The Panah is located in the darkness of the underground, giving the women a "twilight life" (45). Night-time can therefore prove liberating, furnishing a much-needed cover for these marginalized figures.

## Women and rebellion

Shah limns social rebellion as liberating some victims of a diseased society, which has become increasingly isolationist and exclusionary following a pandemic. The women in the Panah refuse to submit to political corruption. Their reluctance slowly seeps out into virtual networks as they encourage other girls to follow them. They rebel against the experiments on their bodies, refusing to act as compliant "incubators" (Shah 2018, 63) within a fertility-obsessed patriarchal society. Sabine had spent years imagining her mother's traumatic inability to conceive more children, calling her a "martyr to infertility" (113). Eventually she realizes that her trailblazing mother faked her barrenness to create a nuclear family. At the time, psychological counsellors reported that her mother, driven by mental ill health, had made an "impulsive, impetuous decision" to kill herself (114). But Shah implies that Sabine's mother didn't really kill herself but was instead "eliminated" by the authorities because she refused to take another Husband. The mother had rebelled against patriarchal policies, which are grounded on women's subordination as an "essential" precondition for reconstructing the society ravaged by a woman-killing Virus.

The women in the Panah start their non-compliance from a young age. Seeking out ways to evade their parents' watchful gaze, they "resorted to things that had become almost obsolete; scrawled notes dropped in places only girls would search" (Shah 2018, 21). Gestures of subtle and overt insurgence are evident, from Sabine's ripping of toilet paper in a hospital's bathroom (148) to Lin's declaration on first meeting Reuben that "I refuse to be part of your system" (135). Acts of rebellion are fostered in youth. Some young girls grow up to join the Panah, stubbornly refusing to be chattels in an exploitative system. Early on, from Sabine's focalization, readers are told: "We do not consent to their conspiracy, first to decimate us, then to distribute those of us who remain [ … ] as if we were cattle or food" (12). The women's rebellion puts them in constant danger from the authorities, who threaten renegades with strict punishment or "elimination" (35). Yet their dissension also creates a fragile sanctuary where the women can form strong bonds.

In her voice notes for Lin, Ilona criticizes "the prison of their so-called peace and security" most of Green City's denizens choose to remain in, commenting on the hypocrisy that if caught, "it's the Wives who would shout for our execution the loudest. We pay for their complacency, for the complicity of both men and women in a system that is as unjust as it is unnatural" (Shah 2018, 36). In an instance of what Deniz Kandiyoti (1988, 274) calls the patriarchal bargain, this society has encouraged women to internalize the rhetoric that they are irreplaceable objects of fertility for the recovery of post-pandemic Green City. Lin describes Green City's women as "winsome puppets" who attest to "the happiness and success of their blended families" through "breathless, saccharine testimonials to the perfection of life in Green City" (Shah 2018, 170). The women moulded by the Bureau to reinforce its policies' value are powerless marionettes. The patriarchal voice is ventriloquized through them, and they are controlled not only by their Husbands but also the city's leadership.

The Panah's women, by contrast, forego any hope of security. Instead, they revel in small moments of solidarity, autonomy, and power, seldom enjoyed by women outside their community. However, even the Panah has extremely strict and limiting rules. Rupa, a sensual and sceptical member of the Panah, regards these laws with disgust. She thinks scornfully that the other women in the refuge have "swallowed all the restrictions and the secrecy without question. The rules have become a part of their bodies, clinging as leeches do to their flesh" (Shah 2018, 50). She pushes against the Panah's regulations through small acts of rebellion like flouting its dress code by wearing a nose pin and larger ones such as having a sexual relationship with a Client. The latter she must keep secret for fear of censure and punishment. Even within the Panah's secretive sanctuary, it remains debatable whether the women are free at all.

Comparably, during COVID-19 stringent rules have protected many citizens against the spread but simultaneously raised questions over how far personal liberties should be curtailed. These rules have proved controversial, as lockdowns endanger the economy and separate families. The reverse, however, could be much worse, as early relaxation of restrictions results in spikes in deaths and hospital admissions. However, the social restrictions imposed in 2020 and 2021 have exposed the fragility of many women's social and economic stability since more women than men have caring responsibilities or face financial precarity at home (Berkhout and Richardson 2020).

One of Green City's initiatives, aimed at stabilizing and strengthening its society, deems pregnancy indispensable to society's survival. Pregnant women are "treated with the reverence assigned to only the most complicated, challenging diseases" (Shah 2018, 97), handled with extreme caution and care due to the need for children to bolster the population. Contrastingly, COVID-19 measures have resulted in a media focus on pregnancy being undervalued, with women sharing their experiences of giving birth with limited support. Furthermore, women have expressed anger over IVF treatments being delayed, evidencing growing levels of perinatal depression and anxiety. In Pakistan and elsewhere, during the pandemic women have faced not only threats to their reproductive rights but also other dangers. These first attach to their maternal health and second relate to a repressive and sometimes violent domestic sphere. Baig, Ali, and Tunio (2020) state that both physical and sexual abuse can be common in Pakistani marriages, as abuse is "considered a private family matter" and thus not often prosecuted (525). The COVID-19 lockdown measures, which have increased the amount of time people spend at home, mean that women in Pakistan and across the globe face "a lethal virus outdoors and abusers at home" (525). This is similar to how Shah's characters confront both the aftermath of physical disease and a debilitating, diseased social order. Demonstrating the threatening environment facing women, seen both in Shah's text and in its context, Baig, Ali, and Tunio give the sobering statistic that there were 399 women murdered in domestic cases in Khyber Pakhtunkhwa, the northwest Pakistani province, after the first lockdown was announced in March 2020. Despite this high number, only a few calls were made to the relevant authorities (525). Moreover, as Abdullah Sarwer et al. (2020, 1307) highlight, gynaecology and obstetrics have become health services of secondary importance during the pandemic in Pakistan. This gives both maternal and infant mortality rates the potential to increase, with an especially detrimental impact on rural communities that lack sufficient access to healthcare facilities such as hospitals.

Analysing the way political leadership often revolves around women and their bodies, Aneela Zeb Babar draws on multiple examples of famed Pakistani women to paint a picture of both gendered oppression in Pakistan and feminist resistance to it. There are tensions between women who oppose gender discrimination and those who endorse a tightening of Shariah law (Babar 2017, 2–3). One example of the latter is Apa Nisar Fatima, a religious scholar who campaigned for "the state to curb her personal liberties and those of fellow Pakistani women as they were vulnerable to temptation and vice" (4–5). By contrast, Benazir Bhutto, the slain former prime minister, became the first world leader to give birth while in power and defied narrow conceptions of decorous female behaviour. These two Pakistani women embody a dual aspect to constructions of femininity, encompassing traits in opposition to one another: passive and active, weak and strong, obedient and rebellious. These dichotomies are often personified in Shah's novel through her different women characters. For instance, Sabine's quiet gratitude to the Panah contrasts with Rupa's rebellious spirit, and Lin's fortitude opposes the sad passivity of many of Green City's women. Through polarities, Shah shows how women's bodies, manipulated and coerced in the novel, are subject to constant political (mis)interpretation.

Despite the disturbing landscape of contemporary South Asian politics, explored in an upsurge in dystopian texts, there are signs of positive advances which resonate with Shah's protagonists' courageous rebellion. These are reflected in the hopeful ending of her novel, which seems to allow her protagonists an escape from violence and oppression. As Sabine contemplates finally escaping Green City, she suggests that her last word should be sorry. "I have broken every rule", she admits, "transgressed every limit" (Shah 2018, 246). Sabine feels the urge to apologize, as she has been conditioned to obey strict rules to keep the Panah's dangerous secrets. Nevertheless, she drives the ambulance in which she and an unconscious Julien escape at speed towards the Semitia Border. Sabine is determined to be imprisoned no longer by either the Panah's subterranean precarity or her current fugitive status, thinking: "I've had enough of cages" (246). This final act of rebellion secures Sabine and Julien their freedom, and it is executed by the woman while her man lies asleep. Therefore, despite its dystopian framework, Shah's novel offers hope for its protagonists' future, as Sabine finally breaks away from the violence and oppression she previously faced.

Arguably, Shah's women rebels have fled a world in which most people bury themselves in legacies of hatred and accept the violent imposition of oppressive restrictions. However, in the Panah these women gravitate towards seeking new avenues for dissent and creating a sanctuary in which they find some measure of liberation even as they construct new hierarchies.

## Conclusion

Shah's novel explores the residues of rampant disease, exposing durable negative aftershocks for women within the affected populations. In particular, it pinpoints sleep as a source of defiance, illness, and anxiety, making night-time a focal point. Even after the Virus has diminished and reality has started to return, Green City society remains diseased, its flaws on display like a patient on the operating table. As a symptom of this ongoing disease, women's fertility is maximized and manipulated, forcing the novel's female characters to seek furtive passages towards autonomy. Our present pandemic, similarly, is encouraging micromanagement, corruption, and inequalities to proliferate. COVID-19 is reversing women's hard-won rights because of the types of service work, caring responsibilities, and emotional labour women tend to shoulder (Chambers and Gilmour 2020; Preskey, Gallagher, and Hall 2021). Fitting its dystopian genre, the novel warns that unless we act soon, the pandemic's afterlife will be post-apocalyptic. Even when the virus has long disappeared, we may be left with systemic oppression, intrusion, and inequality infecting society at its heart.

## Note

1. Throughout this article, the capitalization of words such as "Virus", "Wives", "Husbands", and "Clients" follows the conventions of the novel. In *Before She Sleeps*, Shah draws attention to her dystopian storyworld's unusual social relations by using capital letters. References to "Husbands" and "Wives" indicates the importance Green City accords to polyandry (just as the countercultural Panah gives "Clients" primacy), while the "Virus" indicates this contagion's potency as well as its metaphorical aspect.

## Disclosure statement

No potential conflict of interest was reported by the authors.

## References

ActionAid. 2021. "Climate Change and Gender." *ActionAid*, 17 November. Accessed 19 January 2022. https://www.actionaid.org.uk/our-work/emergencies-disasters-humanitarian-response/climate-change-and-gender

Ahmed, Leila. 2012. *A Quiet Revolution: The Veil's Resurgence, from the Middle East to America.* New Haven, CT: Yale University Press.

Alderman, Naomi. 2016. *The Power.* London: Viking.

Arendt, Hannah. 1958. *The Origins of Totalitarianism.* New York: Meridian Books.

Atwood, Margaret. 1996 *The Handmaid's Tale.* London: Vintage.

Babar, Aneela Zeb. 2017. *We are All Revolutionaries Here: Militarism, Political Islam and Gender in Pakistan.* Los Angeles: SAGE.

Baccolini, Raffaella. 2004. "The Persistence of Hope in Dystopian Science Fiction." *PMLA* 119 (3): 518–521.

Baig, Mirza Altamish Muhammad, S. Ali, and N. A. Tunio. 2020. "Domestic Violence Amid COVID-19 Pandemic: Pakistan's Perspective." *Asia Pacific Journal of Public Health* 32 (8): 525–526. doi:10.1177/1010539520962965.

Bauman, Zygmunt. 2004. *Wasted Lives: Modernity and Its Outcasts.* Oxford: Polity.

Berkhout, Suze G., and Lisa Richardson 2020. "Why Is COVID-19 a Disaster for Feminism(s)?" *History and Philosophy of the Life Sciences* 42 (4): 1-6.

Booker, M. Keith. 1994."Women on the Edge of a Genre: The Feminist Dystopias of Marge Piercy." *Science Fiction Studies* 21 (3): 337–350.

Chambers, Claire. Forthcoming. *Decoronial Writing: Pandemics, Public Health, Prose.* Albany, NY: Liverpool University Press (under contract).

Chambers, Claire, and Rachael Gilmour. 2020. "Covid's Metamorphoses." *Journal of Commonwealth Literature* 55 (2): 139–143. doi:10.1177/0021989420933703.

Domingo, Andreu. 2008. "'Demodystopias': Prospects of Demographic Hell." *Population and Development Review* 34 (4): 725745. doi:10.1111/j.1728-4457.2008.00248.x.

Hafiz, Saad. 2012. "Is Pakistan Descending into Dystopia?" *NewAgeIslam.com: Islam and Politics.* Accessed 20 January 2021. https://www.newageislam.com/islam-and-politics/by-saad-hafiz/is-pakistan-descending-into-dystopia/d/8078

Hobsbawm, Eric, and Terence Ranger, eds. 2014. *The Invention of Tradition.* Cambridge: Cambridge University Press.

Jolly, Margaretta. 2011. "Lamenting the Letter and the Truth about Email." *Life Writing* 8 (2): 153–167. doi:10.1080/14484528.2011.554162.

Kamal, Nudrat. 2018. "Fiction: Building the Walls." *Dawn*, October 28. Accessed 21 January 2021. https://www.dawn.com/news/1441854

Kandiyoti, Deniz. 1988. "Bargaining with Patriarchy." *Gender and Society* 2 (3): 274–290. doi:10.1177/089124388002003004.

Kirkus Reviews. 2018. "Shah, Bina. *Before She Sleeps.*" *Kirkus Reviews*, June1. Accessed 17 January 2022. https://www.kirkusreviews.com/book-reviews/bina-shah/before-she-sleeps/

Kristeva, Julia. 1982. *Powers of Horror: An Essay on Abjection.* Translated by Leon S. Roudiez. New York: Columbia University Press.

Lai, Larissa. 2018. *The Tiger Flu.* Vancouver: Arsenal Pulp Press.

Lim, Thea. 2018. *An Ocean of Minutes.* London: Quercus.

Ling, Ma. 2018. *Severance*. New York: Macmillan.

Maguire, Susan. 2018. "*Before She Sleeps*. By Bina Shah." *Booklist* 114 (21): 14.

Manne, Kate. 2018. *Down Girl: The Logic of Misogyny*. New York: Oxford University Press.

McCartney, Margaret. 2020. "The Art of Medicine: Pandemics Past and Dystopian Futures." *The Lancet: Perspectives* 396 (10250): 526–527.

Minico, Elisabetta Di. 2019. "Spatial and Psychophysical Domination of Women in Dystopia: *Swastika Night, Woman on the Edge of Time and The Handmaid's Tale*." *Humanities* 8 (1): 1–15. doi:10.3390/h8010038.

Patai, Daphne. 1984. *The Orwell Mystique: A Study in Male Ideology*. Amherst, MA: University of Massachusetts Press.

Pérez-Carbonell, Laura, Imran Johan Meurling, Danielle Wassermann, Valentina Gnoni, Guy Leschziner, Anna Weighall, Jason Ellis, Simon Durrant, Alanna Hare, and Joerg Steier. 2020. "Impact of the Novel Coronavirus (COVID-19) Pandemic on Sleep." *Journal of Thoracic Disease* 12 (2): 163–175. doi:10.21037/jtd-cus-2020-015.

Preskey, Natasha, Sophie Gallagher, and Harriet Hall. 2021. "The Pandemic of Inequality: How Coronavirus Is Setting Women's Rights Back Decades." *The Independent*, March 5. Accessed 1 April 2021. https://www.independent.co.uk/life-style/women/coronavirus-womens-rights-pandemic-b1813019.html

Sarwer, Abdullah, Bilal Javed, Erik B. Soto, and Zia-ur-Rehman Mashwani. 2020. "Impact of the COVID-19 Pandemic on Maternal Health Services in Pakistan." *The International Journal of Health Planning and Management* 35 (6): 1306–1310. doi:10.1002/hpm.3048.

Scott, James C. 1987. *Weapons of the Weak: Everyday Forms of Peasant Resistance*. New Haven, CT: Yale University Press.

Shah, Bina. 2017. "How I Came to Write a Dystopian Novel about Life in South Asia." *Delphinium Books*, June 23. Accessed 18 January 2021. https://www.delphiniumbooks.com/came-write-dystopian-novel-life-south-asia/

Shah, Bina. 2018. *Before She Sleeps*. Santa Monica, CA: Delphinium Books.

Shah, Bina. 2020. "Déjà Vu in Pakistan." *Noēma*, December 1. Accessed 1 April 2021. https://www.noemamag.com/deja-vu-in-pakistan/

Shah, Bina. 2021. *Email Interview with the Authors*, March 29.

Sherin, Akhtar. 2020. "Preparedness and Response of Pakistan for Coronavirus Disease 2019: Gaps and Challenges." *KUST Medical Journal* 12 (2): 79–80.

Singh, Malvika. 2018. "The Curious Case of Pakistan's Democracy." *Global Risk Insights*, September 20. Accessed 5 February 2021. https://globalriskinsights.com/2018/09/curious-case-pakistans-democracy/

Sontag, Susan. 1977. *Illness as Metaphor: Decoding Discussions on Disease*. London: Picador.

Tarlo, Emma. 2010. *Visibly Muslim: Fashion, Politics, Faith*. Oxford: Berg.

United Nations. 2020. *Policy Brief: The Impact of COVID-19 on Women*. New York: UN Women Headquarters.

Waterman, David. 2014. "Saudi Wahhabi Imperialism in Pakistan: History, Legacy, Contemporary Representations and Debates." *Societal Studies* 6 (2): 242–258. doi:10.13165/SMS-14-6-2-02.

World Trade Organization. 2020. "The Economic Impact of COVID-19 on Women in Vulnerable Sectors and Economies." *Covid-19 Reports* 10: 1–9. doi:10.30875/74a82a3d-en.

Zakaria, Fareed. 2020. *Ten Lessons for a Post-Pandemic World*. London: Allen Lane.

# The Adivasi and the undead: From (post)colonial carnage to Necrocene apocalypse in *Betaal* (2020)

Johan Höglund ⓘ

**ABSTRACT**

In conversation with work by Mahasweta Devi, Arundhati Roy and Jason W. Moore, this article shows how the 2020 Indian Netflix zombie miniseries *Betaal* aligns British colonial-capitalist oppression with the neocolonial-capitalist violence performed by Indian soldiers on India's indigenous Adivasi community. Merging the (post)colonial with the post-apocalyptic in spectacular and violent ways, *Betaal* tells the story of elimination of an Adivasi community that resists capitalist exploitation of their lands, accidentally releasing a pandemic in the form of undead British soldiers once in the employ of the East India Company. The extractive violence that these two entities perform destroys not only people and traditions, it exhausts the land itself and can thus be considered an element of what Justin McBrien calls "the Necrocene". The zombie pandemic that erupts in Betaal is an attempt to render the apocalyptic violence and death that unregulated capitalism performs on ecology and precarious communities.

[C]olonialism and capitalism are pandemics. If you look at the way colonialism has consumed everything, how could you not compare it and late-stage capitalism to a cannibal that devours everything in its sight mindlessly?

(Barnaby 2020, n.p.)

The God thou serv'st is thine own appetite.

(Graham and Mahajan 2020)

From Mahasweta Devi to Arundhati Roy, Indian postcolonial fiction has frequently addressed both the oppressive history of the British Empire in India, and the failure of India to live up to the promises of social, economic, and ecological justice that decolonization harboured. The long and ongoing history of continued violence directed at Dalit communities and marginalized ethnicities such as the indigenous Adivasi has been an important concern of postcolonial studies since the 1970s. The field has identified many different reasons why such inequality keeps haunting Indian society, from the persistence of Eurocentric epistemologies in Indian political and social life, to the insidious nature of a Hindu caste system that predates colonialism by millennia. More recently, postcolonial scholars such as Neil Lazarus (2011) and the Warwick Research Collective ([WReC] 2015) have redirected attention to the role that capitalism plays in postcolonial nations, as well as in the rest of the world.

When considering the fact that the violence done to Adivasi communities serves as a preliminary to enclosing, privatizing, and extracting natural resources from this land, and to making these resources available to a global industrial market, it should become clear, as Immanuel Wallerstein (1979) has argued, that capitalism is a world-system and that what is happening to the Adivasi is part of a global economic development. Further, if one views the human and planetary violence done to the people and land in India and in other places as an element of the ongoing and global climate emergency, capitalism appears not simply as a world-system, but as what Jason W. Moore (2015) terms a world-ecology: a system designed to make the planet available for extractive capitalism. To highlight the central role that capitalism has played in the history of the climate emergency, Moore eschews the term "Anthropocene" – the most common denominator for our current geological epoch – and instead suggests "the Capitalocene". Focusing the ongoing era of world-destroying ecological crisis produced by an extractive and unregu-lated capitalism intimately entangled with early colonialism, Justin McBrien (2016) has proposed a related concept: "the Necrocene".

This article reads the Indian postcolonial Netflix series *Betaal* as a Necrocene narra-tive. *Betaal*, I argue, explores precisely this capitalist, ecological, medical, and cultural crisis. Merging the (post)colonial with the post-apocalyptic in spectacular and violent ways, *Betaal* tells the story of how Indian Special Forces soldiers, contracted to eliminate an Adivasi community that resists capitalist exploitation of their lands, accidentally release a pandemic in the form of a horde of undead British soldiers once in the employ of the East India Company. From this vantage, the article argues that the series aligns British colonial-capitalist carnage with the neocolonial-capitalist violence performed by Indian soldiers in the employ of capital in the present, in the process revealing how both British colonial rule and the current Indian postcolonial/neo-liberal regime exhaust people and land. I will furthermore claim that the pandemic spread by the undead colonizers and that turns all people into the voracious undead in *Betaal* is not so much a metaphor for extractive capitalism as an attempt to accurately describe the apocalyptic violence and death that unregulated capitalism can engender in precarious communities.

## Postcolonial studies, material history, and the planetary emergency

Postcolonial studies and (neo-)Marxist analysis have been uneasy bedfellows at best. Since its formation, the Subaltern Studies Group (SSG) has emphasized the need to rid India of Eurocentric modes of thinking, and of the paralysing epistemic and physical violence these modes continue to reproduce in the present. Emerging out of a European philosophical tradition, Marxist theory has been perceived as casting the long, culturally complex, and diverse history of the colonization of India, the Indian freedom movement, and Indian independence, as simply a chapter in the evolution of European capital and labour. In the words of Gyan Prakash (1992), writing in the immediate wake of formative contributions to postcolonial theory by Gayatri Spivak, and Homi K. Bhabha (but also in the strange shadow cast by the ceasing of the Cold War and the emergence of Francis Fukuyama's (1992) end-of-history thesis), nationalism and Marxism both "operated with master-narratives that put Europe at its centre" (8). Against such universalizing and inherently Eurocentric intellectual tendencies, postcolonial studies was understood to seek "to undo the Eurocentrism produced by the institution of the west's trajectory, its appropriation of the other as History" (8).

This line of thinking has been very influential for postcolonial studies generally and, arguably, for literary postcolonial studies in particular. Scholars of Indian postcolonial literary writing, as well as many postcolonial authors, have thus been attentive to the way that fiction produces Indian pasts and presents, and how it constructs the racial, ethnic, gendered, religious, and cultural categories out of which Indian identities are built (and against which European identities take form). However, since Prakash's discrediting of Marxist analysis in 1992, a series of global events and developments in India have served to re-energize the Marxist current within postcolonial theory. These international developments and events include the first Gulf War of 1991, the war on terror and the second Gulf War beginning with the invasion of Iraq in 2003, the global economic depression that followed this invasion, and the reliance on a deregulated neo-liberal economy to resolve issues of poverty worldwide (see Kiely 2007). In relation to this development, it is important to note that much of what Rob Nixon (2011) has termed "slow violence" that is eroding the multi-species ecologies in which many postcolonial people live their lives is caused by multinational, capitalist enterprise. Inside India, the appearance of a nationalist and populist state that organizes against the notion of non-Hindu Indian identity, that encourages capitalist exploitation of land and workers, and that assists in the creation of ever larger economic gulfs between rural and urban communities, and between salaried and wage labourers, also suggests the usefulness of a Marxist-oriented analysis. As a consequence, in India as in other parts of the world, the image of the subaltern, ground beneath the heel of imperial and nationalist epistemologies, has partially given way to that of a growing surplus precariat, produced and kept poor by a global neo-liberal capitalist order that has supplanted the direct rule of the old colonial powers (see Hardt and Negri 2000; Standing 2011; During 2015; Scully 2016 for related accounts of this development).

It is not surprising that the role that capitalism plays in postcolonial nations and for planetary ecology has become a concern for many postcolonial writers. In *Capitalism: A Ghost Story*, Arundhati Roy (2014) makes the crucial point that Indian capitalism, as a part of globalized, neo-liberal society, is having a massively detrimental impact both on Indian lives and on (Indian) ecology. Indian post-independence capitalism is thus described by her as having "impoverished and dispossessed" 800 million people and forced 250,000 debt-ridden farmers to commit suicide (8). In addition to this, she importantly notes, it also produced "poltergeists of dead rivers, dry wells, bald mountains, and denuded forests" (8). In other words, capitalism erodes not only human lives but also ecology.

By connecting capitalism to the violence done to Indian people and the land on which they live, Roy joins the vital and important trend in ecocritical and eco-socialist scholarship that identifies the origin of the climate crisis not in humanity as a species but in the emergence of capitalism in the 16th century. Moore is one of the most significant proponents of this direction in environmental humanities, but it also includes Elmar Altvater (2007), Kathryn Yusoff (2018), and Andreas Malm (2016). Central to their writing is that capitalism, colonialism, and the climate emergency are inextricably folded into each other. Considering the relationship between colonialism, capitalism, and the rise of the fossil-fuel complex that is now bringing on global warming, Andreas Malm and Alf Hornborg (2014) make the point that

> [the] rationale for investing in steam technology [ ... during the 19th century] was geared to the opportunities provided by the constellation of a largely depopulated New World, Afro-American slavery, the exploitation of British labour in factories and mines, and the global demand for inexpensive cotton cloth. (63)

Further focusing on the death that the capitalist/colonial project brought to those driven from the land enclosed for extraction, to those used in the process of extraction, and to the land being extracted, McBrien (2016) argues that capital "does not just rob the soil and worker [ ... ] it necrotizes the entire planet" (116). In McBrien's analysis, the accumulation of capital is also the accumulation of extinction. What is being made extinct is not just the biological species (although it is importantly this too):

> It is also the extinguishing of cultures and languages, either through force or assimilation; it is the extermination of peoples, either through labor or deliberate murder; it is the extinction of the earth in the depletion fossil fuels, rare earth minerals, even the chemical element helium; it is ocean acidification and eutrophication, deforestation and desertification, melting ice sheets and rising sea levels; the great Pacific garbage patch and nuclear waste entombment. (116–117)

The death of so many essential creatures, practices, cultures, waters, soils, and ecologies as an effect of (neo-liberal) capitalism and (neo)colonialism prompts McBrien to suggest the name Necrocene for the current moment in the geological history of the planet.[1] In this way, McBrien – as well as Malm and Hornborg, Yusuff, Moore, and Altvater – provides a material history and a theoretical framework that speaks clearly to the issues that Roy discusses in her book.

## *Betaal* and the Adivasi in the Necrocene

Co-written by Patrick Graham and Suhani Kanwar, co-directed by Graham and Nikhil Mahajan, and produced by Blumhouse Television for Netflix, *Betaal* (Graham and Mahajan 2020) constitutes a relatively new type of Indian postcolonial, speculative narrative.[2] Unlike the anglophone postcolonial novel by writers such as Salman Rushdie, Michael Ondaatje, or Rohinton Mistry, *Betaal* was produced for an Indian audience with actors speaking Hindi. At the same time, because of Netflix's global spread and the availability of subtitles, it is an Indian fiction that has travelled widely and is available in a number of nations. *Betaal* is also different from more traditional postcolonial fare in that it is a collaborative fiction, co-funded, co-produced, co-written, and co-directed by European, American, and Indian parties and individuals. It should be noted that, as a net-streamed horror series, *Betaal* lacks much of the sophistication of literary postcolonial writing. However, this lack of subtlety may be precisely what allows the series to speak very plainly about the material capitalist and colonial history of the planetary emergency and the pandemic, and to so clearly connect the violence performed on the Adivasi in India to this history and emergency.

Graham has previously been involved in two similar undertakings for Netflix. His first major project was the three-episode series *Ghoul* (Blum and Ashyap, 2017) for the Indian market and he also assisted Urmi Juvekar and Suhani Kanwar in writing the Netflix adaptation (Mehta 2019) controversial, postcolonial, and dystopian climate-fiction novel *Leila* in 2019. Through the speculative register, *Ghoul* and *Leila* explore the same dark side of postcolonial history that Roy and other vocal critics of Indian politics have investigated; politically motivated violence against Muslim communities and the resurgence of caste-oriented and religious apartheid in the wake of the spreading of Hindu nationalism. *Betaal* also recognizes the existence of these tensions in Indian postcolonial society, but focuses most intensely on the deadly connection between British 19th-century colonialism and capitalism, and modern-day Indian neocolonialism and capitalism. In particular, it investigates the ongoing violence against indigenous Adivasi communities that inhabit regions rich in the natural resources coveted by Indian and international capitalist enterprise.

The culturally diverse communities that make up the Adivasi have a troubled history. On the margins of British colonial, Hindu, and Muslim societies, the Adivasi have long fought a multi-front battle against land-grabbing and physical and cultural erasure. Traditionally referred to by the British as part of the "Depressed Classes" and by the Indian constitution as "Scheduled Tribes" (alongside "Scheduled Castes"), they have existed "at the lowest rungs of the social hierarchy and fare even worse than Dalits" (Das 2018, 31). These Indigenous communities began to unite around a common political agenda through the formation of the Adivasi Mahasabha or "the Great Council of Adivasi" in 1938. In the wake of the United Nations Declaration on the Rights of Indigenous Peoples in 2007 this effort has further intensified, often in collaboration with other indigenous communities across the world (see Rycroft and Dasgupta 2011). The SSG has furthered an image of the Adivasi as a community that has resisted the turn towards capitalist modernity which the post-independence Indian national government has encouraged. As Spivak (1981) notes in the introduction to her translation of Mahasveta Devi's short story "Draupadi", this resistance has sometimes taken militant form, as in 1967 when Adivasi farming communities in the Naxalbari area formed a Maoist guerrilla rebellion and began fighting government agents. The bloodshed that followed this still ongoing resistance has sometimes functioned as the excuse to invade and evict various Adivasi people from their ancestral lands. This is the topic of Roy's (2011) provocative *Walking with the Comrades*. Written in conversation with Adivasi people and Naxalite rebels, Roy's book claims that the government anti-insurgency operation targeting Naxalite resistance, codenamed Green Hunt, is essentially an attempt to clear the land of indigenous people so that the substantial deposits of bauxite valued (in 2011) to up to four trillion US dollars on the international market can be extracted by various Indian corporations.

*Betaal* tells this very story with the help of hyperbole (zombies) and euphemism (road-building through mountains instead of fracking). Interestingly, it also connects the violence performed in India on Adivasi communities to the long and violent history of British colonialism and capitalism. The series thus opens with a quotation from the fictional journal of Lt Col John P. Lynedoch, a British officer and agent of the British East India Company.[3] Dated June 17, 1857 this entry reads:

"We came to help these people. But they resist. The mutiny has reached us. How dare they? I will use their own guardians against them. I will harness the Betaal's curse, and ground these savages into the dirt . . . It seems there are rebels in the tunnel. I must go. (Graham and Mahajan 2020)".

The "mutiny" referred to here is of course the widespread Indian rebellion that began in May 1857 and was finally struck down in 1859. The quotation directs attention to the epistemologies of empire that cast indigenous people as needing the assistance of white Europeans, but equally to the extractive and violent nature of British colonialism in India. In addition to this, it recognizes the Adivasi's contribution to the early Indian independence movement. This contribution is further enhanced in the series opening by Brahmic script which warns the reader to "[t]read silently outside the tunnel", because those who inhabit it "will be hungry when they wake". This ominous beginning is then followed by a smattering of dark imagery and sound that clearly references the opening credits of Zack Snyder's dark and popular zombie horror film *Dawn of the Dead* (Snyder 2004), a remake of George Romero's 1968 seminal film by the same name. This opening thus introduces the political, historical, and cultural framework against which this pandemic horror series plays out.

In the scene that follows, we see present-day Adivasi people performing an arcane ritual intended to keep Lynedoch and his hungry men asleep in the "tunnels". The immediate threat envisioned by the narrative thus seems to be that the British break out of their prison to colonize India yet again. Yet what transpires next is not a confrontation between the zombified agents of a resurgent British Empire and the free Indian nation. Instead, the series focuses on a military anti-terrorist unit termed the "Baaz Squad", a part of the Counter Insurgency Police Department (CIPD). While far from a direct match, this unit is most likely modelled on the Commando Battalion for Resolute Action (CoBRA) tasked with fighting Naxalite resistance in India in the real world. The leader of the imaginary paramilitary unit is Commandant Tyagi and we understand, from media and from flashbacks, that she has taken bribes to eliminate Adivasi communities from areas of interest to a company named Surya Development. However, the (right-wing) media channel that reports on this insidious action responds to critics by asking a question that directly recalls Lynedoch's claim that the British are in India to help: "people who are cut-off from civilization don't deserve a shot at development and progress?" (Graham and Mahajan 2020). On the same news show Tyagi self-assuredly declares that the CIPD has "marched into battle with the likes of Mangal Pandey, Bhagat Singh, and Subhash Chandra Bose" (Graham and Mahajan 2020), central figures in the history of the Indian decolonial struggle.

Commandant Vikram Sirohi, Tyagi's second in command and the protagonist of the series, idolizes his leader and he would love to be counted among the patriotic heroes of the Indian independence movement. Yet the memories that intrude into his waking life are not of him and his squad nobly resisting Maoist guerrillas, but of how he faces, gun in hand, a pre-pubescent Adivasi girl, bloodied among dead bodies.[4] Her face is haggard, and her eyes big and frightened. This is an image that recurs throughout the series and each iteration reveals more of what transpired during that particular encounter.

After the Baaz Squad has been introduced, we learn that the next assignment is to ensure the safety of Surya Development which is in the process of building a motorway through a mountain belonging to an Adivasi community. To save time and money, Ajay Mudhalvan, the person in charge of the operation, plans to open up a tunnel constructed by the British at the time of the Indian Rebellion, after which it was walled up. This is, of course, the same tunnel in which Lynedoch and his undead army is confined. The Adivasi villagers, reluctant to give their land up to the corporation and knowing the horror that hides in the mountain, resist the operation through sabotage and demonstrations. Pressed for time, Mudhalvan plants explosives to make it seem that the villagers are Naxalite rebels. Provoked by the explosions, the Baaz Squad opens fire, massacring the Adivasi villagers and opening up the land and the mountain to exploitation. With the Adivasi out of the way, the tunnel is unsealed, releasing a horde of undead British redcoats into the land. In zombie-like fashion, they begin biting and feeding on the unsuspecting crew and soldiers, spreading the zombie curse in the processes. What remains of the Baaz Squad, together with Mudhalvan, his wife, and young daughter, must flee the area and seek shelter in an old British barracks. There, they encounter a young Adivasi woman, Puniya, and her elderly husband.

The appearance of flesh-eating zombies in a postcolonial narrative may appear distracting, but the insertion of this particular element of horror is better understood as a device that reveals the uncanny and disturbing connections that exist between capital, colonialism, and land, and that makes plain and accessible the slow and fast violence that capitalism is capable of wielding. In turning to non-realist modes of representation, the series in fact joins a notable trend in world literature that explores capitalism and the ecological crisis. In *The Great Derangement*, Amitav Ghosh (2016) observes that most fiction that engages with the planetary emergency to explore the futures that may result if the present emergency is not (miraculously) averted eschews the realist register. Realism, Ghosh argues, is in fact designed to elide the very notion of (natural, chthonic, human-produced) disaster from fiction. The narratives that probe the climate crisis instead belong to "those generic out-houses that were once known by names such as 'the Gothic', 'the romance', or 'the melodrama', and have now come to be called 'fantasy', 'horror', and 'science fiction'" (24). In other words, Ghosh observes that speculative fiction is able to describe, narrate, and make plain the enormous and catastrophic effects that human activity has on the environment, and of the human beings inherently and forever folded into this environment.

Michael Niblett (2012) and the WReC (2015) have also influentially proposed that speculative texts are better able than realist fiction to narrate the ongoing climate emergency. However, unlike Ghosh they theorize the speculative text as emerging out of a conjoined lack of economic and ecological justice. In other words, the non-realistic narrative is a response to the death-dealing inequities and ecological erosions produced specifically by capitalism. Niblett and the WReC have adapted Michael Löwy's (2007) concept of "irrealism" as a descriptor of the aesthetics that rises out of, and makes visible, the experience of being caught in the web of precarity and death created by capitalism.[5] Unlike the realist bourgeoise novel, which tends to occlude the violence of capitalism and colonialism, the irrealist text is thus capable of narrating both the horrific violence that extractive capitalism produces for humans living located outside the affluent strata of global capitalist society, and the strain that extraction puts on an ecology already on the ropes.[6]

When zombified British soldiers from the middle of the 19th century erupt out of a mountain to feed on, and turn against Indian special forces soldiers, Adivasi people, and Indian civilians, *Betaal* makes use of this irrealist register. It is not in spite of this horror element, but through irrealist horror, that the text is able to connect the consumption of Adivasi people and land by the British, to the consumption of Adivasi people by Indian neocolonial and capitalist agents. The zombie pandemic thus becomes a way to identify the parallels between the British colonial and capitalist invasion and occupation of India, and the present-day Indian capitalist assault on indigenous land. In *Betaal*, Lt Col Lynedoch is simultaneously a representative of the British Empire and of capitalism in the shape of the East India Company. He has come to India to profit from the riches this land contains, and couches this endeavour in the language of benevolence as expressed in the opening of the series: "We came to help these with people." Mudhalvan, as an agent of contemporary Indian capitalism, is involved in the very same project. His invasion of Adivasi lands is also imagined as an act of benevolent development, as an attempt to give the Adivasi "a shot at development and with progress", but to him and the Necrocene capitalism he represents, the Adivasi are an expendable part of the land he seeks to prime for extraction.

This parallel becomes even more prominent as the zombie illness begins to spread among the members of Baaz Squad. Several of the soldiers/police have already been infected, including Commandant Tyagi whose hair has turned white and whose mind is slowly being invaded by the undead Lynedoch. Joined by the two surviving Adivasi villagers, Vikram has come to understand that his squad is beset by an out-of-control evil firmly rooted in the British Empire. This comprehension is deepened through an interrogation of a partially zombified and chained solder, and through discovering and reading Lynedoch's old journal, hidden in the barracks where they have taken shelter. From this source they understand that Lynedoch's "greed drove him crazy" and that he intended to become "the sole emperor of British India" (Graham and Mahajan 2020). Trapped in the mountain through which his regiment was building a tunnel, he even sacrificed his own son to the Betaal to gain immortality. This is how Lynedoch turned into the patient zero of the zombie epidemic that the Baaz Squad has unwittingly let out of the mountain where it has been trapped. Yet the Betaal is merely the tool of this transformation. As the diary declares, the god that Lynedoch serves, and that is the true origin of this symbolic and violent epidemic, is not the Adivasi demon Betaal, but Lynedoch's "own appetite".

While Vikram and Puniya are revolted by this revelation, Mudhalvan, as the agent of Indian capitalism, becomes intrigued. If Vikram has (unsuccessfully) pretended that he is an agent of the Indian nation and that he has been fighting the rebels rather than killing innocents inhabiting mountains of great monetary value, Mudhalvan harbours no such illusions. The entrepreneur thus explains to Vikram and the Baaz Squad: "Do you really think you run this country? Money runs the country. The country doesn't run on ideologies – it runs on money." When Commandant Tyagi begins to channel the spirit of Lynedoch – appearing as a dark figure looming just behind her head – Mudhalvan learns that to escape the mountain, the British commander needs a sacrifice much like the one he once performed on his son, but this time preferably "from the female sex", "before she has bled" (Graham and Mahajan 2020). Mudhalvan has access to precisely such a potential sacrifice in the form of his daughter. Symbolically merging his own destiny with Lynedoch's, he proposes a deal whereby he gives up his daughter if Lynedoch agrees to share the terrible power he now possesses. Like Lynedoch, then, Mudhalvan's god is his own appetite. The capitalist hunger for accumulation permeates his being as thoroughly as it does Lynedoch's. With the help of Vikram, now also possessed by Lynedoch, Mudhalvan exits the barracks with her daughter to sacrifice his daughter.

## Conclusion: Apocalypse

> *Betaal* was released in May 2020, a few months into the COVID-19 pandemic, and although conceived long before the new virus emerged, it speaks to this pandemic and its origins in capitalism and colonialism in thought-provoking ways. The spring of 2020 was a time when societies across the world were shutting down to avoid contagion. For large sections of the privileged Global North, and in affluent communities in the Global South, the arrival of the virus was thus also the advent of a novel precarity where endemic ill-health and imminent death, as well as job-loss and homelessness, became real possibilities. Media in many parts of the world thus projected the notion that the pandemic was something new, and also something universal because, as the editors of *Business & Society* put it, "what appears fairly certain is that individuals are equally vulnerable" (Bapuji et al. 2020, n.p.). In the months that followed, this myth began to erode. The COVID-19 virus was no more egalitarian than Ebola or HIV or, for that matter, the influx of pathogens that accompanied the colonial project in America and that killed an estimated 87–92 percent of all indigenous people on the American continent by the year 1600 (Koch et al. 2019, 22).

Indigenous and poor communities have always suffered more than other groups from the health crises caused by epidemics and ecological degradation. Anthropologist Paul Farmer (1996; 2004) has influentially argued that these groups are exposed to a "structural violence" (Farmer 2004) that accelerates suffering. Focusing on Haiti, Farmer insists that this violence has an often-neglected necrotic material history and that it emerges out of a "transnational tale of slavery and dept and turmoil" (2004, 305). The COVID-19 pandemic thus reinforces the understanding of illness as a product of capitalism and colonialism, and of indigenous people as the most vulnerable both to the detrimental effects that the virus has on the body, and to the secondary, social, and economic effects produced by the pandemic.[7] When viewed as such, it also becomes clear that if the pandemic is an apocalypse, this began centuries ago for indigenous people.

Postcolonial and indigenous literature has been telling apocalyptic stories for a long time. Canadian First Nation's author Waubgeshig Rice (2018) spells it out clearly in *Moon of the Crusted Snow*. In this novel about climate upheaval, death and American indigenous people, an elder explains that

> [t]he world isn't ending [ ... ] It already ended. It ended when the Zhaagnaash [white people] came into our original home down south on that bay and took it from us. That was out world [ ... ] Yes, apocalypse. We've had that over and over. But we always survived. We're still here. And we'll still be here, even if the power and the radios don't come back on and we never see any white people again (149).

Ultimately, this is also the story that *Betaal* tells. The Adivasi community in *Betaal* have lived in the shadow of the British zombie pandemic for 170 years. When the Indian soldiers (as mercenaries of capitalism) accidently release this contagion, they bring on suffering and death that seem novel and absurd to the soldiers and the agents of capitalism, but that are not a new experience to the Adivasi community. That the Adivasi have long suffered is brought out in a number of ways, but most strongly through the recurring image of the bloodied and abandoned Adivasi girl that haunts the daydreams of Vikram. In the final episode we understand that Vikram shot this girl in the back as she tried to run away from the village where her family had been massacred by the Baaz Squad. As in the Canadian mountains where *Moon of the Crusted Snow* plays out, the apocalypse is an unravelling process rather than a sudden and inexplicable event. Like the COVID-19 pandemic, it appears as new only because the violence done to people and land has reached such proportions that it also spills over into affluent worlds.[8]

It is by telling this story of how an uneven and dispersed apocalypse erupts, time and time again, out of a long colonial and capitalist history, that *Betaal* narrates the Necrocene. The invasion and rendering asunder of bodies that rise up again and again, animated by the sheer force to accumulate more death, has a systemic colonial and capitalist history. The violent pandemic thus illustrates capitalism's universal relationship to land and people: its necrotic potential to produce universal, extinguishing death. In this way, *Betaal* makes horribly plain how British colonialism and capitalism, and then Indian capitalism, have engaged in what McBrien describes as the "extermination of peoples, either through labour or deliberate murder" (2016, 116–117). The series leaves no doubt that the colonial/capitalist system introduced by the British and then inherited by Indian capitalist agents ultimately produces extinction. As argued by McBrien, the "logic of accumulation is not capable of outrunning extinction because accumulation and extinction cannot be decoupled" (135). In this way, the joint process of colonialism and capitalism is like a zombie pandemic: it wills towards extinction and universal apocalypse.

Yet *Betaal* also offers a certain hope. At the climactic end of the series, the guilt Vikram experiences because of his wilful murder of the Adivasi girl is mobilized as resistance. He refuses to sacrifice Mudhalvan's daughter to the hungry Lynedoch. This allows the Adivasi Puniya and the Baaz Squad soldier Assad Akbar (whose name signals his Muslim background) to bring the daughter out of the tunnel and away from the mountain. While accumulation and extinction cannot be decoupled, the "human being *can* be decoupled from Capital", Mc-Brien argues. "Capital is extinction. We are not" (Mc Brien 2016, 135). In the final scene, the Muslim man, the Adivasi woman, and the Hindu girl, all located in the peripheries of the Indian nationalist state and just decoupled from the extinction occurring in the catastrophic contact zone in the mountains, drive back towards the city. However, as they travel they realize that, despite the rescue of Mudhalvan's daughter, the catastrophe remains imminent. Ancient British sailing ships have been spotted on the horizon. The apocalypse has not been averted; indeed the violence engendered by colonialism and capitalism now threatens all of India. Even so, the prospect of a future that is not extinction remains. The three people driving away from the mountain and towards even greater cataclysm personify the type of resistance capable of dismantling extinction. This is the thin sliver of hope conjured by the series. In a world where ongoing capitalist violence continues to erode ecology, indigeneity, and other precarious communities, a final victory over the zombified agent of empire and capitalism would have been an absurd ending. Hope is thus located, in the series as in the present moment, instead in the margins; where unity can take form across cultural, religious, and class-related gulfs. This is where "we" cease to be extinction.

## Notes

1. See also "Thanatocene" as defined by Christophe Bonneuil and Jean-Baptiste Fressoz (2016).
2. Blumhouse has made a name for itself as an American production company that explores American racism through drama films such as Spike Lee's (2018) *BlacKkKlansman* and via provocative horror such as Jordan Peele's *Get Out* (Peele 2017) and *Us* (Peele 2019).
3. Director Patrick Graham's full name is John Patrick Lynedoch Graham and according to the Internet Movie Database (IMDb) he is a descendant of Thomas Graham, 1st Baron Lynedoch who fought in the Napoleonic wars (https://m.imdb.com/name/nm3318887/trivia). In naming the main British villain of the series "Lynedoch", Graham thus connects the narrative to himself and to his own British imperial history.
4. Vikram is also a reference to the Indian king Vikramāditya who managed to trap a Betaal or vampiric spirit in Indian folklore legends.
5. See also Rebecca Duncan (2020).
6. Elizabeth DeLoughrey (2019) uses the concept of Benjaminian allegory to explain a similar turn in postcolonial, ecocritical writing to unrealistic narrative.
7. See Rebecca Duncan and John Höglund (2021) for a detailed discussion of this understanding of the COVID-19 pandemic.
8. This spillover does not mean that the system as such is collapsing. Capitalism, as Naomi Klein (2007) observes, thrives on crises and uses them to deregulate, to move its positions forward, and to project the sense that it alone can restore society to its former imagined glory.

## Acknowledgments

I am very grateful to the Swedish Foundation for the Humanities and Social Sciences (Riksbankens jubileumsfond) for the research funding that made the writing of this article possible. I am also greatly indebted to the Linnaeus University Centre for Concurrences in Colonial and Postcolonial Studies and to members Rebecca Duncan and Mike Classon Frangos for crucial feedback during the writing process.

## Disclosure statement

No potential conflict of interest was reported by the author.

## Funding

This work was supported by the Riksbankens jubileumsfond [SAB20-0015].

## ORCID

Johan Höglund ⓘ http://orcid.org/0000-0003-3293-6324

## References

Altvater, Elmar. 2007. "The Social and Natural Environment of Fossil Capitalism." *Socialist Register* 43: 37–59.

Bapuji, Hari, Frank G. A. de Bakker, Jill A. Brown, Colin Higgins, Kathleen Rehbein, and Andrew Spicer. 2020. "Business and Society Research in Times of the Corona Crisis." *Business and Society* 59 (6): 1067–1078. doi:10.1177/0007650320921172.

Barnaby, Jeff. 2020. "Decolonizing the Zombie Apocalypse: An Interview with Jeff Barnaby about His New Film *Blood Quantum* [Conducted by Sean Carleton]." *Canadian Dimension.* https://canadiandimension.com/articles/view/decolonizing-the-zombie-apocalypse-an-interview-with-jeff-barnaby-about-his-new-film-blood-quantum

Blum, Jason, and Anurag Ashyap, dirs. 2017. *Ghoul.* Miniseries. Los Angeles, CA: Blumhouse Productions.

Bonneuil, Christophe, and Jean-Baptiste Fressoz. 2016. *The Shock of the Anthropocene: The Earth, History and Us.* London: Verso.

Das, Budhaditya. 2018. "Adivasi Identity and Livelihoods in Contemporary India." *Economic & Political Weekly* 53 (30): 31–34.

DeLoughrey, Elizabeth. 2019. *Allegories of the Anthropocene.* Durham, NC: Duke University Press.

Duncan, Rebecca. 2020. "Writing Ecological Revolution from Millennial South Africa: History, Nature, and the Post-Apartheid Present." *ARIEL: A Review of International English Literature* 51 (4): 65–97. doi:10.1353/ari.2020.0028.

Duncan, Rebecca, and Johan Höglund. 2021. "Decolonising the Covid-19 Pandemic: On Being in This Together." *Approaching Religion* 11 (2): 115–131. doi:10.30664/ar.107743.

During, Simon. 2015. "Choosing Precarity." *South Asia: Journal of South Asian Studies* 38 (1): 19–38. doi:10.1080/00856401.2014.975901.

Farmer, Paul. 1996. "On Suffering and Structural Violence: A View from Below." *Daedalus* 125 (1): 261–283.

Farmer, Paul. 2004. "An Anthropology of Structural Violence." *Current Anthropology* 45 (3): 305–325. doi:10.1086/382250.

Fukuyama, Francis. 1992. *The End of History and the Last Man.* New York: Free Press.

Ghosh, Amitav. 2016. *The Great Derangement: Climate Change and the Unthinkable.* Chicago: University of Chicago Press.

Graham, Patrick, and Nikhil Mahajan, dirs. 2020. *Betaal.* TV Series. Written by Patrick Graham and Suhani Kanwar. Los Angeles, CA: Blumhouse Television for Netflix.

Hardt, Michael, and Antonio Negri. 2000. *Empire.* Cambridge, MA: Harvard University Press.

Kiely, Ray. 2007. "Poverty Reduction through Liberalisation? Neoliberalism and the Myth of Global Convergence." *Review of International Studies* 33 (3): 415–434. doi:10.1017/S0260210507007589.

Klein, Naomi. 2007. *The Shock Doctrine: The Rise of Disaster Capitalism.* New York: Picador.

Koch, Alexander, Chris Brierley, Mark M. Maslin, and Simon L. Lewis. 2019. "Earth System Impacts of the European Arrival and Great Dying in the Americas after 1492." *Quaternary Science Reviews* 207: 13–36.

Lazarus, Neil. 2011. *The Postcolonial Unconscious.* Cambridge: Cambridge University Press.

Lee, Spike, dir. 2018. *BlacKkKlansman.* Los Angeles, CA: Blumhouse Productions.

Löwy, Michael. 2007. "The Current of Critical Irrealism: 'A Moonlit Enchanted Night'." In *Adventures in Realism*, edited by Matthew Beaumont, 193–206. Oxford: Blackwell.

Malm, Andreas. 2016. *Fossil Capital: The Rise of Steam Power and the Roots of Global Warming.* London: Verso Books.

Malm, Andreas, and Alf Hornborg. 2014. "The Geology of Mankind? A Critique of the Anthropocene Narrative." *The Anthropocene Review* 1 (1): 62–69. doi:10.1177/2053019613516291.

McBrien, Justin. 2016. "Accumulating Extinction: Planetary Catastrophism in the Necrocene." In *Anthropocene or Capitalocene? Nature, History, and the Crisis of Capitalism*, edited by Jason W. Moore, 116–137. Oakland, CA: PM Press.

Mehta, Deepa, dir. 2019. *Leila*. Miniseries. Mumbai: Open Air Films, LLP.

Moore, Jason W. 2015. *Capitalism in the Web of Life: Ecology and the Accumulation of Capital*. New York: Verso.

Niblett, Michael. 2012. "World-Economy, World-Ecology, World Literature." *Green Letters* 16 (1): 15–30. doi:10.1080/14688417.2012.10589097.

Nixon, Rob. 2011. *Slow Violence and the Environmentalism of the Poor*. Cambridge, MA: Harvard University Press.

Peele, Jordan, dir. 2017. *Get Out*. Los Angeles, CA: Blumhouse Productions.

Peele, Jordan, dir. 2019. *Us*. Los Angeles, CA: Blumhouse Productions.

Prakash, Gyan. 1992. "Postcolonial Criticism and Indian Historiography." *Social Text* 31 (31/32): 8–19. doi:10.2307/466216.

Rice, Waubgeshig. 2018. *Moon of the Crusted Snow*. Toronto: ECW Press.

Roy, Arundhati. 2011. *Walking with the Comrades*. London: Penguin.

Roy, Arundhati. 2014. *Capitalism: A Ghost Story*. London: Verso.

Rycroft, Daniel J., and Sangeeta Dasgupta. 2011. *The Politics of Belonging in India: Becoming Adivasi*. Abingdon: Routledge.

Scully, Ben. 2016. "Precarity North and South: A Southern Critique of Guy Standing." *Global Labour Journal* 7 (2): 160–173. doi:10.15173/glj.v7i2.2521.

Snyder, Zack, dir. 2004. *Dawn of the Dead*. Los Angeles, CA: Strike Entertainment.

Spivak, Gayatri Chakravorty. 1981. "'Draupadi' by Mahasveta Devi." *Critical Inquiry* 8 (2): 381–402. doi:10.1086/448160.

Standing, Guy. 2011. *The Precariat: The New Dangerous Class*. London: Bloomsbury Publishing.

Wallerstein, Immanuel. 1979. *The Capitalist World-Economy*. Cambridge: Cambridge University Press.

Warwick Research Collective. 2015. *Combined and Uneven Development: Towards a New Theory of World-Literature*. Oxford: Oxford University Press.

Yusoff, Kathryn. 2018. *A Billion Black Anthropocenes or None*. Minneapolis, MN: University of Minnesota Press.

# Septopia and the wastialized Other: Allegorizing neo-liberalism in the age of COVID-19

Aleks Wansbrough


**ABSTRACT**

Sepsis, septic tank, septum – these terms help to locate phantasmatic representation of waste spaces in cinema, which is here termed "septopia". Those who inhabit septopia are positioned as broken, fractured, or discarded identities. Amid COVID-19, septopia becomes more relevant to political realities, where people rebel against sanitized spaces and lockdown policies. Using Fredric Jameson's concept of the political unconscious and theorization of allegory, this article navigates how media and film can map anxieties and clashes surrounding pandemic measures. It first explains the concepts of septopia as a mode of political commentary in the 2000s post-apocalyptic movies: *Wall-E, District 9*, and *Land of the Dead*. It then explores how "septopia" and wastiality contribute to expressions of the political pandemic's unconscious, superstructurally mediating peoples' responses to lockdown. The article argues that attempting to understand why people protest against COVID measures can help avoid counterproductive responses and counter increased social abjection.


Using Fredric Jameson's interconnected theorizations of the political unconscious and allegory, this article examines a subset of 2000s Hollywood speculative fiction films. The films examined here all have narrative elements now linked to COVID-19: contamination, tracking, and sanitized spaces, and explore a sort of "wastial" othering and fracturing of identity along race and class contours. The article proposes that these films, *WALL-E* (Stanton 2008), *District 9* (Blomkamp 2009), and *Land of the Dead* (Romero 2005), all explore what could be termed "septopia": spaces inhabited by those deemed insufficiently white or middle class, who are segregated, even *abjected*, from cleaner, efficient spaces. While these films take aim at George W. Bush's administration, they also highlight issues of neo-liberal precarity (Standing 2011) that have come to the fore amid the pandemic, and therefore have a renewed relevance. Moreover, the article will contend that these films help to understand those who protest against COVID-19 restrictions.

## Jameson, allegory, and wastial abjection

In *The Political Unconscious*, Jameson (2002) argues that works of fiction both reveal and conceal the reality of exploitation and political struggle. Operating at the level of ideology, works of art/entertainment are interpretations of the present, which itself has a history. Any fictional story is ultimately a reflection of a larger history (4). Thus, according to Jameson, it is in "restoring to the surface of the text the repressed and buried reality of this fundamental history, that the doctrine of a political unconscious finds its function" (4). To explain this idea, Jameson quotes the *Communist Manifesto*'s claim that the history of the world is the history of class struggle (4). For Jameson, texts – and culture more generally – reflect but also refract the historical situation of exploitation and economic production. Jameson (1991) maintains that fiction is therefore historically situated to the extent that even speculative fiction, far from predicting the future, echoes the past (283) and absorbs the present. In short, "the repressed and buried" of historical struggles become the basis for a text's meaning. Struggle, then, can be depicted in the texts, but there is also a struggle within the text itself, a sort of unconscious struggle between rejecting and submitting to the current conditions. As the term "allegory" intimates, these narratives conceal and undermine their own emancipatory potential (Jameson 2002, 2020). Thus, by drawing out this struggle, one can participate in it (at least on a textual level), highlighting and identifying social and economic inequalities.

Although texts express their historical situation, exploitation is both historical and transhistorical. As such, texts seem prophetic because their meaning is recontextualized so that their authors can "predict" the present crises, which themselves echo past crises and struggles. Through this Jamesonian prism (Jameson 2002, 17–18) we can see how Hollywood speculative fiction 2000s cinema responds to then-contemporary crises in such a way that they can frame COVID-19. While Jameson focuses on class, this article will highlight the intersection with race (Crenshaw 2017), with a focus on neo-liberalism. The selection of Bush-era films facilitates a demonstration of this recontextualized relevance, as these films stress issues of surveillance, class, and race disparities, and the existence of septic and anti-septic zones. The article will contend that some forms of abjection, here called "wastiality", can then also be understood in a Jamesonian way; as related to symbolically expelling the used-up and redundant worker. "Wastiality" and "wastial" are used throughout to connect class and race with symbolic and economic processes of categorizing contaminants (for the intersections between race, waste, and class, see Mascarenhas, Grattet, and Mege 2021). In this vein, the term "septopia" is my attempt to capture interrelated phenomena: illness and contamination (sepsis and sep-toria), expulsion and division (septum), and segregation as waste, requiring septic containment.

Crucially, each film follows an *abjected* Other, an Other regarded as wastial; a subject who elicits disgust, viewed as a contaminant. This disgust is distinctive in its relationship to social, political, and economic systems. Disgust can be used to justify persecution and exploitation and to scapegoat concerns onto the Other (think Nazi Germany's blaming of the phantasmatic Other of the Jew, or Stalin's demonization of the Kulak). However, the sort of wastializing abjection that this article will focus on is an abjection ascribed to the Other along class and race contours: as no longer able to be integrated into the functioning of society or the economy, and, thus, as replaceable. There is even a neo-liberal accent to this concept of wastiality since neo-liberalism stresses competition and precarity rather than Fordist integration.

The wastialized subject is an inefficient, discarded, uncompetitive subject. Russell West-Pavlov (2018) captures this quality well, when he writes that "persons as laborer-objects become commodities for producing commodities; they become things, or even nothings. Ultimately, they may be reduced to detritus akin to the waste products into which commodities are also transformed at the moment of their obsolescence" (149–150). One can further understand this process of abjection through psychoanalysis. Julia Kristeva (1982) argues that the abject, while biological and affective, also has a symbolic dimension that is an affront to law, order, and linguistic categorization (in Lacanian psychoanalysis, the symbolic order). On a symbolic level, this defiance means mean-inglessness itself, or, as Kristeva puts it, the "thing that no longer matches and therefore no longer signifies anything" (4). Abjection is then that which can no longer be processed further within a schema. As such, the wastial Other goes from the inside to the outside of the social order, as Zygmunt Bauman's (2004) "wasted", precarious worker is excreted out, becoming an affront to value and order.[1]

There are strong racial connotations to this abjection. The link between abjection and race has often been explored in studies of black abjection (Kee 2015), but also studies of whiteness, too, that frame white resentment as a fear of encountering black abjection and thus being designated as "white trash", of losing whiteness (Wray 2006; Wilson 2002; Kirkland 2016; Metzl 2019). After all, both the concepts of black abjection and white trash share a focus on othering as having a *wastial* association with race, with "white trash" being used to designate those who are not quite white, who while having white privilege still fail to attain white middle-classness. One merit of these films is that they provide a sort of cinematic sympathy for their wastialized protagonists and the possibility of sympathy between racialized, indeed wastialized, subjects. The movies *WALL-E*, *District 9*, and *Land of the Dead* imagine septopias that are openly and consciously disdainful of neo-liberalism – cinematically depicted as corporations replacing the authority of gov-ernments and creating partitioned spaces between the wealthy white and the under-privileged "not white" Other. But as this article also contends, these films conceal as they reveal: they do not commit to exploring the realities of the intersections between class and race.

## Septopia in speculative fiction

The movie *WALL-E*, directed by Andrew Stanton, depicts the earth as unliveable and cluttered by waste. The movie encapsulates ecological concerns that were stymied by the Bush administration's anti-environmental policies (see Kellner 2009, 79–80). Abandoned by a rotund and consumerist human race, the earth is submerged by garbage. Nothing lives there but cockroaches, and a single robot, WALL-E, who must clean up the garbage engulfing the planet. The ground itself has been rendered infertile. However, the spaces of *WALL-E* may recall the underdeveloped, over-exploited countries – evocative of shanty towns. Imperialism and neo-liberalism are thereby gestured to, and perhaps equated with each other within the film as the Global North's rubbish processing often takes place in the developing nations of the Global South (here allegorized as the earth itself).

WALL-E is an almost *wastial* entity, inhabiting the septopia that is earth. The very name, Wall-E, stands for Waste Allocation Load-Lifter: Earth-Class. "He" works tirelessly to clean up planet earth. This entails his identity being literally reconfigured. His parts cease to work, and he must cannibalize other robots to survive and continue his mission – perhaps evoking the sort of flexibility required to survive as a member of what Guy Standing (2011) calls the precariat. Extending the possible class dimension, in which workers experience themselves as machines, constantly having to be updated to remain functional, Wall-E must survive through ingenuity. Although attesting to his mental agility and underscoring his green recycling credentials, Wall-E's tendency to cannibalize may suggest a despondency or psychical fracture as he does not mourn the deceased, once sentient robots. They are mere parts.

Class is then obfuscated. Although the machines are unpaid workers, the film confuses class in a way that would obscure's the film's own critique of neo-liberalism. For instance, the film is evidently criticizing consumerism (while consumerism existed long before neo-liberalism, the marketplace is neo-liberalism's conception of democracy) – we see humans as obese consumers, literally carried and cared for by machines. They live medicalized, dependent lives. The film further stages a critique of neo-liberal rhetoric in terms of how the space mission is conceived. After all, neo-liberal rhetoric insists that markets are more democratic than elected government and so businesses rather than governments should solve social problems through "market solutions". The movie takes aim at this "let the market sort it out" attitude by showing that it is a corporate chief executive officer (CEO) that convinces humans to give up dwelling on the earth. But here class is confused. We see robots as themselves operating along class contours whereas the humans on board the ship have no real power. Humans, passive consumers, are not exploited workers or victims, per se. But while the machines and robots are workers, they are also in charge – indeed some robots know more about what is really going on with the ship's mission than other robots – namely that the plan was never to return to earth. The human captain of the ship is just a figurehead without power who is unaware of the real plan to stay in space forever. Robots therefore are not quite exploited workers, but also not quite wealthy capitalists – so while the film clearly mocks consumerism and corporate power (space colonialism), its critique becomes obscured.

Indeed, one could argue that the film itself presents a Utopia on board the human colony of the ship, a sort of "fully-automated luxury consumer communism" (Bastani 2019), whereby human exploitation is exchanged for automation, money is abolished, and humans can relax in luxury. If a postcapitalist future were to eventuate, there would still be issues of waste, but focusing on consumption, as *Wall-E* does, can reinforce a blame on the individual rather than the lack of regulations on corporations. Similarly, the film both registers and confuses concerns about racial and class intersections. Some robots seem smart and powerful, and those robots are literally white – emulating the sleek design of Apple computers, but also simulating a sort of racial hierarchy. Other, more menial robots, such as Wall-E, are more yellow-brownish, and toil amid waste. In one scene, Wall-E finds himself inside the spaceship. Everything is clean but Wall-E leaves a trail of filth that is cleaned up by white robots who view Wall-E as a contaminant. There is perhaps a note of racial disgust, and Wall-E's lack of whiteness clearly makes him stand out. But it is unclear if Wall-E is a person/robot of colour. He is not necessarily black, brown, or Asian, and so what could be a critique of race and class – and how the two converge in relation to waste surroundings – is dampened. Viewers may unconsciously register racial abjection, but they are not invited to think about it too hard. We see, for instance, that WALL-E's movements are surveilled, and tracked as he and EVE are identified as "rogue robots", which may recall echoes of the Patriot Act, but could be also seen to predict how immigrant, "not white" communities during COVID-19 faced increased surveillance and restrictions in some countries (see Evans and Elhaj 2021). As with WALL-E, immigrant communities are often approached as potential contaminants in the Global North.

Perhaps, at a stretch, one could view WALL-E's friendship with the white robot EVE as an act of solidarity, EVE overcoming "her" prejudice to work together with WALL-E. She seems to look down on him. Indeed, part of Wall-E's abjection is that he is seen as not correctly functioning (on board the ship), or because his function or value as a workbot is unclear. After all, we see EVE incinerate the waste that Wall-E has been so carefully stacking, rendering the need for his onerous activity redundant. We later discover that EVE herself is irrelevant to the real mission – EVE is meant to retrieve samples of organic life on earth so that humans can recolonize it. While EVE discovers a plant and takes it on board the ship, the plant is stolen (by other robots – as the robots in charge have no desire to return to earth). EVE is then treated as malfunctioning since she could not produce the plant and is, in a sense, "lumped" in with Wall-E. She even resents Wall-E for this, believing he lost the plant. The friendship between EVE and Wall-E could be a sign that intersecting experiences can build solidarity and empathy, working together against an impersonal system. But it could be understood as obfuscating the intersections of race and class.

Slavoj Žižek (1989, 24–26; 2007) has argued that ideology is not overt politicization but rather a sort of abyss that one can project pre-existing prejudices upon. Such a claim buttresses Jameson's (2002, 2020) contention that texts both reveal and conceal through their open-endedness. In this case, however, while *Wall-E* may seem to be a parable against neo-liberalism, the film itself reigns in its potentially radical critique. Understood through Jameson's and Žižek's interpretation of ideology, the processes of re-terraforming the earth – human and robot working side by side – could express solidarity, but also obscure the way that racial resentments are stoked in the first place. After all, studies indicate that during economic crises there is a renewed blame of asylum seekers (Isaksen 2019). Further, the very notion of terraforming can be linked to "tidying up spaces", and these also have associations with gentrification and policing. Black Lives Matter protests were rekindled amid COVID-19 in the wake of the murder of George Floyd' and so we may be reminded how cleaning up the streets has a racial register. Moreover, the way that waste is consigned to certain areas where people are regarded as not white or upwardly mobile is not apparent from the film. In the US, for example, researchers Michael Mascarenhas, Ryken Grattet, and Kathleen Mege (2021) have found that "race and class oppression are manifested in the siting of hazardous waste facilities" (109). Closer to capturing this racial quality of waste is the movie *District 9*.

*District 9* (2009), directed by Neill Blomkamp, is set and made in South Africa and fuses critiques of colonization and neo-liberalism. The film imagines a world where aliens are real and segregated from human society into separate zones. Appearing repugnant to humans (and referred to as prawns), they are heavily policed in shanty towns engulfed by trash in a manner redolent of the extreme measures associated with colonial rule. The very title of the film borrows from District Six in Cape Town: a once multi-ethnic metropolitan area that in the 1960s was declared whites only. People were mercilessly evacuated from their homes, which became part of an area of wealth accumulation. Black Africans were not allowed to own any property. Their new "homes" were squalid and designed for easy policing as the war journalist Scott C. Johnson (2009) observes in his review of the film:

> Each dormitory community had one entrance and exit, so as to further contain the inhabitants inside. Houses were small and poorly designed. The sewage system could regulate the waste of no more than 300,000 people, but soon the Flats were home to almost a million. (n.p.)

Frantz Fanon's (1963) description of the merciless barbarity of the colony is fitting: "The cause is the consequence; you are rich because you are white, you are white because you are rich" (40).

The racializing and brutal segregation in the film captures this barbarity as we see that alien technology is being stolen and co-opted, while aliens like the black Africans have their property stolen. The aliens are condemned to live amid rubbish. Such a process could gesture to dispossession, whereby once powerful aliens have their means of subsistence stolen from them just as indigenous peoples around the world had their lands and bodies stolen from them. This could almost be understood along the lines of "primitive accumulation" – a concept borrowed from Marx but reconfigured by post-colonial and black sociological scholarship (see Federici 2004; Robinson 1983). Such scholarship argues that the combination of controlling and subjugating human bodies and the theft of land, considered here as primitive accumulation, remains part of ongoing modernizing practices, rather than a stage prior to capitalism or an early stage of capitalism – and continues to have racialized dynamics. (One could, for instance, think of the dependence on undocumented migrant labour within some professions, net-worked and global sex trafficking, or the lucrative of establishment of new markets amid war and regime change, or even the brutal, forced labour of the Uyghur populations in China.)

A connection between labour, land, borders, and an expelled workforce is gestured to in the film. Its documentary aesthetic allows us to see an excerpt of an interview with an entomologist who states: "What we have stranded on Earth in this colony is basically the workers. They don't particularly think for themselves. They will take commands. They have no initiative" (Blomkamp 2009). Thus, the image of an out-of-work, easily con-trolled blue-collar, "low skilled" workforce is acknowledged within the metaphor. Further, the protagonist, Wikus, a decidedly white-collar worker/bureaucrat, is employed by the military contractor Multi National United (MNU), to oversee aliens signing eviction notices. In one scene, Wikus explains to his colleagues that "the prawn doesn't really understand the concept of the ownership of property. So, we have to go there and say 'listen, this is our land. Uhm please will, will you go?' " Such a remark buttresses Stuart Hall's argument that "race is the modality in which class is lived" (Hall et al. 1978, 394). The handheld camera in the scene gestures to the irony of a white man saying this as the camera pans to show the reaction of black African colleagues. In this way, the racism (coded as speciesism via the term "prawn") buttresses a policy of both neocolonization and neo-liberal gentrification as public housing is replaced with private housing. It is worth underscoring the history of colonization here. Indigenous peoples from around the world were displaced using the pretext that they did not "own the land", or even their own bodies, as they allegedly lacked a Lockean conception of liberty. One could even think of Australia where *terra nullius* was central to British colonization. But people being forced out of their houses may also evoke the threat of eviction, that was prominent in the 2007–08 global financial crisis.

Although the aliens in *District 9* are another species, the barely sublimated reality of humans bestialized by economic and racializing procedures is gestured to throughout the film alongside a nearly Marxian idea of dead labour (Marx [1857]–[61]). The term "dead labour" in Marx refers to technology sapping the living labourer, through mechanization. Technology threatens to maim the workers and allows them to be exploited to an inhuman level. Wikus is a human transformed into an alien through technologization, in a way that affords his hyper-exploitation. The alien is then the product of engineering and of technological form, indicated in part by the fact that it is the alien's fuel which turns Wikus into a hybrid being. We see Wikus undergo a sort of Cronenbergian transformation as his body is torn apart; his hand, an instrument for labour, transforms into a claw, able to wield alien technology, emulating a sort of workerization of the human form. He is then experimented on by the evil corporation and military contractor, MNU, which conducts inhumane tests. In one scene it even attempts to vivisect him and harvest his organs, further accentuating that as a workerized alien-hybrid form, Wikus is no longer seen as a human being, but rather a divisible resource.

Wokerization is evidently racial, following the metaphor of the alien as the Other. In a sense, Wikus becomes both transracial and biracial. He is human and alien, white and non-white. Indeed, it is worth noting that the fuel that transforms his skin is appears black or brown as does his vomit – a self-*abjecting* process. His very body tries to expel the alien, overwhelmed – in defecating and vomiting up blood (Wikus mentions that he has "shat" his pants). Moreover, when MNU views Wikus as a resource, he is not considered revolting, as he remains useful. It is Wikus as resister that is viewed as a disgusting, abject entity, vilified through miscegenation (he is accused of having sex with aliens). Indeed, part of Wikus's abjection is the fact that he is viewed by his father-in-law – a figure high up in the MNU – as useless, ineffectual, and unmasculine – thus suggesting a sort of intersection between "the native other", the effeminate man, and the unproductive worker.

In a sense, the aliens are just a stand-in for the extremely othered and the extremely exploited. The concept of the intergalactic alien clearly echoes "alien residents", immigrants too-often called "illegals". After all, the Bush administration established US Immigration and Customs Enforcement (ICE), and the film also directly alludes to Nigerian refugees in South Africa in 2004. But of course, the film also gestures to how black Africans were treated during colonial rule. As such, Wikus must – as someone who is not quite white, like WALL-E – contend with extreme forms of surveillance as his location is tracked and he is hounded and demonized as a threat. However, using intergalactic aliens as a stand-in for "othered" populations (whether black, immigrant, or unemployed) has its limits. The movie cannot convincingly show how the intergalactic aliens are surplus, wasted labour; aliens suggesting an order exterior to economic relations, rather than a group excreted by society. As with *WALL-E*, the very metaphoric device obscures the relationship between neo-liberalism, contemporary racialized resentments, and waste. While it is clear that the aliens have been denied their own technology that would allow them to thrive, this critique of colonialism is distorted as there is little allusion to the Global North.

Nevertheless, the film remains relevant amid the aftermath of Trump's presidency, a presidency in part defined by images of children in cages. Having built on racist claims such as "Mexican rapists" ("Drug Dealers, Criminals, Rapists" 2016), Trump further weaponized these tactics with COVID-19, using terms like "China Virus" and promoting the need for harsh borders ("President Trump" 2020). Unfortunately, Trump's wastializing of migrants has not gone away. Biden's administration has continued expelling undocumented immigrants, potentially matching or exceeding Trump (Valverde 2021), while COVID–19 serves as a smokescreen.

Returning to fiction, other inhabitants of segregated, waste-filled spaces include zombies. In George A. Romero's film *Land of the Dead*, there is a curious class division between zombies, humans, and rich humans. The zombies are contrasted and compared with the humans in the film in a way that highlights labour. We even see zombies behave as wannabe workers, with one zombie in particular filling up cars with petrol at a gas station. These zombies seem like they were laid-off workers – aimless, despondent, and performing unnecessary tasks. But within the gated human stronghold, we human workers are separated from the corporate elite. Both the poor humans and the zombies will band together separately within their respective grouping to fight against the rich. Studies of zombie films often trace how their popularity in the 1980s coincided with neo-liberal policies and de-industrialization (Blake 2015; Domingo 2018; Castillo et al. 2016). Neo-liberal de-industrialization induced wastial conditions as communities that were hotbeds of production saw their livelihoods disappear while being excluded from the "smarter" gig economy. At the same time, neo-liberal policies furthered different kinds of wastial conditions in the Global South as factory and textile production engendered zones of pollution and immiseration. This type of dead labour is literalized by zombies, who are stand-ins for obsolete workers. Zombification is itself implied to be a sort of virus, and the virus is equated with neo-liberalism.

However, there is a way that *Land of the Dead* is especially relevant for our own times. The zombies as laid-off, blue-collar workers (the zombie leader/organizer literally wears a blue uniform) contrast with the working-class humans in the film who perform chores for the rich, emulating the so-called "self-employed" contractors of the gig economy. As a consequence of COVID-19, the precarity of the gig economy became especially highlighted. In a sense the film predicts this situation: poorer humans perform errands for the rich and risk being infected by the zombies in a way that cannot but seem reminiscent of the gig economy. Amazon delivery services and food delivery workers among other professions are particularly at risk of catching COVID-19.

Yet the film remains problematic along the lines that Jameson (2002, 4) highlights, where texts disavow their own critique. Cinematic zombification implies a capitalistic logic of blame towards the so-called inefficient workers, who are no longer part of the middle class. Zombies, historically slow-moving, catch those who are not fast enough on their feet, not competitive enough. Zombies exist amid zones abandoned by capital, zones of de-instustrialization and waste. Zombies are presented as waste products – literally dead, useless humans. While zombies were once a metaphor for slaves (Lauro 2015; McAlister 2012), by the 1980s zombies had become a metaphor for a precarious working class who sustain themselves on cheap consumer goods. In the film, Romero goes further in exploring the possibility that these two groups of workers (the blue-collar unemployed zombies and the human gig-economy precariat) could resist the rich together. However, this possibility is undercut by the contradictions with the genre as zombies must live off humans, becoming a metaphor for parasitism as well as consumerism: zombies are often slow-moving creatures living off fast(er) food (Newbury 2012).

The image of the zombie is confused further as we see in closed-circuit television (CCTV) footage of the zombies that almost emulates the surveillance of post-9/11 America. The zombies could be read as terrorists who must be surveilled. This points to a common problem that can be seen between these three films. Each film, in some way, targets the Bush administration, ultimately critiquing a (neo)conservative, hawkish neo-liberalism. The films offer a critique of neo-liberal sensibilities as often as they do of the economic process at work. As such, these movies fail to register the way that more progressive neo-liberals (Fraser 2019) are also part of the problem. According to Nancy Fraser, progressive neo-liberals tend to blame the state as the instigator of injustice and so view corporations and markets as requiring only notional technocratic management, since markets are considered ways of fighting old reactionary prejudices and structures. The proper place of the state remains enforcement and crime prevention, and a bare-bones means-tested (and therefore punitive) social safety net. Liberals often of a progressive neo-liberal bent, for instance, often fail to take seriously the concerns of anti-lockdown protestors.

As good liberals, we know that there is a need for anti-septic, sanitized spaces, equipped with literal sanitizer, as well as masks and social distancing. As such, it is hard not to react with disgust to those who protest these measures. After all, they employed gross antics; and it is not hard to have disgust at their consumerist mentality – think of the clips of people in the US irately demanding haircuts ("Armed Protestors" 2020). We hear about protestors being abusive to reporters, sometimes spitting on them. Given the threat to general health, well-being and safety, there is a "naturalness" to the disgust, accompanied by a desire to deride those not obeying social distancing or mask-wearing edicts. But cinematic depictions of septopia also furnish liberals with an easy way of equating the worst of the protestors with unclean, brain-dead, contaminating zombies. Take, for example, the photographs and videos circulating of people flouting COVID-19 restrictions. These videos and photos have captions and comments comparing them to zombie hordes. As *Slate* magazine reported:

> In Columbus, Ohio, a group of about 100 protesters of the state's conservative stay-at-home policies showed up outside the statehouse during Gov. Mike DeWine's daily COVID-19 briefing. Reporters Anna Staver and Cole Behrens covered the protests [ ... ] and their story was topped by a striking photo of the protesters, pressed up against glass doors, mouths open in snarling anger. [ ... ] You've probably seen it around, juxtaposed with stills from *Shaun of the Dead* or captioned with jokes like "The final season of *The Walking Dead* sucks". (Onion 2020, n.p.)

While liberals on social media attacked the protestors as brainless zombies, the image's photographer, Joshua A. Bickel, tried to contextualize the image – stressing the protestors' humanity and right to protest (Onion 2020).

Lumping of the protestors in with waste – as undead contaminants – is not helpful. It is counterproductive and makes it easy to overlook the issue of class, or else to indulge in a classism that has a racial and even *wastial* tinge – whereby white protestors are regarded as white trash. While COVID-19 is a health crisis, it is also an economic crisis as businesses go bust, endangering the livelihoods of workers and small business owners alike. At least in part, some of the protests are related to this precarity. As such, we should focus on how policies can alleviate alienation and precarity. Responses of disgust, if anything, give these protestors something to organize around, as they start trying to "trigger" and provoke liberals, to garner reactions. Such reactions only confirm to them that liberals want to eject them, and their abjection becomes a resistance, a clogging of the corporate-feudal state. Since these protestors think they are living in a medicalized, corporate dystopia, watching films about such dystopias can encourage understanding and provide a shared reference point.

## Wastializing the Other amid COVID-19

These movies narrate worlds where corporations are in charge, and zones of cleanliness are enforced. The wastial (an intersecting category of class, race, and waste) "Other", whether WALL-E (in the eponymousfilm), the aliens, or thealien-ified Wikusin *District* 9, and the zombies relentless recorded on CCTV from *Land of the Dead*, are all tracked and surveilled – abjected from a white middle-class existence. All three films show a world in which the corporate and capitalist class have replaced the government, thus indicating a sort of neo-liberal turn towards neofeudalism (Dean 2020). Such a situation is hastened in our own time as Big Tech's profits have grown amid the pandemic.

It is worth noting how readily the more hysterical protestors against COVID-measures sound as though they fear being victims of colonization. They openly describe the state and big business as Nazi, and opine that not being able to go to restaurants without proof of vaccination is a form of segregation. As historian David Barber (2020) writes,

> [w]hite supremacy is not only white over black, it is also the small number of rich whites over the much larger number of poor and working class whites. In return for a guarantee that the latter group of whites will suffer the many calamities of life afflicting working people in a capitalist society less intensely and less frequently than do black people and people of colour, the poor and working class whites will not challenge the rule of the rich. (n.p.)

Much research backs up the view that "whiteness" actually hinders white workers, often leading white workers to vote against their best interests (Metzl 2019). How then could these films be interpreted for our times? In part, these films help us to understand what some of the more conspiracy-inclined protestors think they are protesting. They think they are *othered* (in some ways they are, but not to the extent that they believe), and they see the embrace of Big Pharma, the soaring profits of Big Tech during the pandemic, and government mandates as all interrelated (again, in a sense they are, but not in the sense that these conspiracists believe).

Throughout these films, there is a fear of sanitized and pristine spaces. These spaces are void of grit and texture and life – people are literally alive there but lack a sense of life's importance. In *District 9* we see laboratories and beige offices, as spaces that are lifeless. In *WALL-E*, there is something sinister about the anti-septic spaceship, carrying human colonies, living virtual lives. And the cold corporate building of *Land of the Dead* contrasts with the trash-filled spaces that ordinary human survivors must put up with. The protestors against COVID-measures often feel that this emphasis on health and cleanliness is itself a type of tyranny, a type of war against them. The cleanness of politics that progressive neo-liberals advocate for understandably appears to COVID-restriction protestors as Big Business and Big Government working side by side. In Toronto, a group protesting vaccines dressed as medicalized zombies (TMZ 2020). They wore white face masks and hazmat suits but shuffled and moved like Romero's zombies – intimating that medicalized responses were somehow zombified. They played a recording, satirizing what they took to be the current anti-septopian dystopia:

> Thinking for yourself endangers the common good. Body contact causes suffering. Facial expression is excessive. Solitary confinement is safe. Closeness is dangerous. Sterility is essential. Aloneness is the answer. Restrictions are freedom. [ ... ] Big business is essential. Big government is essential. (TMZ 2020).

In short, the protestors against COVID-19 government measures fear being erased. They fear becoming "othered" by elites and the "ruling classes". They see, in some ways correctly, that there is indeed already a fusion between Big Business and Big Government. At the same time, many of the protestors cleave to quite preposterous and repugnant views. At demonstrations against COVID-19 measures (vaccine mandates, lockdown, social distancing, masks, surveillance with QR codes, heavy-handed policing), there are often QAnon followers and other reactionary groups. There is a fear of replacement. Many protestors may be against sanitized spaces but many still equate the Other with filth. One of the merits of films about septopia is that they attempt to engender empathy with those subjected to living amid trash and those abjected by, and from, neo-liberal society. These films point to possible alliances and the need for solidarity among those who are designated as potential contaminates.

These films also highlight themes very relevant to today and COVID-19. Jameson has argued that the political unconscious can be used to re-politicize texts and critique the present. Neo-liberal handling of the crisis has been critiqued throughout the pandemic. The focus on markets by Britain, Sweden, and the US in 2020 saw COVID-19 cases skyrocket. We see that the crisis has laid bare the very inhumanity that can be generated by market-first approaches to policy, supplemented with a punitive state. In many nations, the most vulnerable immigrants and poor have been treated by governments and the press as requiring more policing to prevent the virus from spreading. Policies and approaches that "other" the poor and ethnic minorities do precede neo-liberalism and are arguably inheritances from colonialism. But progressive neo-liberals stress the way that the market fights racism, sexism, and classism. Even if true, COVID-19 shows the failure to overcome these inheritances. And so long as these troubling inheritances continue, white fears, or the fears of not being white, will persist. In this sense septopia is the unconscious of the pandemic: the repressed fears of becoming a wasted being. Part of the reason after all to hoard toilet paper is to separate oneself from waste, to hold onto sanitary comfort and prepare for the potential post-apocalyptic dystopias that populate the Hollywood screen.

## Conclusion: Septopian films

Amid COVID-19, septopia becomes more relevant to political realities, where people rebel against sanitized spaces and lockdown policies. While Bush-era films explored heavy policing in a war "against"/(of) terror, and racial and class disparities, COVID-19 has also been compared to war conditions, and has exacerbated racial and class tensions, renewing the relevance of the films *WALL-E, District 9*, and *Land of the Dead*. Septopian films allegorize neo-liberalism under warlike conditions, whether the fight is against terror or the pandemic. But these films also reinforce the very concerns that COVID-restriction protestors decry. This itself can aid in understanding these protestors' concerns and not reacting moralistically to their "performed" wastiality, their attempts to "trigger the libs". Although at times obscuring these issues, the three films illustrate the way that racialized policies intersect with class and people deemed not "white". Depictions of waste zones, of septopia, help to remind viewers that government and corporate policies often target minorities and reinforce the idea that immigrants, the poor, and workers are *abjected* as contaminants. As such, a Jamesonian understanding provides a (re-)politization of these concerns, both in texts and in life.

## Note

1. The horrific conditions in India in 2020, where workers were forced to make their way home by foot, often travelling across state lines and struggling to find shelter for the night, captures something of this sense of labour's violent expulsion. India, however, is too complex to discuss here due to its relationship between neo-liberal precarity, statism, class, and caste.

## Disclosure statement

No potential conflict of interest was reported by the author.

## References

"Armed Protestors Demand an End to Michigan's Coronoavirus Lockdown Orders." 2020. *The Guardian* video, April 16. https://www.theguardian.com/global/video/2020/apr/16/armed-protesters-demand-an-end-to-michigans-coronavirus-lockdown-orders-video
Barber, David. 2020. "Renouncing White Privilege: A Left Critique of DiAngelo's 'White Fragility'." *CounterPunch*, August 3. Accessed 6 December 2021. https://www.counterpunch.org/2020/08/03/renouncing-white-privilege-a-critique-of-robin-diangelos-white-fragility/
Bastani, Aaron. 2019. *Fully Automated Luxury Communism*. London and New York: Verso.
Bauman, Zygmunt. 2004. *Wasted Lives: Modernity and Its Outcasts*. Cambridge: Polity Press.

Blake, Linnie. 2015. "'Are We Worth Saving? You Tell Me': Neoliberalism, Zombies and the Failure of Free Trade." *Gothic Studies* 17 (2): 26–41. doi:10.7227/GS.17.2.3.

Blomkamp, Neill, dir. 2009. District. 9. Calver City, CA: Sony Pictures Releasing.

Castillo, David R., David Schmid, David A. Reilly, and John Edgar Browning, eds. 2016. *Zombie Talk: Culture, History, Politics*. Hampshire: Palgrave Macmillan.

Crenshaw, Kimberlé. 2017. *On Intersectionality*. New York: The New Press.

Dean, Jodi. 2020. "Neofeudalism: The End of Capitalism?" *Los Angeles Review of Books*, May 12. Accessed 6 December 2021. https://lareviewofbooks.org/article/neofeudalism-the-end-of-capitalism/

Domingo, Andreu. 2018. "Analyzing Zombie Dystopia as Neoliberal Scenario: An Exercise in Emancipatory Catastrophism." *Frontiers in Sociology* 3 (July): n.p. doi:10.3389/fsoc.2018.00020.

2016. "'Drug Dealers, Criminals, Rapists': What Trump Thinks of Mexicans." *BBC News*, August 31. Accessed 20 December 2021. https://www.bbc.com/news/av/world-us-canada-37230916

Evans, Rachel, and Robin Elhaj. 2021. "Common Ground Residents Demand Compensation for Harsh Lockdown." *Green Left* 1319: n.p. September 16. Accessed 6 December 2021. https://www.greenleft.org.au/content/common-ground-residents-demand-compensation-harsh-lockdown

Fanon, Frantz. 1963. *The Wretched of the Earth*. Translated by Constance Farrington. New York: Grove Press.

Federici, Silvia. 2004. *Caliban and the Witch*. New York: Autonomedia.

Fraser, Nancy. 2019. *The Old Is Dying and the New Cannot Be Born: From Progressive Neoliberalism to Trump and Beyond*. London: Verso.

Hall, Stuart, Chas Critcher, Tony Jefferson, John Clarke, and Brian Roberts. 1978. *Policing the Crisis*. London: Macmillan Press.

Isaksen, Joachim Vogt. 2019. "The Impact of Financial cCisis on European Attitudes toward Immigration." *Comparative Migration Studies* 7 (24): n.p. doi:10.1186/s40878-019-0127-5.

Jameson, Fredric. 1991. *The Postmodern Condition*. London: Verso.

Jameson, Fredric. 2002. *The Political Unconscious*. London: Verso.

Jameson, Fredric. 2020. *Allegory and Ideology*. London: Verso.

Johnson, Scott C. 2009. "The Real District 9: Cape Town's District Six." *Newsweek*, November 6. Accessed 6 December 2021. https://www.newsweek.com/real-district-9-cape-towns-district-six-78939

Kee, Jessica Baker. 2015. "Black Masculinities and Postmodern Horror: Race, Gender, and Abjection." *Visual Culture and Gender* 10: 47–56.

Kellner, Douglas M. 2009. *Cinema Wars*. West Sussex: Wiley-Blackwell.

Kirkland, Ewan, ed. 2016. *Shades of Whiteness*. Oxford: Inter-Disciplinary Press.

Kristeva, Julia. 1982. *Powers of Horror: An Essay on Abjection*. New York: Columbia University Press.

Lauro, Sarah J. 2015. *The Transatlantic Zombie: Slavery, Rebellion, and Living Death*. New Brunswick, NJ: Rutgers University Press.

Marx, Karl. 1857–61. *Grundrisse*. Accessed 6 December 2021. https://www.marxists.org/archive/marx/works/1857/grundrisse/

Mascarenhas, Michael, Ryken Grattet, and Kathleen Mege. 2021. "Toxic Waste and Race in Twenty-First Century America." *Environment and Society: Advances in Research* 12 (1): 108–126. doi:10.3167/ares.2021.120107.

McAlister, Elizabeth. 2012. "Slaves, Cannibals, and Infected Hyper-Whites: The Race and Religion of Zombies." *Anthropological Quarterly* 85 (2): 457–486. doi:10.1353/anq.2012.0021.

Metzl, Jonathan. 2019. *Dying of Whiteness: How the Politics of Racial Resentment Is Killing America's Heartland*. New York: Basic Books.

Newbury, Michael. 2012. "Fast Zombie, Slow Zombie: Food Writing, Horror Movies, and Agribusiness Apocalypse." *American Literary History* 24 (1): 87–114. doi:10.1093/alh/ajr055.

Onion, Rebecca. 2020. "These People Aren't Zombies. They're People." *Slate*, April 16. Accessed 6 December 2021. https://slate.com/human-interest/2020/04/ohio-protester-zombie-photo-coronavirus-interview.html?via=rss_socialflow_twitter

2020. "President Trump Calls Coronavirus 'Kung Flu'." *BBC News*, June 20. Accessed 6 December 2021. https://www.bbc.com/news/av/world-us-canada-53173436

Robinson, Cedric J. 1983. *Black Marxism*. Chapel Hill, NC: University of North Carolina Press.

Romero, George A., dir. 2005. *Land of the Dead*. Universal City, CA: Universal Pictures.

Singh, Nikhil Pal. 2016. "On Race, Violence, and So-Called Primitive Accumulation," *Social Text* 34 (3): 27–50.

Standing, Guy. 2011. *The Precariat: The New Dangerous Class*. London: Bloomsbury.

Stanton, Andrew, dir. 2008. *WALL-E*. Burbank, CA: Walt Disney Studios Motion Pictures.

TMZ. 2020. "COVID 2020 Zombies Protest Vaccines: 'Questioning Vaccines Is Murder'." *TMZ Online*, December. 26. Accessed 20 December 2021. https://www.tmz.com/2020/12/26/toronto-covid-19-coronavirus-vaccine-protest-hazmat-suits/

Valverde, Miriam. 2021. "Fact-checking Claims about Deportations in Biden's First Month." *PolitiFact* February. 26. Accessed 21 February 2022. https://www.politifact.com/article/2021/feb/26/biden-backtracking-deportation-promise-social-medi/

West-Pavlov, Russell. 2018. *The Global South and Literature*. Cambridge: Cambridge University Press.

Wilson, Jacqueline Zara. 2002. "Invisible Racism: The Language and Ontology of Whiteness." *Critique of Anthropology* 22 (4): 387–401. doi:10.1177/0308275X020220040101.

Wray, Matt. 2006. *Not Quite White: White Trash and the Boundaries of Whiteness*. Durham, NC: Duke University Press.

Žižek, Slavoj. 1989. *The Sublime Object of Ideology*. London: Verso.

Žižek, Slavoj. 2007. "'Ode to Joy', Followed by Chaos and Despair." *New York Times*. December. 24. https://www.nytimes.com/2007/12/24/opinion/24zizek.html

# Fragmentations, phantom limbs, re-memberings: Negotiating bodies, representation, and subjectivity in Caribbean British writing

Silvia Gerlsbeck ⓘ

**ABSTRACT**

This article examines representations of corporeality in Caribbean British writing and focuses on two novels in particular: George Lamming's *The Emigrants* (1954) and David Dabydeen's *The Intended* (1991). After outlining relevant insights from the field of body studies and discourses of the body in Caribbean literature, it argues that the novels focus on the body to voice similar concerns about writing, representation, and knowledge. The novel aspect of this article lies in its rereading of the texts' foregrounding of issues of corporeality. Where corporeal imagery in postcolonial literatures has mostly been conceived as a symptom of the racialization and feminization of the "other" body as a legacy of colonialism, this article shifts the focus towards seeing the novels' employment of the body as a negotiation of discourses of representation and subjectivity. In probing and problematizing constructivist and materialist conceptions, they furthermore negotiate important shifts in approaching "matter" in literary theory.

## Discourses of the body in Caribbean literature

Following the "corporeal turn" in the humanities and the social sciences in the 1990s, and particularly in the last decade, the body as locus of meaning(s) has become a central subject of analysis in many disciplines. Here, literature can offer new epistemological frames, as Hillman and Maude (2015) state: "[i]n confronting us with the legible materiality of the body", it offers "forms of resistance to socially instituted perceptions and demands" and is able to challenge disciplinary regimes (4–5). And while the interest in "body matters" remains undiminished in literary and cultural studies, there are some lacunae in this regard in the field of Caribbean writing. Particularly, this concerns interrogations of bodies and body discourses in Caribbean literature that go beyond seeing them predominantly as metaphors for a national (Caribbean or British) body politic and social belonging. This article looks at two Caribbean British novels, George Lamming's *The Emigrants*, published in 1954, and David Dabydeen's *The Intended* from 1991, and their representations of the body as a site where inscriptions of different modes of subjectivity are negotiated. It draws on insights from feminist, post-structuralist, and new materialist theories to inquire into the texts' complex portrayals of corporeality and embodiment and their interaction with theories of subjectivity and writing.

In *Body Work*, Peter Brooks (1993) emphasizes the importance of the body for the subject, but likewise its ambiguous status: "[o]ur bodies are with us, though we have always had trouble saying exactly how. We are, in various conceptions or metaphors, in our body, or at one with our body, or alienated from it" (1). Elizabeth Grosz's (1994) feminist reconceptualization of the body describes it as the locus of social, political, cultural, or geographic inscriptions, productions, and constitutions (23). Drawing on Jacques Lacan, she argues that the image of the body as whole, as it emerges in the mirror stage, also indicates "the meaning that the body has for the subject, for others in its social world, and for the symbolic order conceived in its generality (that is, for a culture as a whole)", as both "an individual and collective fantasy" (39–40). Grosz's statement points to the body as cultural product and metaphor – "bound up in the order of desire, signification, and power" (19) – that is, as providing the imagery for describing a whole culture or parts of it, rather than mere biological matter. This is not surprising, as matter per se is only tangible through representations and subject to mediation through language.

Yet, while acknowledging the body's discursive formation, theorists like Grosz also strive to consider the body's irreducible and fracturing dimensions (Grosz 1994, 13). Jean-Luc Nancy ([1992] 2008), in a similar vein, urges us to conceive of the body not just as a conceptual trope, but to pay attention to its materiality: "[l]et there be writing, not *about* the body, but the body itself. [...]. Not signs, images, or ciphers of the body, but still the body" (9). Nancy's work marks a radical return to matter, his view transcends the body's dematerialization, its function as a sign only, and, instead of unity and coherence, emphasizes its interminability.

These positions criticize the body's presence "as an object of discourse [...] [while] the body *itself* remains largely undertheorized" (De Clercq 2013, 79; emphasis added) and are anticipating a recent shift in academia towards a renewed concern with materiality, which originated in the field of sociology and has increasingly gained traction in literary and cultural studies as well. Works by new materialists and material feminists, in particular, have initiated a turn to the agency of matter to counter effects of dematerialization, seen as a by-product of the linguistic turn (Barad 2007; Alaimo 2010; Coole and Frost 2010), and their insights and urges to "take account of material constraints and conditions once again without reinscribing traditional empiricist assumptions" (Barad 2007, 152) are crucial for attesting to narrative moments where language fails to account for embodied experience.

While these positions foreground the relevance of the body and materiality in general, the importance corporeal matters carry varies in light of differential categories such as gender, sexuality, or race. Thus, it is not surprising that the emphasis on matter – as a negotiation of historical inscriptions onto the "other" body – is so conspicuous in postcolonial literatures. In western philosophy, the idea of the neutral, disembodied subject that emerged in the 18th century and its claim to universality always needed the "other('s)" body – differentiated through its race, ethnicity, sex, gender, or class – as a demarcation for the self. The Cartesian privileging of mind over matter has for a long time relegated the body to the margins and, consequently, begotten the white, male, able body as invisible norm. The "other", marked body has subsequently been represented as *just* body; its heightened physicality often bordering on the grotesque (Ahmed 2002, 51–53). Scholarship on the black female body in particular has foregrounded the burden of intersecting processes of gendering, sexualization, and racialization and the ideologies behind framing the body as a "grotesque" foil for the European self (Ahmed 2002; Newman 2018).

The body that is marked by difference emerges as hyper-visible, serving as the hegemonic subject's essential abject that stabilizes the norm and solidifies identity, albeit always only tenuously, as Judith Butler (1990) states: "[t]he boundary of the body as well as the distinction between internal and external is established through the ejection and transvaluation of something originally part of identity into a defiling otherness" (133). The body of the "other" and its abjection are entangled in processes of subjectification: following Michel Foucault (1982), this specific order of knowledge of the body constitutes a "form of power" (781) that structures "different modes by which, in our culture, human beings are made subjects" (777). The body becomes a locus where different, often contradictory, knowledges are inscribed, but also where they can be contested. In this vein, analyses of the female body also attest to the subversive and decolonial potential of representations of black bodies; for instance, the potential to rupture the imaginary coherent nation body (Tate 2015).

In a Caribbean context, Michael Dash (1989) speaks of the "lost body" (17) of the Caribbean subject and finds that for many writers, the body becomes a site where constant cultural change and psychological alienation manifest:

> The imaginative concern with the subject [...] is responsible for a system of imagery in Caribbean literature whose centre is the body. The body is an endlessly suggestive sign through which the process of "subjectification" is mediated and expressed. [...] The ever shifting, unstable relationship between body and non-body, between dis-membering and re-membering, is a continuous aesthetic and thematic concern. (20)

The notion of absent and present bodies and their "dis-membering" as a prerequisite for "re-membering" are crucial for my reading as well, and this becomes even more prevalent in the context of diaspora: in Britain, it was the bodies of the *Windrush* generation and their descendants that were conceived as a challenge to the national body politic.[1] The denigration of the immigrant body as detrimental to the social body goes back centuries and is visible in the plethora of imaginations of racialized bodies, which have served to restrain those marked as "other" but have, at the same time, always also been marked by ambivalence.[2] Particularly, it is the male, racially marked body which, as a constant object of fear and desire, is arguably even more ambivalently received than the female "other" body; in cultural representations simultaneously hyper-sexualized and effeminized and also at the centre of discussions surrounding the integrity and health of the national body. These observations resonate with Frantz Fanon's insights: the fixing of the "other" body under the white gaze in a phantasmatic image and the knowledge this yields, he argues, is dependent on a historically racialized schema; that is, historical and racist dimensions are inscribed under the body's surface, a fact that Fanon ([1952] 2008) calls the "epidermal racial scheme", which determines its occupation of and orientation in space (92).

It might hence not come as a surprise that Caribbean literature and theory frequently employ images of corporeal fragmentation, dismembering, or dis-*membrane*-ing – that is, shedding one's skin. Thus, the stereotype of the fragmented culture of the "Caribbean periphery" – vis-à-vis a supposed coherence of the "metropolitan centre" – is, for instance, tellingly expressed in Derek Walcott's Nobel lecture. Commenting on the performance of an epic drama in Trinidad, Walcott criticizes perceptions of the Caribbean as lacking history through the metaphor of the fragmented body:

> The purists look on such ceremonies as grammarians look at a dialect, as cities look on provinces and empires on their colonies. Memory that yearns to join the center, a limb remembering the body from which it has been severed, like those bamboo thighs of the god. In other words, the way that the Caribbean is still looked at, illegitimate, rootless, mongrelized. [...] Fragments and echoes of real people, unoriginal and broken. (1992, 26)

Yet writers also emphasize corporeality to subvert racialization or stereotypes of ahistoricality and to envision new modes of writing. This is prominent, for instance, in the work of Wilson Harris and best captured in his notion of the "phantom limb". Harris considers the bodily contortions of the limbo dance, an element of West Indian carnival, and the dance's metaphorical reassembly of "dismembered" memories and stigmata of the Middle Passage as an example of a shared Caribbean phantom limb (Harris [1970] 2008, 10–14). This expresses experiences of cultural dislocation, yet also implies (artistic) renewal and compensation – issued "from a state of cramp to articulate a new growth" (13).

Processes of and ideologies behind racialization, dislocation, and fragmentation are then questioned and undermined in Lamming's and Dabydeen's novels. Following Lacan's notion of the dismembered body as signifying the "real" and thus the outside of the symbolic order and dominant representations, the authors negotiate this "unbearable knowledge" of the body – that is, a poetics that fixes the subject via specific projections of the body – and show its cultural fabrication. Yet while in recent years the body has been omnipresent, there is a neglect in analyses of corporeality in Caribbean British literature that especially spurs my interest in rereading these texts: when the body does receive attention, it is mostly regarding processes of racialization and feminization, as outlined above, as a perpetuation of or resistance to colonial epistemologies. What has been neglected so far and what is a major interest of this article is the novels' use of the body to question representational regimes and theoretical conceptions of corporeality and subjectivity. My analysis of *The Emigrants* and *The Intended* sees the texts' fragmentation of bodies as signs that indicate a shift in mediating memory and rendering history and as a consciously employed trope that problematizes knowledge altogether. This pertains to notions of engaged literature, but also to theoretical conceptions of subjectivity that are variously emphasizing embodiment or discursivity. In this sense, my reading goes beyond analyses that are concerned with notions of identity and are oftentimes somewhat essentialist. Rather, it aims to illustrate that these texts anticipate and reflect major shifts in conceptions of subjectivity, specifically radical constructivist perspectives that envision the dissolution of the subject that will become the major paradigm in literary theory in the second half of the 20th century.

On the other hand, corporeal metaphors also point towards the "intransigence" (Coole and Frost 2010, 1) of matter and the inability of language and representation to fully capture it. This is pertinent in Lamming's novel, which in 1954 portrays bodily fragmentations that signal the emptying out of conventional signs – which can be read as anticipatory of postmodern theories of subjectivity – and bodies that "speak" their own language without being intelligible. Dabydeen's novel, published in 1991, makes use of the body to negotiate the racialized subject's problematic position between a belief in the discursive constructedness of identity and an awareness of the weight of the body's materiality and lived reality, something feminist theorists often emphasize. In both novels, discourses of the body are also simultaneously manifestations of discourses of authorship.

## Dismembering bodies: George Lamming's *The Emigrants*

Lamming's ([1954] 1994) novel *The Emigrants* depicts the departure for and arrival in Britain of a group of emigrants from the West Indies and is a key text for the experience of the *Windrush* generation. Tracing the arrival of the emigrants in three chapters, the novel strongly emphasizes the "othering" of the migrants' bodies and, I argue, employs the body to question forms of representation: its emphasis on fragmentation, rather than mourning a loss of identity, can also be read as anticipating a post-structuralist "erasure" of the material body and an emphasis on its discursive shaping to defy notions of universality.

In this context, the character Collis as the novel's writer figure is important, being charged with representing the emigrants' experience, as the fellow emigrant only known as "Strange Man" tells him: "[y]ou're a writer [...] You're articulate not only for yourself, but thousands who'll never see you in person but who will know you because the printed page is public property" (Lamming [1954] 1994, 100–101). Yet in the novel it is often the body itself that is figured as barrier and limit for writing the subject and making it legible, functioning as an obstacle to incorporate the "other" into epistemological frameworks that have theorized their inferiority. Collis's interaction with fellow traveller Dickson is most telling here, as it is often Dickson's body that prevents Collis from "knowing" him:

> [H]e felt [Dickson's] rigidity. The passage between their bunks was the space of two bodies, yet Collis felt that he had filled it completely. [...] [H]e felt that Dickson's body was speaking, warning that it shouldn't be touched, fearing its action if it had been touched. [...] His eyes had kept the line of direction with Dickson's back, but they weren't seeing. [...] [S]hocked by the sudden turn of Dickson's body[, Collis] dropped his glance and half turned. The bodies seemed to communicate in a way neither could interpret. (30–31)

The emphasis on corporeality in this excerpt is striking and indicates a breakdown in representation: Dickson's body prevents Collis from scrutinizing – "seeing" – Dickson and, as a writer, turning him into literary material, into "public property". The body stands as a barrier against a *littérature engagée*, a form of writing that rests on essentialist conceptions of the postcolonial subject, serves to make it convenient for a metropolitan audience, and entails its commodification in a western literary market. The passage's emphasis on emotions that highlight the materiality of the body and its extra-linguistic, affective dimension ("felt", "fearing", "shocked") shows a pre-empting of representation on the level of language and a resistance of the body to materialize according to dominant discourses of gender and race, as the meaning of the bodies' language eludes Collis.

Collis's attempt to "see" the other passengers on the ship is one attempt at infusing bodies with meaning the novel presents – and prevents. At times, the scopophilic, fragmenting absorption of his fellow travellers' bodies is portrayed as unsettling the gazing subject: trying to see "what kind of figure he cut", Collis scrutinizes the character known as Governor and his "thick legs, hard calves and short, stubborn toes" and "dense bush of hair that covers his chest" (Lamming [1954] 1994, 38). In a melange of desire and threat, the predetermined inscriptions on the emigrants' bodies cause Collis to experience anxiety regarding his own subjecthood as both masculine and heterosexual and evoke the body as the realm of the "real": "[e]very limb [of the Governor] seemed an assertion of loud masculinity. Collis recoiled into the space, trying to avoid his eyes" (38–39).

An alternative view that refrains from imposing an interpretation on other bodies and conceives the body as affective entity – as locus of pleasure, beyond the inscriptions of difference – emerges in a dancing scene in the dining hall of the ship. The perspective here is not attributable to a specific character and eschews an authoritative account of the meaning of the episode:

> [E]njoyment required no special accommodation, but was a condition of the body, issuing from within the body whose resources were infinitely greater than the person understood. [...] The other had been annihilated. There was only the body which was the dance itself, regulated, informed, nourished and dictated not only by its blood, but by some pervasive, measureless source of being that was its own logic of receptivity and transmission [...] Its form, shape, movement, the physical discharge of itself constituted an open secret which everyone saw but could not read. [...] [T]hen[,] exhausted and broken by its own desire, it fell. (Lamming [1954] 1994, 93–94)

Resonating with Harris's phantom limb and the collectivity inherent to the limbo dance, Lamming's commentary on the tension between discursive and material dimensions of the body becomes most visible in this scene: foregrounding the impenetrability of the body – as an "endlessly suggestive sign" (Dash 1989, 20) – constitutes a refusal to re-enter it into existing discursive formations. Yet its free flow of desire ultimately collapses, "falls", indicating that the subject's break from the symbolic order can only be temporary, being "within and outside itself simultaneously" (Lamming [1954] 1994, 93), a *hors-corps* – borrowing from Derrida's (1967) famous *hors-texte*[3] – and thus an outside of discourse is impossible. Yet Lamming's attempt to write the body itself, not *about* it (as Nancy envisioned it), for once creates an intermediary space where the distinctions between self and other are momentarily suspended. As a theoretical comment, this necessitates acknowledging the body as discursively produced but at the same time implies another origin, thus hinting at an extra-linguistic, ineffable dimension – "part of the source of its being and at the same time its being" (Lamming [1954] 1994, 93). Moreover, the bodily affects portrayed potentially also affect readers, who rely on the heterodiegetic narrator's explanation of the bodies' meaning for their own interpretation. Frustrating these expectations amounts to an ethical gesture, as it urges the shedding of body knowledge and thus preconceived notions of the "other".

The "forgetting" of the body in this passage reverberates through the novel and has its effect on Collis as well: his attempts to narrate – to "literarize" – his fellow passengers culminate in his loss of sight and the impossibility of coordinating signifier and signified. His vision dis-members: "[h]e wouldn't recognize the nose as nose, or the eye as eye. The organs kept their form, but somehow lost their reference. They became objects" (Lamming [1954] 1994, 219). While the theme of vision in the novel has been analysed either as a negotiation of colonial violence and the ensuing alienation or as resisting against it,[4] I read blindness as reversing the assumption of a specular image in the mirror stage; that is, as probing the dissolution of the imaginary, whole body as a discursive object, and the evocation of the "real" as a signal for a new style of writing and thinking that extends to all subjects. Collis's gaze on Frederick, the white Englishman, who also dissolves in his vision, speaks to that: "Collis was looking for his eyes but it seemed that he had forgotten what an eye was. He saw the objects of dull glass evenly balanced on either side of Frederick's nose, but he could no longer recognise Frederick's eyes" (224). The imaginary anatomy, as "internalized image or map" of the body's meaning (Grosz 1994, 39–40), is fragmented, the function of speech and discourse for subjectivity revealed and pre-empted – bodies are constituted in language, and in Collis's fragmentation of the body, his inability to understand it as a sign, the limits of the symbolic order's control over the body are indicated. This *corps morcelé*, following Lacan,[5] stands at the beginning of identification and the subject's quest for wholeness: rather than portraying a paralysis of the colonized subject, Lamming here then envisions a constant returning to the material body in its minutest parts in a spiral movement that plays with drawing on established body knowledge and discarding it, thus foregoing any absolutism. The return to the fragmented body as an "inchoate collection of desires" (Lacan [1956] 1993, 39), moreover, also indicates a moment where the contradictory desires of the subject are yet unorganized and equally valuable; it marks the triumph of the subject's desires over any deceptive imagination of wholeness and societal norms – with Nancy, the body becomes "the end of the signifier" (Nancy [1992] 2008, 75). Lamming's dismembering temporarily liberates the subject from incorporations into rigid confinements (as regards gender, race, or sexuality).

Ultimately, the novel suggests, this liberation necessitates a break with form. In a scene where the character Dickson becomes the voyeuristic object of his landlady, the dissolution of Dickson's body is mirrored in the text's dissolution:

> [The landlady and her sister] devoured his body with their eyes. It disintegrated and dissolved in their stare, gradually regaining its life through the reflection in the mirror.
>
> me. me. me. out them all. me.
>
> He couldn't recollect what had happened. [...]
>
> out of them all. me. the man is mad. out of them all. me. me. (Lamming [1954] 1994, 266)

Dickson's psychological disintegration and becoming "other", "the man", in this scene and the loss of his body – afterwards, "[h]e had to make sure he was there, under his clothes" (267) – is paralleled by the fragmentation of his thoughts, due to the degradation experienced, and by the fragmentation of the text's "body" itself. This marks another instance where Lamming ambivalently portrays "losing" one's body as a prerequisite for new affiliations, a new solidarity and communal vision beyond the individual's isolation: while acknowledging the situation's traumatic quality, the text also portrays Dickson's "shattering" experience as a cause for him to look "for some kind of help. He wanted to make his peace with someone, to ask for admission into the lives of others" (267). *The Emigrants* thus sketches new subject positions based on vulnerability and empathy. On a formal level, these new affiliations coincide with Lamming's disembodying of the narration: narrative instances shift and often remain uncertain, as do focalizers and character identifications, and chronology is only loosely adhered to, amounting to a narrative that seems to spring from a collective body in which, however, many different perspectives coexist.

Lamming's emphasis on the fragmented body, then, is not (just) expressing a mournful view on the unbelonging, alienation, or loss of identity experienced by the *Windrush* immigrants. In a move anticipatory of post-structuralist ideas of subjecthood, the text's evocation of the *corps morcelé* hints at the conflicting task of the writer to create imaginary, whole subjects, to assume writerly responsibility without resorting to a textual form that reinscribes, to cite Barad again, "traditional empiricist assumptions" (2007, 152) or false teleologies and causalities. Ultimately, the text suggests, writers must fear their own authority, perpetually return to the fragments, with every composition existing always only temporary. This makes Lamming such an intriguing case study, as the text so staunchly defies contemporary demands, where attempts to emancipate the formerly colonized subject necessitated essentializing strategies of emphasizing presence, sameness, and recovering cultural identity and history.

## Negotiating epidermal meanings: David Dabydeen's *The Intended*

The body as epistemological category and the relation of body, memory, and writing is also a central if critically neglected topic in Dabydeen's first novel *The Intended*. Designed as a coming-of-age story and, following a *Bildungsroman* trajectory, formally less experimental than Lamming's text, the novel blends the unnamed narrator's childhood memories from Guyana, where he grew up, with episodes from his adolescence in Balham in the 1970s with his friends Shaz, Patel, Nasim, and Joseph, and culminates with his departure for the University of Oxford. The narrator, a self-described "Indian West-Indian Guyanese" (Dabydeen [1991] 2010, 8), in remembering his own story constantly reinscribes bodies with colonial knowledge. The internalization of the "white gaze" leads to the different "shades" of "the brownness of our skins" (8) becoming a measuring tool for propriety and respectability. The narrator's wish to be white – "I'm dark-skinned like them [the West Indians] but I'm different, and I hope the whites can see that and separate me from that lot" (127) – as a result of "lactification", the epidermalization of a sense of inferiority (Fanon [1952] 2008, 80), represents more than a striving for assimilation: being an aspiring author, shedding his racialized body, which has historically been associated with "nature" rather than "culture", resonates with a wish for disembodiment and existence as pure mind, his denigration of the West Indian's supposed sole interest to "dance and breed" vis-à-vis his respect for "good manners, books, art, philosophy" and a shared civilization with the whites (Dabydeen [1991] 2010, 127) attests to that.

Body knowledge in the novel is influenced by the legacy of empire and its exploitation of "others", particularly women. The voyeuristic gazes the narrator and his friends train on women are frequently turned around and set back on themselves. The narrator, for instance, becomes his girlfriend's object when she buys him a shirt: "[s]he turned me round again and again, screwing up her eyes and peering intently. I felt like one of Shaz's whores, or a slave on an auction block" (Dabydeen [1991] 2010, 171). Equating the hyper-visible body of the woman and the racial "other", the text lays bare that both, in western Cartesian ontology, have been marked as *only* body. Yet more so, it probes how to circumvent a reinscription of this – or any authoritative – knowledge and foregrounds the fragmented body as a trope that signals a continuous questioning of authorial methods. This happens, I argue, by rehearsing various discourses of representation that manifest on the body and often centre on "skin": one enquires into the body's function and value as an (artistic) commodity, another into its role in a humanist conception of writing, and a third into the ramifications of post-structuralist fragmentations of the body for the subject.

Representational discourses, for once, are embodied by the narrator's friends Patel and Shaz. The latter, while "really wanting to be artistic", has to succumb to his family's wishes to become a businessman. At the same time "obsessed with bodily functions" (Dabydeen [1991] 2010, 107), he joins Patel in turning bodies into another form of art by making pornography to cater to a predominantly white, English, working-class audience, who are in turn also solely defined by the satisfaction of their bodily instincts: "they're lazy, good-for-nothing, they live for their bellies, from day to day [...]. Eat and drink and watch videos and play football" (142). Patel's claim is an ironic use of a Victorian discourse that racialized the working class to strengthen class distinctions,[6] both the white working class and the racial "other" are configured as *only* body. With the commodification of bodies, Shaz and Patel also reference a genealogy of exploitation through empire and turn it around: instead of black, white bodies – female and male – are now commodified:

> He was putting up a new poster advertising some trashy film, "Night Angel", or some such title. It displayed a beautiful woman lying on white satin sheets [...]. A man loomed over her, his shadow darkening the whiteness of her thighs. (162–163)

The exaggeration of the colour symbolism also marks a parodic, postmodern turn, where the fear of the hyper-sexualized "other" has already been commodified and become part of the logic of the market. In the struggle to survive, all existence is reduced to corporeal facts, so far that the body itself only signifies as capital: in a clever twist on the commodification of human bodies in the colonies, for Patel, his clients are "[w]alking banknotes. Their skin is pale and shiny like coins" (142). In the larger body politics of the nation, Patel, while abjected from the nation body, even by the narrator – "[white people] are better than us Pakis" (142) – comes out on top: "I'm a rich Paki, a happy Paki, [...] and they [the whites] wish it was their shop, they're full of envy" (142–143).

The narrator, as aspiring author and influenced by his role models William Blake, Joseph Conrad, or John Milton, has outwardly subscribed to a humanist ideal of *Bildung*, and envisions a Cartesian disembodied existence as pure intellect. Yet he, too, returns to the body to initiate creation: striving to write an epitaph for his landlord's sister, Mrs Ali, the narrator cannot look beyond the meaning of her body: he imagines her "coughing all over her entry forms" and emitting a "thin spray of blood and spittle" (Dabydeen [1991] 2010, 102), only able to count "according to the number of fingers and toes", "her mouth [...] barely consolidating some remaining teeth", "the echoes of her vomiting" resounding in his memory (103). It is precisely this abject quality of her body that prevents the narrator from inscribing her into a universal and aestheticized frame of representation: the persistent materiality of Mrs Ali's sick and fragmented body, emphasized in imagining her as body parts only, encroaches on his memory and indicates the limits of western knowledge and representation, as it ultimately cannot be enclosed in an epitaph based on Blake's "Tyger" and Milton's "Lycidas", as he intended (104–107).

This points to the danger of fixing the "other" in representation and neglecting historical dimensions and epidermalizations of the black body. Tellingly, it is also a *dead* body that the narrator is meant to describe, which resonates with Fanon's notion of the (pseudo-)petrification of colonized cultures: in *The Wretched of the Earth*, Fanon describes this as an imagined bodily and mental arrest that serves to signify simplicity and coherence and contrasts with the "dynamism" of the colonizer's actions ([1963] 2007, 14–17). Continuously repeating and reinscribing this "petrified" body, then, confines and restricts individual embodiment. Thus, it is only after death – leaving the body, breaking from its state of petrification – that Mrs Ali is transformed: "now she was moving freely above clouds, seeing with an astronaut's eye the eeriness of the earth beneath" (Dabydeen [1991] 2010, 102), able to "utter the most fluent songs, [she] could quote from a thousand books of literature at will, could speak innumerable languages" (102). Left deliberately ambiguous and foreclosing any definite interpretation, this "new", disembodied existence, the text suggests, should not be qualified and reinscribed through stereotypes.

The novel further complicates matter as epistemological category; for instance, through the reciprocal personification and technologization of things and humans: the attractions of the fairground, where the friends work during the summer, are infused with human activity, one-armed bandits "relieve [...] themselves" into the owner's collection bag (Dabydeen [1991] 2010, 57–58), and the prostitute the friends visit drops money "into her bosom, like the robot hand at Battersea Fun Fair" when "activated by a shilling" (130). As authorial comment, this confusion of images can be understood as negotiating and probing new corporeal conceptualizations, particularly the affiliation with technology and non-human matter – as post-human bodies – that question the hegemony of the "human" and have become central in the field of body studies in the last decades.[7] Here, it also points towards the necessities that inhere in a theoretical return to matter, especially the need to acknowledge its specific relevance for those othered in terms of gender, sexuality, race, or other, who are also those most crucially reduced to it.

The notion of disembodiment that filters through the narrator's descriptions, as in Mrs Ali's case, culminates in the artistic vision of his friend Joseph. Being illiterate and lacking formal education, he is the most marginalized of the friends. With Joseph, I argue, the text rehearses post-structuralist negotiations of subjectivity that manifest in his conception of bodies, which, even though Joseph dies, have the most long-lasting ramifications and leave the strongest impression. Feeling the fragmentation of his own body most acutely and misrecognizing himself due to internalized stereotypes – "[w]hen I was in borstal I was rumour. They look at me and see ape, trouble, fist. [...] You can't even see yourself, even if you stand in front of mirror, all you seeing is shape" (Dabydeen [1991] 2010, 74) – he is also aware that this is only a mythic construction: "but you know you is nothing, atoms, only image and legend in their minds" (74). In a search for new means of representation for this dilemma, for writing a "different kind of book" (77), Joseph turns to film as a medium that, paradoxically, serves to transcend the immanent materiality of bodies and things, as it helps him to express his "interest in nothingness, colourlessness, the sightlessness of air, wind, the pure space between the trees" (97). Engaged in filming Patel's pornography, Joseph's focus on the immaterial undermines this project that rests on the sheer materiality and capitalist value of bodies. Turning away from the whole bodies in action and focusing on "the spaces between one rib and the next" (167), Joseph foregrounds – and dismantles – the body as sign by highlighting the arbitrary coordination of signifier and signified and the endless metonymic shifting of meaning:

> He focused on the contours of letters in BOOBY TRAP [the name of the pornographic film], the way the B curved in semi-circles like breasts, leading to rounded O's, the shape of lips perhaps, or the space inside an open mouth, before forming breasts again and the Y-like cleavage of thighs. It was as if he was more fascinated by the suggestions made by letters, the subtleties and abstraction of their form, than by the gross actuality before him. (166)

Joseph's art deconstructs the coherence of the body and matter by performing *différance* – abandoning presence for absence, wholeness for fragmentation, identity for subjectivity. As himself inevitably epidermalized and petrified, Joseph consequently can only escape his own body through self-immolation and thus dissolve the boundaries between identity categories, "purifying hisself of all the shame and desire by burning off his black skin", leaving only "molten flesh, meat that could have been that of a white man, or an animal" (140).

I have stated that the novel endorses Joseph's radical constructivist conception of bodies, and the strongest claim for this, even though Joseph dies, is that he continues to signify for the narrator – in his absence, his ideas are most present, as he returns as a spectre that accompanies the narrator to Oxford: "[h]e stalks me even here, within the guarded walls of the library [...] where centuries of tradition [...] conspire to keep people of his sort outside the door" (Dabydeen [1991] 2010, 139). The "shape" Joseph sees in the mirror, a foreshadowing of his later burned, shapeless, skinless body, remains with the narrator as a reminder of another self within him (140), and fittingly, the novel then ends with the narrator performing his *own* dissolution in metaphorical flames:

> I wait under the street lamp, wanting to be visible, but the light flames upon my head, flames upon my skin and I have to step back into the shade. Soon the black cab will come scuttling along the road like a beetle. Its bright eyes will pick me up like prey, and soon I'll be gone [...]. One last breath, then I'll climb in and be gone. (173)

## Conclusion: Writing bodies, reading bodies

The body as a nexus of varying, conflicting discourses has, in Caribbean British literature post-*Windrush*, moved centre stage for negotiating issues of oppression and inferiorization, but also of cultural participation, questions of representation, and theorizations of subjectivity.

While the separation of "body" and "mind" has long become obsolete and the body "our general medium for having a world", as Merleau-Ponty ([1945] 2002, 169) states, this assertion takes on a somewhat different relevance in the context of Caribbean, black British, or postcolonial writing in general. As the analysis has shown, the lived experience in epidermalized and "petrified" bodies necessitates a fragmenting, dismembering of the body, that means dismantling it as a sign and removing it from the symbolic order, to shed oppressive corporeal epistemologies. Haunted by the spectre of essentialism, the texts shy away from rephrasing matter and employing new authoritative forms of representation. Lamming's text here probes ways of writing and speaking the "other" and the "self" by evoking the body as extralinguistic sign, standing for itself alone, and constant fragmentation to continuously subvert the creation of whole, yet essentialized subjects. Dabydeen's novel, on the other hand, published in 1991 and thus more reflective of the caveats regarding constructivist ideas of subjectivity, still maintains fragmentation, particularly through skin-related imagery, as a necessary paradigm while indicating the problematic political aspects of eradicating the notion of the subject altogether, as Joseph's death shows.

The body as deliberate "blank canvas", as repeatedly dis- and re-membered, however, is evoked to affect readers, who are urged to interrogate and reorient their own knowledge. Thinking of writing as, following Nancy, "not the monstration, the demonstration, of a signification but a gesture toward *touching* upon *sense*" ([1992] 2008, 17; original emphasis), this, possibly, marks the only ethical way to "write" the body.

## Notes

1. Ashley Dawson (2007), for instance, provides an overview over post-*Windrush* politics and debates surrounding a "pure body politic" in his introduction to *Mongrel Nation* (16).
2. This has been most prominently voiced in Homi K. Bhabha's ([1994] 2004) work on the ambivalence of colonial discourse, where the colonizers' fixing of the "other's" body via fetishist stereotypes is a simultaneous indicator of their desire for it (117).
3. *Il n'y a pas de hors-texte* (Derrida 1967, 227; original emphasis).
4. For these differing interpretations, see, for example, Sarah Pouchet Paquet (1982) and John Clement Ball (2004).
5. Lacan ([1949] 2006, 97) originally develops this idea of the "fragmented body" and an "orthopedic" fantasy of totality in his lecture on "The Mirror Stage as Formative of the *I* Function".
6. This is most prominent in Henry Mayhew's (1851) *London Labour and the London Poor*, where he describes the lower classes as "vagabond savage[s]" (320). Anne McClintock (1995), in her analysis of advertisements for Pears' soap, likewise emphasizes the similarities in representations of the working-class and the immigrant body as "dirty others" to the middle-class's "clean", white body (211).
7. Especially in the work of Donna Haraway, Rosi Braidotti, or Cary Wolfe.

## Disclosure statement

No potential conflict of interest was reported by the author.

## ORCID

*Silvia Gerlsbeck* (iD) http://orcid.org/0000-0001-7905-5503

## References

Ahmed, Sara. 2002. "Racialized Bodies." In *Real Bodies*, edited by Mary Evans and Ellie Lee, 46–63. Basingstoke: Palgrave Macmillan.

Alaimo, Stacy. 2010. *Bodily Natures: Science, Environment, and the Material Self.* Bloomington, IN: Indiana University Press.

Ball, John Clement. 2004. "Towards a Transcultural London: Early West Indian Fiction and the Metropolis." In *Bridges across Chasms: Towards a Transcultural Future in Caribbean Literature*, edited by Bénédicte Ledent, 117–126. Liège: Liège Language and Literature.

Barad, Karen. 2007. *Meeting the Universe Halfway: Quantum Physics and the Entanglement of Matter and Meaning.* Durham, NC: Duke University Press.

Bhabha, Homi K. [1994] 2004. *The Location of Culture.* Abingdon: Routledge Classics.

Brooks, Peter. 1993. *Body Work.* Cambridge, MA: Harvard University Press.

Butler, Judith. 1990. *Gender Trouble: Feminism and the Subversion of Identity.* New York: Routledge.

Coole, Diana H., and Samantha Frost. 2010. "Introducing the New Materialisms." In *New Materialisms: Ontology, Agency, and Politics*, edited by Diana H. Coole and Samantha Frost, 1–44. Durham, NC: Duke University Press.

Dabydeen, David. [1991] 2010. *The Intended.* Leeds: Peepal Tree Press.

Dash, Michael. 1989. "In Search of the Lost Body: Redefining the Subject in Caribbean Literature." *Kunapipi* 11 (1): 17–26.

Dawson, Ashley. 2007. *Mongrel Nation: Diasporic Culture and the Making of Postcolonial Britain.* Ann Arbor, MI: University of Michigan Press.

De Clercq, Eva. 2013. *The Seduction of the Female Body.* Basingstoke: Palgrave Macmillan.

Derrida, Jacques. 1967. *De la grammatologie.* Paris: Éditions de Minuit.

Fanon, Frantz. [1952] 2008. *Black Skin, White Masks.* Translated and edited by Richard Philcox. New York: Grove Press.

Fanon, Frantz. [1963] 2007. *The Wretched Of The Earth.* Translated and edited by Richard Philcox. New York: Grove Press.

Foucault, Michel. 1982. "The Subject and Power." *Critical Inquiry* 8 (4): 777–795. doi:10.1086/448181.

Grosz, Elizabeth. 1994. *Volatile Bodies.* Bloomington, IN: Indiana University Press.

Harris, Wilson. [1970] 2008. "History, Fable and Myth in the Caribbean and Guianas." *Caribbean Quarterly* 54 (1–2): 5–38. doi:10.1080/00086495.2008.11672333.

Hillman, David, and Ulrika Maude. 2015. "Introduction." In *The Cambridge Companion to the Body in Literature*, edited by David Hillman and Ulrika Maude, 1–9. New York: Cambridge University Press.

Lacan, Jacques. [1949] 2006. *Ècrits: The First Complete Edition in English.* Translated and edited by Bruce Fink. New York: Norton.

Lacan, Jacques. [1956] 1993. *The Psychoses, 1955–1956: The Seminar of Jacques Lacan, Book III.* Translated by Russel Grigg, edited by Jacques-Alain Miller. New York: Norton.

Lamming, George. [1954] 1994. *The Emigrants.* Ann Arbor, MI: University of Michigan Press.

Mayhew, Henry. 1851. *London Labour and the London Poor: A Cyclopaedia of the Condition and Earnings of Those that Will Work, Those that Cannot Work, and Those that Will Not Work. Vol. I: The London Street-Folk.* London: George Woodfall and Son.

McClintock, Anne. 1995. *Imperial Leather: Race, Gender, and Sexuality in the Colonial Contest.* New York: Routledge.

Merleau-Ponty, Maurice. [1945] 2002. *Phenomenology of Perception.* Translated and edited by Colin Smith. London: Routledge.

Nancy, Jean-Luc. [1992] 2008. *Corpus.* Translated and edited by Richard A. Rand. New York: Fordham University Press.

Newman, Brooke N. 2018. *Dark Inheritance: Blood, Race, and Sex in Colonial Jamaica.* New Haven, CT: Yale University Press.

Pouchet Paquet, Sarah. 1982. *The Novels of George Lamming.* London: Heinemann.

Tate, Shirley Anne. 2015. *Black Women's Bodies and the Nation: Race, Gender and Culture.* Basingstoke: Palgrave Macmillan.

Walcott, Derek. 1992. "The Antilles: Fragments of Epic Memory." *The New Republic* 207 (27): 26–32.

# Flattening the curse: Cooling down with Zadie Smith's *Intimations*

Pallavi Rastogi


**ABSTRACT**

Zadie Smith's latest collection of non-fiction, *Intimations* (2020), walks her readers through the burning blaze of the pandemic with what this article calls "cooling down". Embracing both aesthetics and affect, the concept of cooling down is not new to Smith's oeuvre. Indeed, its signature characteristics that include a calm authorial voice, controlled pace of prose, a self-aware narrator, and an insistence on reflection appear in all of Smith's work, including novels such as *White Teeth* (2000) and *Swing Time* (2017) and non-fiction, such as *Changing My Mind: Occasional Essays* (2010) and *Feel Free* (2019). This article examines narrative structure, affective appeal, and political commentary as the three cooling-down registers deployed in the "pandemic" essays of *Intimations*. Reading against the organizational grain of the collection, the article is organized by discussing them out of sequence to emphasize an alternative juxtaposition that renders Smith's intervention through form, affect, and/or politics most accessible.


> Experience – mystifying, overwhelming, conscious, subconscious – rolls over everybody. We try to adapt, to learn, to accommodate, sometimes resisting, and other times submitting to, whatever confronts us. But writers go further: they take this largely shapeless bewilderment and pour it into a mold of their own devising. (Smith 2020, 6)

What were you doing in those hazy floating dream-like days before the pandemic shut life down, stilled movement, and confused thought? How did you feel when the fog seemed to lift but, instead of lucidity, each day brought new unknowns? When even public health messaging on "social distancing" and "flattening the curve" prompted more questions rather than promised scientific certitude? And everything you read or heard sounded like a prophecy about how the world would end: not with a bang or even a whimper, but with the feverish convulsions of sickened humanity. How did you survive the explosion of the apocalypse? How will you move through the slow burn of the post-apocalyptic world?

The pandemic has perpetuated the first three letters of its generic name, sowing *pan*ic and *pan*demonium globally, and forcing a reflection on individual and collective health as well as on the future of the human race itself. We are never alone in our contemplation of existential crisis, though. Literature and culture provide desperately needed anchors in times of collective suffering. Over two years after the first round of shutdowns due to COVID-19, the world is still ablaze, and we still turn to writers and thinkers for comfort, clarity, and grace.[1]

Zadie Smith's latest collection of non-fiction essays, *Intimations* (2020), was composed during the first few months of the pandemic. Smith navigates the apocalypse (now!) through what I call "cooling down". Both aesthetic and effect, cooling down is not new to Smith's considerable oeuvre. Its signature characteristics include the calm authorial voice, the controlled pace of prose, self-aware narrators, and insistence on reflection that appear in all of Smith's work. These include novels such as *White Teeth* (2000) and *Swing Time* (2016), and non-fiction such as *Changing My Mind: Occasional Essays* (2009) and *Feel Free* (2018).[2] Smith's maximalist aesthetic – the literary gesture writ large – is discussed by Cătălina Stanislav (2018) who states that "her rich, ambitious novels encompassing a plethora of characters and a multicultural reality have been incredibly popular at the end of the twentieth century and well into the twenty-first century" (37). Maximalist features also surface in *Intimations*, amongst Smith's most minimalist works, which includes a wide range of characters and the multicultural worlds they inhabit. However, *Intimations* consists of essays written or edited during the pandemic. The collection is also subject to the unique imperatives imposed on literature during a sudden onset of ongoing disaster, especially the need to disseminate information quickly and to prioritize truth-telling, but without reducing literary narrative into mere documentation.

In *Postcolonial Disaster: Narrating Catastrophe in the Twenty-First Century* (Rastogi 2020), I argue that sudden onset disasters, such as the Sri Lankan tsunami in 2004, often create new forms of writing that reflect the rupture of the disastrous event in form and theme:

> Given the tsunami's recent date and its sudden occurrence, fiction dealing with this catastrophic tidal wave has been able to process the oceanic disaster only through short poetry or nonliterary fiction such as children's literature and the "nobrow" novel. The diversity of genre here [shows] that disaster fiction can be written in forms other than highbrow literary fiction. The readerly eye requires training to recognize that fiction can provide important interventions in disaster relief while at the same time setting the stage for more complex narratives written in the wake of temporally distant disasters. (33)

The worldwide declaration of COVID-19 as a pandemic in March 2020, and the rapid implementation of the mitigation measures of lockdown and social distancing, have placed similar pressures on writers today. Most of the literary work in the ever-evolving pandemic genre consists so far of short-form non-fiction, stories, or poetry – brief bursts of art – often published in blogs or news outlets.[3]

Brevity is also an identifying characteristic of the essays in *Intimations*. Smith deploys some of the literary strategies necessitated by a cataclysm, most obviously by writing a very short collection of very short personal essays. *Intimations* shows how literary narration can come close to (but never neatly align with) describing the indescribable – sometimes through brief, oblique, fragmented, and multiple perspectives, sometimes through compassion and connection to create community, and sometimes through a stinging censure of the political malignancy exacerbating the effects of the pandemic. This article examines cooling down as both an aesthetic *and* an affective aspect of Zadie Smith's post-pandemic writing. Cooling down is often a step back to calm emotions that may rage out of control. It is also temporal – like telling someone to "count to ten before you react". Cooling down is associated with working out when we pause from intense exercise to stop sweating and get our heartrate back to its normal rhythm. My use of the term is as capacious as the many manifestations of its meaning. Although the narrative necessities of a sudden-onset disaster – especially the urgency to get the word out quickly and in short digestible bites – may restrict Smith to brief essays, cooling down also reduces intense explosion to slow-burn reflection. I identify narrative structure (form), affective appeal (emotion), and political commentary (ideology) as the three most dominant registers of cooling down in *Intimations*. While these registers triangulate in each of the short pieces some essays foreground one aspect more than others. Reading against the organizational grain of the collection, I juxtapose the essays out of sequence to emphasize an alternative structure rendering form, emotion, and/or ideology most transparent.

The disciplined writing, the brevity of each essay, and the measured unruffled tone thus emulate the attempt to control and manage the world during a medical conflagration and healthcare collapse. Smith repeatedly disavows the ability of language to make sense of the nonsense of catastrophe. Yet *Intimations* seeks to impose order on a disorderly world.[4] Smith's calm and collected – pun intended – prose graphs a straight line through the multiple axes of literature, disease, and public health, and walks us through the flames of suffering into the ashes of the post-apocalyptic future. While cooling down may appear cold and elitist, Smith recognizes it as the privileged position of a wealthy writer for whom social distancing and lockdown do not result in the loss of income, insurance, and education that it does for others. Cooling down maintains a crucial, but never over-whelming, acknowledgement of the writer's distance from the heat of the explosion.

## Cooling down as narrative structure

Diffuse and free-flowing though they may initially appear, the essays in *Intimations* bind an inchoate catastrophe into a tightly organized narrative. In a typically ironic, what we can even playfully call a "Smithsonian" vein, she states: "for reasons of convenience we have settled into this symmetrical pattern. It is not the only false symmetry" (Smith 2020, 42). Yet Smith still creates a seemingly false symmetry through narrative form. She recognizes at once the necessity of literary structure and scaffolding in times of crisis. The formal registers of cooling down are manifested through literary characteristics such as epigraphs, paradoxes, temporal distance, brevity, symmetry; a steady, but ironic, narrative voice; italics to separate the high emotion of other people from the cool tones of the narrator; multiple "snapshots" or character sketches; and the use of allegory, metaphor, and oblique rendition to dance around the depiction of the virus than render this medical disaster only through mimetic representation.[5]

Although *Intimations* is Smith's most direct and concise book yet, and the needs of the time require brevity, not one but two epigraphs precede the introductory text:

The first:

It stares you in the face. No role is so well

suited to philosophy as the one

> you happen to be in right now.
>
> MARCUS AURELIUS

The second:

> My vocabulary is adequate for writing notes
>
> and keeping journals but absolutely useless
>
> for an active moral life.
>
> GRACE PALEY

The Roman philosopher and military commander Marcus Aurelius was inspired by Stoicism to lead a life of fortitude and resilience. *Memento mori* ("Remember, you die!"), his best-known injunction, declares life as endurance and death as its inevitable end. US writer Grace Paley wrote short stories reflecting on gender, race, and class. The two epigraphs preview the themes of the essays that follow. Throughout the collection, Smith emphasizes the need for stoicism during a crisis, the inevitability of death, and the nexus of class, race, and gender in the management of a pandemic.

While the epigraphs reveal Smith's usual erudition, the juxtaposition of these particular lines from Aurelius and Paley demonstrates the conundrum all cultural producers face when reflecting on an ongoing crisis. On the one hand, as the opening lines of the Aurelius quote indicate, the moral responsibility "stares you in the face": in a crisis, it is ethically incumbent to make meaning out of the incomprehensible experience of the pandemic. On the other hand, the writer also recognizes that their vocabulary is insufficient to capture the magnitude of a crisis. Smith understands the paradox all too well: of being burdened with the imperative to philosophize even as all the linguistic felicity in the world leaves her "absolutely useless" to live up to this obligation. Yet inadequacy in the face of such a daunting task never negates the necessity of attempting to control chaos, if only as "something to do" (as another essay in the collection is titled). Paradox, thus, establishes itself as an important characteristic of the formal/literary aspect of cooling down. It reveals self-awareness; it challenges certitudes; it displaces from the horror of the Real. Moreover, the gap between Aurelius and Paley and Smith creates a crucial distance of time, race, nation, subject, history, and culture. Smith may not have temporal distance from this particular pandemic but reading works on other catastrophes can guide her to understand the importance of the writer, and the open-ended and partial value of the words they offer in a crisis-riven world. Literary form, here the use of two well-chosen epigraphs, provides a cooling-down clarity through paradox and temporal distancing.

*Intimations* is no *White Teeth*, *Swing Time*, or *NW* in size. At only 97 pages, it is divided into six essays:

(1) "Peonies"
(2) "The American Exception"
(3) "Something to Do"
(4) "Suffering Like Mel Gibson"
(5) "Screengrabs (After *Berger*, before the virus)"
(6) "Intimations"

"Screengrabs" consists of six shorter vignettes and a post-script:

(1) "A Man with Strong Hands"
(2) "A Character in a Wheelchair in the Vestibule"
(3) "Woman with a Little Dog"
(4) "A Hovering Young Man"
(5) "An Elder at the 98 Bus Stop"
(6) "A Provocation in the Park"
(7) "Postscript: Contempt as a Virus"

My replication of the table of contents seeks to highlight the optical effect of the neat symmetry of six essays, including one essay consisting of six small pieces. The pandemic necessitates brevity as word must get around fast. Yet the *number* (6 short essays and 6 shorter sub-essays in 97 pages) conveys the pain, suffering, and regeneration (and even beauty) of the *multiple* groups afflicted by the pandemic. The symmetry of "six within six" provides a pleasing, albeit conventional, pattern of order and wholeness. In numerology, for example, six is associated with balance and the idea of symmetry itself is often associated with beauty.[6] Smith extracts catharsis from brevity and symmetry as early as the table of contents, even as the postscript reminds us of the "false symmetry" of the six within six pattern. While formal arrangement is an enduring characteristic of her writing, organization becomes even more necessary during crisis when the structure of everyday life collapses. Cooling down is a commitment to restoring narrative order during a medical disaster when the social order as we know it – going to work or sending our children to school – is thrown into disarray.

Writing in the immediate wake of a disaster often produces shorter narratives to capture and quickly circulate as many ideas, experiences, and reflections as possible in a constantly changing situation. Even the "Foreword" warns the reader about the brevity of the collection.

Smith claims that Intimations is not a "historical, analytical, political," comprehensive account of 2020. Instead, it is an attempt to

> [ ... ] organize some of the feelings and thoughts that events [ ... ] have provoked in me, in those scraps of time the year itself has allowed. These are above all personal essays: small by definition, short by necessity (Smith 2020, xiii; emphases added).

Smith offers brevity as a structural form in this collection written in "scraps of time" and made up of "small" and "short" pieces. No comprehensive account of a catastrophe as big as a global pandemic is possible in the immediate wake of the crisis; instead, scaling down becomes cooling down, about organization in the midst of chaos.

Smith then proceeds to discuss how she started reading Marcus Aurelius at the start of the pandemic for "practical assistance", asserting that reading and writing can provide ways to negotiate a crisis. From this Roman general, Smith culled "two invaluable intimations. Talking to yourself can be useful. And writing means being overheard" (Smith 2020, xii). Readers familiar with Smith's work will recognize the allusive ironic tone that is the hallmark of her style. The lines from T.S. Eliot's ([1957] 2022) poem "A Dedication to My Wife" ("But this dedication is for others to read: / These are private words addressed to you in public") also resonate here. Both Eliot's poem and *Intimations* highlight another paradox. The etymological root of the word "intimations" suggests intimacy, of the "private words addressed to you in public". The form of those intimate utterances, memorialized forever in a mass-published book or in a poem by a Nobel Laureate, renders the private addressee into a public audience.[7] As with Aurelius and Paley in the epigraphs, Smith obliquely evokes Eliot to situate herself within a literary lineage that momentarily separates her work from the temporal immediacy of the pandemic. Furthermore, the word "intimations", literally meaning a hint offered as a suggestion, is yet another invitation to cool down. Smith *will* utter inconvenient truths about the pandemic, but they will not be the absolute truths. Instead, writerly advice will manifest itself through open-ended intimations on "scraps of paper".

"Screengrabs" reveals this linguistic obliqueness and economy most vividly. Hale (2012) says that

> [i]n *On Beauty* the lives of Smith's socially diverse characters are filled with aesthetic experience, and their individual attempts to understand that experience – through private contemplation as well as through acts of social exchange – highlight the power relations and social alliances that give meaning to even the most embodied sensory perceptions. In Smith's novel, not only is the "felt experience of cognition" shown to be contingent upon social life, but any abstract idea a character might hold about the operation or value of cognition is shown to be inseparable from an individual's social position within a particular cultural formation. (92)

The "individual social position within a particular cultural formation" in this instance always reverberates through the pandemic. Consisting of snapshots, or character sketches of people Smith knows vaguely, the genre of the vignette, highlighting brevity again, mimics the rapidly moving social media feed through which we receive information about what people are doing: usually as a slice of their lives. While possibly reductive – how can the complexity of any individual be adequately represented in a three-paragraph essay? – the screengrabs also lock down their characters in their small frame – conjuring the social distancing of people as well as the containment of the virus. Smith muses on her everyday social interactions before the pandemic here. These "soft" relationships – or the "acts of social exchange" that Hale views as essential to Smith's fiction – were ruptured during the pandemic and replaced with loneliness instead. In writing real people back into her life through words, Smith recuperates the soft social encounters she lost in March 2020. The multiplicity and brevity of "Screengrabs", of multiple short vignettes rather than one long essay on a single life, recreate the casual communities of everyday interaction ripped asunder by the pandemic, and preserves them in almost photographic ways.[8]

Structured like a snapshot of images, the length of the pieces in "Screengrabs" reveals the importance of form in narrating the immensity of the catastrophe. When catastrophe cannot be represented in long-form genres such as novels or epic poetry due to time – not even Zadie Smith can write a 400-page novel in 4 months – shorter narratives attempt the work instead. Thus, instead of including long sections on each character like *White Teeth* or focusing on one individual like *The Autograph Man*, the multiple snapshots, the plurality plus brevity combination, forge an understanding of the different lives struck down by the pandemic. Moreover, in rendering some of the characters anonymous and even abstracting them through the titles of the essays, such as "Hovering Young Man", she shows each character as representing a larger group. *Intimations* shows that community can only be evoked through multiplicity when writing about cataclysmic times *in* cataclysmic times. Smith represents multiplicity in short pieces that gather together as many voices as possible as quickly as possible. Time is truly of the essence here.

Smith regularly uses italics, especially in "Screengrabs", to convey high emotion that cools down rather than fires up. In "In a Character in a Wheelchair in the Vestibule", she calls the eponymous protagonist Myron. The name is derived from a character in her story "Words and Names", as Smith does not know his real name. Toggling Myron between fact and fiction challenges the categories of real and fictional, further emphasizing the storytelling aspect of the collection and distancing the text from the heat of real life. The screengrab ends with Myron yelling into his phone: "*No, No, I ain't running from no cold. I survived worse. I survived WAY worse*" (2020, 46; italics in original). Smith uses italics and upper case to convey the high emotions of other people and to separate them from her own tone, which she keeps as cool, calm, and collected as possible.

In "An Elder at the 98 Bus Stop", Smith's mother tells her about the murder of a woman they know: "*this lockdown is driving people crazy ... [It's] just so sad. And then he set the flat on fire and it's been burning all night*" (202, 64).[9] The short, simple unadorned prose reveals the effects of forced containment on human beings. Smith offers no lines of authorial commentary here. Death, murder, pain, and the destruction of property during the lockdown are depicted in the affectively intense register of italics. Like the post-script in "Screengrabs," the essay concludes with the image of an ongoing roaring conflagration burning on and on, exceeding the pages of the text in which it is confined. Yet, again, the depiction of the high tragedy is separated from the author's voice, which retains its assured tone even in its silence.

The formal registers of cooling down also manifest themselves through a deliberately oblique conjuring of the virus and the destruction it wrought. "Peonies" offers important advice on living in the pandemic through a meditation on a cluster of tulips. In reflecting on the relationship between nature and humanity, Smith never mentions the pandemic directly but often evokes it through elliptical references. The essay opens with the sentence "Just before I left New York" (Smith 2020, 1), suggesting future flight from the pandemic as well as the privilege of being able to embark on that future flight literally and metaphorically. Smith refers to the day as being "cold, bright, blue. Not a cloud between the World Trade and the old seven-digit painted phone number for Bigelow's" (2). She elicits the imminent disaster of the pandemic through the past disaster of the World Trade Center and 9/11, as September 11, 2001 was a cold, bright, blue day too. The looming loss of the old ways of existence is also indirectly prophesied through the now-defunct seven-digit number of a beloved New York restaurant.

When Smith encounters the tulips, she says she was "very well defended" (Smith 2020, 1), an assertion followed by the phrase "[b]ut this was a sneak attack ... by horticulture". The virus, not horticulture, similarly mounted a stealthy invasion on the supposedly "well defended" world. Looking at the tulips on display, Smith finds herself holding onto the bars separating her from the flower shop and "ogling" at the tulips in a "predatory way" (7): this image brings to mind the incarceration of social distancing, lockdown, and curfew even as it subtly articulates the wish-fulfilment of the virus as the predator behind bars.

Yet the virus is never mentioned as the virus, thus creating a distance from the pandemic to cool down and reflect. Oblique evocation is a key formal strategy in the collection as a whole. Even as "Peonies" moves to Nabokov, chimpanzees, *Lolita*, the ageing female body and its depleting fecundity, the pandemic is always present. Thus, when reflecting on the inevitability of submission to menopause, Smith writes: "at the hot core of it there was an obsession with control, common among my people (writers)" (2020, 6–7). The "hot core" returns the narrative to its buried subtext of fevers and pandemics as well as the hot flashes of menopause. Smith encounters the tulips a few days before "the global humbling" and they "served as a tiny, early preview of what I now feel every moment of every day, that is, the complex and ambivalent nature of 'submission' " (7). The varied musings in the essay eventually constellate into some direct advice – "sometimes it is wrong to resist disease and right to submit to the inevitable. And vice versa" (7). Smith shares this direct advice only after she offers a series of intimations. Once she creates the cooling-down distance through oblique evocation in the first essay, the rest of the collection constantly negotiates this ongoing dialectic of resistance and submission.[10]

## Cooling down as affective appeal

According to Ronit Frenkel, "Smith's centralization of affect as both a critical object and perspective [ ... ] facilitates an understanding of the social world and our place within it amid a pandemic" (2021, 216). Smith both shows and uses emotion to offer more direct intimations through the affective register of cooling down. Characteristics of this register include the deliberate use of self-reflection and auto-critique, compassion for the self and other, and a call to create love and community to survive the pandemic. In "Something to Do", Smith acknowledges the necessity of submission, including submitting to the infinite boredom that comes with social distancing, lockdown, and quarantine. She asserts that "everybody finds their capabilities returning to them, even if it's only the capacity to mourn what we have lost" (Smith 2020, 24). Smith then reflects – even mourns – on the nature and value of art in a crisis:

> In the absence of these fixed elements, I'd make up hard things to do, or things to abstain from . . . Running is what I know. Writing is what I know. [ ... ] What a dry, sad, small idea of a life. And how exposed it looks, now that the people I love are in the same room to witness the way I do time. [ ... ] For me the cliché is true: *only way out is through*. (24–25; emphasis added)

The dry small life harks back to the moist largeness of the tulips. The word "exposed" suggests exposure to disease, again evoking the virus in oblique ways. Smith considers the limits of art during a crisis: what power does art have to change the cultural moment in the here and now if it cannot reflect the times in which it is produced? The cooling-down aesthetic encourages self-reflection, mourning, and auto-critique. Yet, again, writing *through* the crisis is the only way out of the crisis.[11] The essay ends with Smith's ringing call to find greater purpose and clarity through love: "Love with a capital 'L', an ideal form and essential part of the universe – like 'Beauty' or the color red – [ ... ] Without this element present, in some form, somewhere in our lives, there really *is* only time" (2020, 27). The turn to Love emphasizes that registering affect and emotion are crucial in the isolation of a pandemic. At the heart of the affective registers of cooling down is amplifying Love, not as a grand passion, but as compassion present *somewhere* in our lives.[12]

"Suffering Like Mel Gibson" shifts the emphasis of affect and the self to affect and the other, particularly through emotions such as empathy and sympathy. Smith urges her readers to distinguish between suffering (which is absolute and real) and privilege: "Everybody learns the irrelevance of these matters next to real suffering" (2020, 31). What is real suffering, though? In bringing to mind the performative suffering of Mel Gibson in *The Passion of the Christ*, Smith concludes that pain is pain no matter the privilege of those who suffer. Suffering is not relative since it appears absolute to the afflicted. Because our suffering seems absolute to us, we should also honour other people's sufferings with the same validity we give to our own sentiments. Indeed, those suffering (with the privilege of time, money, health care, and jobs) must step aside from their own suffering for a small space of time to reach out to others less fortunate. The essay calls for a form of compassion, which is at once radical and simple as well as big-hearted:

> But when the bad day in your week finally arrives – and it comes to all – by which I mean, that particular moment when your sufferings, as puny as they may be in the wider scheme of things, direct themselves absolutely and only to you, as if precisely designed *to destroy you and only you*, at that point it may be worth allowing yourself the admission of the reality of suffering, if not for yourself, exactly, then in preparation for that next painful bout of videoconferencing, so that you don't roll your eyes or laugh or puke while listening to what some other person seems to think is pain. (36)

Smith tasks her readers with managing their emotions during a crisis in order to understand other people's suffering no matter how small it may seem. Like love, sympathy and empathy are important affective registers of cooling down: of lowering the heat of our own self-sympathy to a gentle comprehension of the pain of others.

The penultimate essay in the collection is titled "A Provocation in the Park". During the lockdown, an email about a self-loathing Asian man is sent out to the university. Smith was, and still is, baffled by his burning hatred for himself:

> What is it like to have always seen, in your mind's eye, apocalypse in the streets of New York, and then one day walk out into those streets and find – just as it is in your personal hellscape – that they are now desolate, empty and silent? (2020, 72)

The rhetoric of the apocalypse is shifted to a character here. Smith empathizes with the Asian man who experiences racial dysphoria and what it is to belong to a body that feels unhomed in itself and with the world outside:

> Instead of the complex judgment such a decision requires, I was left with the useless thoughts of a novelist: what is it like to have a mind-on-fire at such a moment? Do you feel ever more distant from the world? Or has the world, in its new extremity, finally come to you? (72)

This is not a reflection on the individual psychosis of the Asian man; instead, the "mind on fire", indicating a feverish delirium, suggests that we are all suffering from the dysphoria the self-loathing man depicts. No one belongs in the time-space continuum the pandemic has imposed on us. In urging compassion for "the angry Asian man" who hates himself, Smith lowers the flames of hatred, of self and other, to the more cooling registers of sympathy and other-centred identification instead.

This other-centred identification is also used to create community. In "A Woman with a Little Dog", Smith describes her neighbour Barbara: "There is an ideal, rent-controlled city dweller who appears to experience no self-pity, who knows exactly how long to talk to someone in the street, who creates community without overly sentimentalizing the concept" (2020, 49). Smith's description of Barbara offers a meta-comment on the affective registers cooling down – to create community without resorting to mawkish emotions. There is no "over-sentimentalizing" of the discourse and no self-pity. Instead, Smith advocates for a compassion for others that does not demand eternal empathy, so creating stability in its very momentariness. Smith represents Barbara as a constant in the ever-shifting cityscape and even her pesky dogs remain the same. Her unchanging New Yorkness gives Smith the constancy and stability she longs for:

> Thing is, we're a community, and we got each other's back. You'll be there for me, and I'll be there for you, and we'll all be there for each other, the whole building. Nothing to be afraid of – we'll get through this, all of us, together. (51)

Smith, too moved to respond in anything but a sibilant murmur, says: "'Yes, we will,' I whispered, hardly audible, even to myself, and walked on" (51). Even the soft interactions – a quick word of comfort from a neighbour or a writer talking to a reader – can create the social exchanges desperately desired in times of anguish and loneliness. Smith reveals the importance of positively interacting with other people through emotions such as compassion and neighbourliness as a way to cooling down via a community. Thus, as Frenkel posits, "Smith can help us to theorize emergent affectivity from inside a pandemic-strained world" (2021, 212).

## Cooling down as political commentary

Nowhere is the intersection of form and affect manifested more clearly than in the essays on politics in which Smith, a citizen of both the USA and the UK, writes her anguish and anger large. "The American Exception" starts with describing the bombastic rhetoric of an unnamed American president. The title itself announces an ironic departure from the historical nomenclature for US exceptionalism with its use of the definite article: *The American Exception*. Rewriting exceptionalism as failure not success, Smith criticizes Donald Trump's mismanagement of the pandemic without ever naming him. Imbuing the former president with messianic qualities, she delivers a stinging set of rebukes:

> He speaks truth so rarely that when you hear it from his own mouth – March 29, 2020– it has the force of revelation: "I wish we could have our old life back. We had the greatest economy that we've ever had, and we didn't have death". (Smith 2020, 11)

Yet the very next line, which is typeset in a different paragraph, switches tone through mere indentation and some droll phrasing: "Well, maybe not the whole unvarnished truth". Using understatement and anonymity, Smith criticizes Trump for misleading a credulous public into believing a return to the old normal is possible. Refusing the possibility of this return, she insists instead on the inevitability of the new normal:

"disaster demanded a new dawn. Only new thinking can lead to a new dawn" (11). As Smith reflects on how she allowed herself for a second to be sold with "snake oil, snake oil, snake oil" (12), she realizes the idea "we never had death" seduced her into picking up the "wormy" apple offered by Trump whom she reduces from messiah to demonic snake in five quick sentences.

After casting Trump as a bad apple, Smith emphasizes that the former president was a symptom but not the cause for a pervasive US malaise. The next paragraph on death takes the form of incantatory recitation: "We had dead people. We had casualties. [ ... ] We had body counts [ ... ]. Wrong place, wrong time. Wrong skin color. Wrong side of the tracks" (Smith 2020 12). Repetition is often a form of healing from trauma, the rocking motion of its rhythm creating a lullaby effect.[13] Indeed, Smith uses the word repetition to move into describing death as repetition. Americans, claims Smith, "attack death as a series of discrete problems. Wars on drugs, cancer, poverty, and so on" (17). Here, Smith argues against the rhetorical displacement of her own style, particularly oblique evocation. Americans have used the language of war, and their own corresponding military might, to constantly postpone a real contemplation on the racialization of death and disease in the US. Smith explains the cavalier attitude towards the pandemic within the larger context of a racial history of the US that extends beyond Trump and into the heart of American self-definition. Ending the essay with Clement Attlee, Smith hopes the "next generation of [writers] might find inspiration" in these quiet lines of courage: "the war has been won by the efforts of all our people, who [ ... ] put the nation first and their private and sectional interests a long way second" (17). Using post-war Europe to reflect on the battlefield of the post-pandemic world, Smith offers universal healthcare as a solution to managing the pandemic: "As Americans never tire of arguing, there may be many areas of our lives in which private interest plays the central role. But, as post-war Europe, exhausted by absolute death, collectively decided, health care shouldn't be one of them" (18). The heat of political indictment is not only cooled down with a referential displacement to post-war Europe, but also with an assertion of resolution – the promise of a panacea through universal healthcare.[14]

The postscript to "Screengrabs" takes on social-political issues more directly despite its allegorical structure. In "Postscript: Contempt as a Virus", the title gestures to brevity through the PS but also creates the affective intimacy of a letter addressed directly to the reader: "You start to think of contempt as a virus. Infecting individuals first, but spreading rapidly through families, communities, peoples, power structures, nations" (Smith 2020, 73). The metaphor pointedly condemns the US for its treatment of Black Americans and the killing of George Floyd. The "contempt" virus has vaccinations available, though, and inoculations consisting of sloughing off the skins of privilege:

> Real change would involve a broad recognition that the fatalist, essentialist race discourse we often employ as a superficial cure for the symptoms of this virus manages, in practice, to smoothly obscure the fact that the DNA of this virus is *economic at base*. (81; original emphasis)

Using social resolution as a strategy to cool down the heat of political prosecution, Smith attaches italics to her voice only when articulating and emphasizing the crux of the problems in the US. Through rendering contempt into a virus, Smith suggests that contempt and COVID are insidious, dangerous, omnipresent, often accidentally and collectively acquired, and that their consequences are the responsibility of the writer and the world to work through. The collection begins with a muted allegorical representation of the virus in "Peonies", moves to anonymizing Donald Trump in the middle, and ends with a searing indictment of US society. Smith refrains from depicting the virus as virus to deflect panic about the disease; instead, high emotion is displaced onto political issues now named more explicitly as causal factors exacerbating the intensity of the disease. Living up to the meaning of its title, *Intimations* thus intimates rather than intimidates.

## Notes

1. I would like to thank Michael Bibler and Alexandra Chiasson for reading this essay. The CFP for this Special Issue of the *Journal of Postcolonial Writing* quotes cultural critic Byung-Chul Han as describing the post-COVID world as a "burnout society".
2. John Williams (2020) sees this as a collection of "ultra-timely essays (several written in the past few momentous months) [that] showcases her trademark levelheadedness".
3. For example, see the many blogs and websites dedicated to publishing poetry in the wake of the pandemic, such as "Mediation Beyond Borders" (https://mediatorsbeyondborders.org/pandemic-poetry-calming-words-in-the-midst-of-chaos/).
4. Indeed, in "Peonies", Smith wryly comments that "the part of the university in which I teach should properly be called the Controlling Experience Department" (2020, 6).
5. My use of the word "dance" deliberately suggests the relationship between direct naming of the catastrophe and its oblique representation – as sashay and counter-sashay within the graceful synchrony of the formal structure of a dance. As Kate Rigby (2015) argues, "one aspect of what it means to dance with disaster [ … is ] to develop modes of *personal and collective comportment* that are no longer premised on *certitude* [ … ] but that instead *presuppose the unforeseeable*. The dance I have in mind in here would therefore have to be largely *improvisational*" (5; emphases added). Terms such as Rigby's "dance with disaster" and "slow-burn" are an extrapolation and expansion of some of the ideas in *Postcolonial Disaster* (Rastogi 2020).
6. Marcus Enquist and Anthony Arak (1994) state that "[h]umans and certain other species find symmetrical patterns more attractive than asymmetrical ones" (169).
7. According to the *Online Etymology Dictionary* (n.d.), "intimations" derives from "Mid-15c., 'action of making known,' from Old French *intimation* (14c.), from Lat Latin *intimationem* (nominative *intimatio*) 'an announcement,' noun of action from past-participle stem of Latin *intimare* 'make known, announce, impress' (see intimate [adj.). Meaning 'action of expressing by suggestion or hint, indirect imparting of information' is from 1530s" (n.p.).
8. In "Hovering Young Man", Smith articulates the necessity of tethering. "It is easy to despise institutions, to feel irritated or constrained by them [ … ] but confronted with the style of Cy I felt glad he was at least tethered to an institution, like a red balloon caught in a tree" (2020, 55).
9. The essay starts from an evocation of female fertility and ends on the death of a young girl, the screengrab circling back to the opening and closing moments of the human life cycle.
10. As Smith says, "is it possible to be as flexible on the page – as shamelessly self-forgiving – and ever changing – as we are in life? We can't seem to find the way. Instead, we write to swim in an ocean of hypocrisies, moment by moment. We know we are deluded, but the strange thing is that this delusion is necessary" (2020, 8).
11. Smith's "whimsy" may be seen as self-critique and an acknowledgement of her own privilege. According to Frenkel, " 'Something to Do' exhibits the privileged positioning of Smith (and others like myself) amid the uncertainties of pandemic life [ … ]. As someone who was not hampered by food scarcity or under-resourced living conditions, Smith articulates a restless languor that marked the COVID-19 affectivity of lockdown" (2021, 215). But since Smith is replicating the very privilege she critiques (of not being an essential worker) in the act of critiquing it, the self-awareness can ring a little hollow.

12. "Although the most powerful art [ ... ] is an experience and a going-through; it is love comprehended by, expressed and enacted through the artwork itself" that animates a work of art. (Smith 2020, 27).
13. See, for example, Arundhati Roy's comment on *God of Small Things* (quoted in Rastogi 2020, 237–238).
14. A Black British writer of Jamaican origin identifying post-war Europe as a model to create an equitable social order is ironic, but also reveals the extent of the malaise in US society. Even post-war Britain did better for its battle-scarred citizenry.

## Disclosure statement

No potential conflict of interest was reported by the author.

## References


Eliot, T.S. [1957] 2022. "A Dedication to My Wife." *The Poetry Hour*. Reading, UK: Josephine Hart Poetry Foundation. Accessed 1 July 2021. https://thepoetryhour.com/poems/a-dedication-to-my-wife

Enquist, Marcus, and Anthony Arak. 1994. "Symmetry, Beauty and Evolution." *Nature* 372: 169–172. doi:10.1038/372169a0.

Frenkel, Ronit. 2021. "Some Speculative Musings on COVID-19 Affectivity, Raymond Williams' 'Structure of Feeling and Zadie Smith's *Intimations*." *English Studies in Africa* 64 (1&2): 212–222. doi:10.1080/00138398.2021.1969125.

Hale, Dorothy. 2012. "*On Beauty* as Beautiful? The Problem of Novelistic Aesthetics by Way of Zadie Smith." *Contemporary Literature* 53 (4): 814–844. doi:10.1353/cli.2012.0033.

Meyer, Lily. 2020. "The Literature of the Pandemic Is Already Here." *The Atlantic*, July 20. Accessed 1 July 2021. https://www.theatlantic.com/culture/archive/2020/07/zadie-smith-decameron-project-pandemic-literature/614458/

Online Etymological Dictionary. (n.d.). "'Intimation'. Intimation | Etymology, Origin and Meaning of Intimation by Etymonline." Accessed 7 February 2022.

Rastogi, Pallavi. 2020. *Postcolonial Disaster: Narrating Catastrophe in the Twenty-First Century*. Evanston, IL: Northwestern University Press.

Rigby, Kate. 2015. *Dancing with Disaster: Environmental Histories, Narratives, and Ethics for Perilous Times*. Charlottesville, VA: University of Virginia Press.

Smith, Zadie. 2020. *Intimations: Essays*. London: Penguin.

Stanislav, Cătălina. 2018. "Establishing a Convention at the Beginning of the twenty-first Century: James Wood's Hysterical Realism and Stefano Ercolino's Maximalist Novel." *Revista Transilvania* 7: 37–42.

Williams, John. 2020. "In *Intimations*, Zadie Smith Applies Her Even Temper to Tumultuous Times." *The New York Times*, July 22. Accessed 1 July 2021. https://www.nytimes.com/2020/07/22/books/review-intimations-essays-zadie-smith.html

# The art of COVID-19

Pramod K. Nayar


**ABSTRACT**

This article examines one strand of COVID art that encodes a heteroclitic cultural imaginary – and is irregular and unsettling. Banksy's murals and paintings parody classical artworks, and are themselves parodied, so as to capture the new cultural realities of the COVID era. In the case of other artists, such as Chiara Grilli, the traditional heliotrope is parodied to convey a similar reality, like Banksy's inversion of the superhero mythology. With the employment of conventional disease-vector images, such as those of rats, Banksy brings into the human 5dwelling a "postnatural wilderness" showing the reversal of the disruption of ecosystems that had rendered animals habitat-less in India, with animals once again entering human spaces. Hence, the pandemic's inversion of spatialized distribution of life can be seen as a decolonial and decolonizing moment. Subsequently, the article highlights how COVID-19 art intervenes through its parodic, kitschy quality, in the discourses around the pandemic.


The aesthetic-cultural imaginary of COVID-19 is embodied in the form of a massive archive – and this is in process, still – of artwork. Instagram created the COVID-19 Art Museum (Instagram 2020), and COVID-19 art festivals – one by the World Health Organization (2020a), no less – were held in some parts of the world. Artists of different traditions, styles, and aesthetic ideals *drew* COVID-19 and its consequences, progression, and mythic symbolism, in their own way (Bruner 2020).

I argue that a strand of COVID-19 art encodes a heteroclitic cultural imaginary, one that is irregular, deviates from established rules of capturing, say, devastation, or in the discourse of disaster, and is therefore unsettling. This also means paying considerable attention to the context – COVID-19 and its social, political, and cultural meanings – of the artwork so that we can see how the artist and the artwork offer us a sideways and tangential glance at the ongoing event that is COVID-19.

It may be important to note that we see the pandemic as a "multiplicity of the Covid-19 pandemic" (Erni and Striphas 2021, 212). This means linking it to the bush fires of Australia, state-sponsored violence in many nations, the murder of Black people by US law enforcement authorities, and the Black Lives Matter movement. In the words of John Nyuget Erni and Ted Striphas (2021), this linking is important "because it refers to a series of crises superimposed with such pressure as to leave one wondering where even to begin at all" (212). The racial, ageist, and classist dynamics that have (re)surfaced in the pandemic have been noted by commentators (Akerkar 2020; Smicker 2021) such that "Covid-19 devastates along established systems of power, rights and values that organize the cultural practices of the everyday" (Silva 2021, 238). They are undoubtedly a constituent of the perceptions, "management", and experience of the pandemic, with a deep impact on the "language" of COVID-19. This article, however, restricts itself to the "arts" of the pandemic in isolation (by which I mean the arts produced in the period of the COVID-19 pandemic).

To Banksy's parody of Vermeer's *Girl with a Pearl Earring* in Bristol someone added a mask during the pandemic (BBC News 2020a). Holly Bess Kincaid rejigged Andrew Wyeth's *Christina's World*. Chiara Grilli invoked Edward Hopper's *Morning Sun*. *Time* magazine thought this development was significant enough to comment on, and contextualized it as follows: "The human drive to engage with culture hasn't diminished, but with cultural institutions closed globally, that desire is manifesting in an alternative way" (Bruner 2020).

These artworks embody a specific version of the parodic. Parody is the "imitation and transformation of another's words" (Dentith 2000, 3). The key feature, Simon Dentith (2000) notes, is the exact inflection and transformation we effect in our appropriation of another's words, and how we have adapted them for the occasion (4). Dentith treats parodic repetition as an instance of intertextuality, alluding (deliberately, explicitly) to precursor texts, but also often a "generalized allusion to the constitutive codes of daily language" (7). It is playful but not necessarily satirical (11). Later, Dentith proposes a more precise and expanded characteristic of the parody: "the polemical allusive imitation of a preceding text that characterizes parody can have its polemic directed to the world rather than the preceding text" (18).[1] The classical and renowned paintings and photographs are employed by the artists in the COVID-19 year to capture in a language at once new and old the trauma of the present. In the process, they also reappropriate the older visual texts. It could also be argued that the COVID-19 year has enabled the creation of a new language, or vocabulary, one which engages with already known visual forms in order to generate a new one.

We can discern two stages in the cumulative parody of the Vermeer in the COVID-19 age. First, in the Vermeer painting, the girl, her head half turned to look at the viewer, wears an oriental turban, and a prominent pearl earring. In Banksy's (2014) parody (*The Girl with the Pierced Eardrum*) the earring, an ornament and fashion accessory, is replaced with a device that has come to characterize the contemporary era of securitization: the burglar alarm (*BBC News* 2020a).[2] Now, Banksy's work is painted *around* the material installation on the walls of the apartment. He thus merges Vermeer's representation of a girl with not only his own representation – we can think of these as discourses – but a material object, the alarm on the wall.

Second, Banksy's parody which is further layered with the addition of the mask is not just a joke (which is the case with "regular" parody, as Robert Hariman [2008] argues) – we can call it "BanksyPlus" – but a heteroclite: anomalous and disruptive. The COVID-19 mask is a parody of a parody when two material objects, the burglar alarm and the mask, enter the "scene", so to speak. The Vermeer scene focuses on a subject – the girl – while the parodies make two objects the eye-catching subjects of the mural. The double-parody, then, is in fact the "narrative elaboration" (Hoskins 2006) of two objects that may well be the material markers of an age. The Vermeer picture has as its subject a girl, but the parody arrests us not because of *this* subject but because of what the subject has *appended* to her: the mask. That is, the parody signals how subjectivity itself may now be contingent upon the appendages that are no longer a matter of choice or taste – unlike jewellery and accessories – but rather a matter of necessity and regulation (the mandate to wear masks in public places).

Banksy's parody is alluding to the Vermeer, of course, but the polemic is directed at the world and not just the Vermeer "text". The mask is a polemical narrative elaboration of a now-ubiquitous object, again directed at the contemporary world crisis, the pandemic. The two narrative elaborations are heteroclitic – a term often used to signify a misfit or an ill-fitting set of elements – because they are disruptive of the commonplace social order, etiquette, and appearance. The alarm disrupts the illusion of a secure society, the mask gestures at the unhealthy environment of social interaction where facial gestures and voice are both interfered with and modified. Neither, therefore, is part of a funny parody: both are deadly serious.

The double-layered parody captures the new cultural realities. Margreta DeGrazia, Maureen Quilligan, and Peter Stallybrass (1996) have argued about early modern Europe that objects "can be made to absorb other evanescent cultural realities especially within the institutionalized contexts of [ ... ] theatrical display, symbolic representation, and ritual observance" (19). The argument applies readily to BanksyPlus (my term for the Banksy additions to the Vermeer) as well. The alarm absorbs the power of the Vermeer in its parodic state, causing a reflection on the classic, and its relevance to the present day. In the process, Vermeer (the painting as artefact) is repurposed in order to capture the current realities: the securitized and "hygienic modernity" (I adapt the term from Ruth Rogaski [2004]) respectively. When incorporated into the artwork, they constitute the heteroclitic parody of the Vermeer.

In Chiara Grilli's (2020a) parodic photograph of Edward Hopper's 1952 painting *Morning Sun*, what is at work is an attempted parody of the heliotrope. Hopper's girl tilts forward just a little bit, towards the sun. Grilli's parody does not. The sunshine per square foot in Hopper is much higher than that in Grilli's version. The fact is: Grilli's version tells a bleaker story than the relatively more open Hopper image. What is seen from Grilli's window is another building, and another window, with bars. In Hopper's we see distance, space, and expanse. There is no sense of expanding space in Grilli, and, despite the sunlight, she offers up an air of claustrophobia, even if we did not know it was "quarantine art". Grilli, who calls it "Quarantinart" (Grilli 2020b), says of this new trend: "I thought that it represented the quarantine-like condition of many of us without using many words, hashtags or mottos" (cited in Bruner 2020, n.p.).

Grilli's parody of Hopper turns the heliotrope inside out. The sun in Hopper shines *outside*, where, as the outwork of the piece tells us, the painting captures a "very quarantine-like atmosphere, catching these days' mood" (Grilli 2020a). The earth turns towards the sun, as does all human technology (see DeLoughrey 2011, 235–251). In Grilli, the sun represents the impossibility of life on the outside. As the pandemic forced people into homes and closed spaces, the sun begins to represent the unattainable: the outside. The passage of time, for instance, was solely driven by clocks, as weather conditions and the sunshine became irrelevant to those incarcerated within their homes.

Jacques Derrida (1982) sees the "heliotrope" as simultaneously a movement turned towards the sun and the turning movement of the sun. He would go on to argue that the entire history of (western) philosophy is in fact a photology, with its panoply of metaphors of darkness and light, of self-concealment and self-revelation. The very idea of truth has traditionally hinged on this photology: of enlightenment and knowledge-as-light.[3]

Now, vision, argues Cathryn Vasseleu (2002), involves touch, when the texture of light caresses the eye for vision to occur. Vasseleu speaks of a "concept of vision that is open to or affected by the touch of light" (12). So one cannot think of vision as an independent sense in which the seer is distanced from the object (12). In other words, there is a certain tactility, or hapticity, to vision. Kelly Oliver (2001), appropriating Vasseleu, writes:

> We must begin with the presupposition that space is full of light, air, language, and the elements that make human life possible before we can imagine a public space in which we can speak to each other and, more importantly, listen to each other. We need to recognize our connection, dependence, and indebtedness to each other as individuals and as social groups. The possibility of love, then, is founded on the possibility of public space as full of the elements that connect us to each other. (75)

All vision, then, involves touch, because light touches us. Vasseleu and Oliver are both working towards the sense of connection, community, and spaces. In Grilli, the heliotrope and its outwork signify a *withdrawal* from contact, connection, and community. The sun falls on places one *cannot* access, people we *cannot* meet, and a community-in-space we must steer clear of. While the vision of the woman staring out of the room, into the sunlight, is a tactile sense, being touched by its light, and even if the seer/object are linked by a sunlit touch, it remains a distancing/distanced situation.

The heliotrope, in its parodic variation and ironic appearance in the Grilli text, is about life-at-a-distance. In this case, the parody not only serves as a polemic about the world, but also fits in with the traditional literary trope where the sunflower – the quintessential heliotrope – "has long been linked to the unrequited devotion of a lover, or to the longing of the earthbound soul for its heavenly home" (Ferber 2007, 212). The heliotrope is less about tactility, connection, and community than it is about distance and the impossibility of belonging and shared spaces. As a heteroclitic aesthetic, it disrupts the *sense* of a heliotrope, and polemicizes the world which has changed so drastically.

Banksy, continuing his parodic art, issued during the pandemic a call for the radical re-evaluaton of the myth and cult of the superheroes who, traditionally, save the earth.

In Banksy's (2020a) painting *The Game Changer*, originally located in Southampton General Hospital in 2020, Batman and Spider-Man are consigned to the garbage bin, and the boy plays with the new superhero: a nurse.[4] The nurse wears a cloak and the COVID-19-era mask. She also wears a red cross on her uniform, where the superhero's hallmark symbol is traditionally figured. Banksy's image extends and reiterates the already existing *state* discourse of the nurse-as-hero that has been circulating since the pandemic.[5] There are several features of Banksy's parodying that arrest our attention. Introducing the child as the chief protagonist enables Banksy to foreground parody as pedagogy: the child learns to discern between superheroes and replace one with another. David Seitz (2011) has argued that "the role-play of parody can also build a stronger ethical awareness of the politics of representation" and hence serves a pedagogic purpose (372). In this process, parody helps us to imagine alternatives to what we have taken for granted (Kenny 2009, 222–224). Superheroes as a "modern mythology" (Reynolds 1994) have been intrinsic to popular culture across the world. The Batman/Superman/Spider-Man mythos has been an indispensable part of the cultural politics around superheroes as well. Jeffrey Brown (2016), in his essay on parodies of superhero films, has argued that

> [s]uperhero parodies do not just model paragons of masculinity as the mainstream super-hero films do, the parodies ridicule it, they criticize it, they invite viewers to laugh at it [ ... ] and then they confirm that it is still a state that even the lowliest of males can and should achieve. (132)

He further proposes: "Superhero films present a very narrow definition of masculinity within a narrative designed to foster viewer identification with the character's empower-ment" (134). Parodies, therefore, work with images of a "failed masculinity" (139).

The hypermasculine superhero is unclaimed and untouched in the garbage bin. The figures are also drawn in postures far less than heroic – Spider-Man appears dead and/or helpless, and Batman is on his back, one leg in the air – a far cry from the pumped-up, high-flying (literally) superheroes. Here we have two who have been grounded, embody-ing a failed masculinity. We may mourn the passing of an era, but we also are amused – as Brown indicates – at the helplessness of the masked superhero, whose masks, super-powers, and abilities are of no use in the pandemic.

Banksy's superhero is a female nurse. Banksy is responding to, incorporating, and subverting the superhero mythos by introducing a new type of superhero even as he bestows a certain profession – medical assistance – with *superheroic* qualities: the nurse may not, like superheroes, save the world, but she saves those who approach her for assistance. Through this, Banksy implies that even the child has discovered – and this is the pedagogic perfor-mative of the figurines and their parody – who the true superhero is: the nurse. From this, by extrapolation, those viewing Banksy's image also get, so to speak, the "true" picture.

Even though parody, like the superhero mythos, is culturally coded, global cultural flows – notably with the huge success and dissemination of Marvel and DC superhero films – have ensured a degree, albeit unquantifiable, of familiarity with the genre. These cultural icons have, as Sangeet Kumar (2012) has argued, developed variants that could be identified as the "hybrid global". This, I suggest, is precisely Banksy's nurse: a hybrid global icon whose provenance in a culturally coded mythography is diminished due to its circulation and topicality in the COVID-19 era. Disruptive and a misfit in the superhero pantheon – and hence heteroclitic – the nurse-as-superhero embodies a new age of superheroes. There are plenty of COVID-19-memes that emphasize the heroism of these workers and healthcare professionals. Banksy's work fits right into this new cultural imaginary and iconography.

But there is more going on in Banksy's parody. The "new" superhero reinforces the hierarchy of superheroes versus ordinary mortals: that is, the new entrant into the superhero mythos does not disturb the world of superheroes as a *world*. It substitutes one superhero for another, while the hierarchy of superheroes and "others" remains effectively undisturbed. Such a parodic "inversion" as Banksy's seems to be at first sight, is what Jeffrey Rush (1990) terms a "hybridized parody", wherein

> [t]he parodied discourse challenges the diegetic frame, the construction of the profilmic world itself, by reasserting its legitimacy against the narrating discourse that is trying to undermine it. There is a constant struggle between transformation and tradition, with the resultant breakdown of a clear hierarchy of discourse. (5–6)

First, the cultural codes integral to the diegetic universe of superheroes do constrain the making of a new superhero who also needs to *fit in* in order to be recognized as a superhero (as Umberto Eco and Natalie Chilton [1972] argued), consistency is the formula for recognition in/for Superman, and, by extension, superheroes: complete with cloak and mask:

> The parodied discourse challenges the diegetic frame, the construction of the profilmic world itself, by reasserting its legitimacy against the narrating discourse that is trying to undermine it. There is a constant struggle between transformation and tradition, with the resultant breakdown of a clear hierarchy of discourse. (Rush 1990, 5–6)

Now, while Banksy's nurse-as-superhero appears to be limited by and to the pre-assigned role and identity qua superhero, he also asks: how have we constructed the very idea of the heroic? Is "saving the world", the standard rationale for superhero action, the same as saving or nursing the sick? Is the latter significantly more important than the former since it has an immediate and localized effect? The nurse, by definition, attached to a service and an institution, battles enormous odds in the COVID-19 era. While her sphere of influence is spatially limited, the nurse represents, I suggest, the very synthesis and embodiment of the term "treatment". I adapt here the work of Lisa Diedrich (2007) who notes the multiple meanings of the term, listing

> "[t]he process or manner of behaving towards or dealing with a person or thing"; "the application of medical care or attention to a patient, ailment, etc."; "a manner or instance of dealing with a subject or work of literature, art, etc."; and, perhaps most important, "discussion or arrangement of terms, negotiation". (viii)

Banksy's nurse encompasses *all* these meanings, if we contextualize what the medical profession has faced in the COVID-19 period. Adapting Diedrich, it is possible to see Banksy's parody of superheroes – which also, it must be noted, is gendered, in his evocation of the woman-nurse, and thus references superheroines like Wonder Woman – as embodying an affective history of COVID-19 and its social consequences. The nurse is a symbol and a material manifestation of the world's "treatment" of the afflicted and the affected. As an instrument of contemporary history, the nurse (and the medical profession in general) has moved people with her work ethic, her risky commitment.[6] It is impossible to "see" Banksy's nurse outside the outwork of the news of the profession's work during the pandemic. Thus, we see Banksy's image alongside thousands of images portraying them as the "real heroes" and accompanying graffiti stating: "not all heroes wear capes – some wear scrubs".[7]

"Treatment", as nurses represent, is at several levels, and they have been admired for it. Banksy's nurse is a hybridized parody, because the work breaks free of the hierarchy that determines what counts as heroism. Moving away from the (super)heroism structured traditionally around "saving the world", national secrets, and military, sometimes inter-planetary operations, towards care and community matters, the Banksy artwork presents the latter as superior and culturally valuable. It codes "treatment" – which includes the multiple layers and meanings that Diedrich (2007) outlines – as heroism.It is hybridized parody because it utilizes the conventions of the superhero trope in order to draw attention to the modes through which the very idea of the heroic has been constructed, and maybe even leveraged (Stokes-Parish et al. 2020).

Banksy (2020c) concluded 2020 with the drawing of a granny sneezing, situated on a sloping road (the outwork tells us it is Vale Street, the steepest street in Bristol).[8] The old lady's dentures fly out with her sneeze, her walking stick and handbag fall away. Now, the stick, the handbag, and the overall appearance present the woman as an instance of what has come to be called "affirmative ageing". Through this, Banksy resists stigmatizing old age with its dominant stereotype of the loss of the sense of the self and identity by drawing an old-ish woman who appears independent and mobile.

Amelia DeFalco (2010) argues, about the legibility of the aged, that "old age renders its subjects both invisible and unmistakable; personhood is often cast into doubt, even imagined as entirely erased, while the body marked by age draws the eye and comment" (4). There is, she proposes, a certain "cultural invisibility" in the aged (4). Banksy is playing off such a "cultural invisibility" against the anxiety-inducing hypervisibility of COVID-19 manifestations (cough, sneezes) in public places. In DeFalco's terms, she is at once a "spectacle" and a "specimen".

First, the frail and therefore vulnerable body is rendered helpless to employ Adriana Cavarero's (2011) distinction: the old lady loses her dentures, her bag, and her walking stick. Her discomfited, off-balance appearance renders her a sorry *spectacle*. The loss of her appurtenances and her dentures renders her doubly so. The spectacle of being discommoded as an individual, as a fragile body, is at the heart of Banksy's painting. Whether such a person, senior in years, would otherwise receive any attention is a moot point. However – and this is the second aspect of Banksy's work – the sneeze immediately alters her visibility quotient. In an age of paranoia around sneezes and coughs, the old woman's sneeze renders her a *specimen*: one who has (perhaps) a COVID-19 infection. The specimen-nature of her being alters her cultural invisibility to hypervisibility (a spectacle). Disrupting the discourse and practice of invisibility around the aged, Banksy's sneezing woman is a heteroclitic intrusion in the behaviour of the street she is traversing at the moment. While not yet, strictly speaking, a patient-body, the old woman is a proleptic symbol of how COVID-19 may hurt/injure/affect the old. She is to be viewed, examined, analysed, her suffering coded as a certain dramatic enactment of a common condition, even as the condition renders her a biomedical entity/specimen, as a possible vector.

Banksy announced that he was working from home, and showed the world his bathroom, peopled now with rats.[9] Rats are a favourite Banksy device for social commentary. As Martin Bull (2015) notes, "[r]ats are assumed to represent the urban underclass", and "rat" is an anagram for "art" (21). Drawn in the year of the pandemic, Banksy's incorrigible rats, which have clearly colonized his bathroom, may be read as an artist's invocation of a historical symbol: rats as the animal vectors for the plague, from the year 1348 through the centuries. Yet, as is typical of Banksy, he repeats the symbol with a difference. The playfulness of the rats in his bathroom – playing on unravelled toilet paper, using the commode, swinging from a towel ring, squishing a toothpaste tube, and so on – are incongruous when we recall the historical association of this creature.

But there is much more. Historians have noted that the plague of 1348 left survivors in states varying from anxiety to despair (Ziegler 1991). Many artists, argues Louise Marshall (1994), drew worshippers and patron saints, worshippers and images in hier-archical relationships as a way of regaining control over their environment. Banksy evades the traditional metaphors around the plague by presenting non-threatening, playful, and pesky rats. However, given the context in which we "read" Banksy, his invocation of rats invokes, in turn, a certain historical repetition of the epidemic as a human condition.

In his study of the "writing" of the English plague, Ernest Gilman (2009) says:

> Descriptions of epidemics and even "firsthand" accounts may be indebted more directly to stories of the same kind than to immediate (and unmediated) experience – whether because [ … ] these "unspeakable" events recur in the form of unassimilable traumatic reenactments or, more generally, because even reports of direct experience have a generic history. Thus, each subsequent account of a plague – including accounts of smallpox, tuberculosis, or aids – will, self-consciously or not, register the history of topoi, sentiments, descriptions, moralizations, and so forth that characterize plague narratives in general. (38)

Even true stories, argues Gilman, "migrate from text to text" (39). Banksy, I suggest, draws in the context of the COVID-19 pandemic on an archive of epidemic representations when depicting the rampaging rats.

Banksy's rats need to be read in the context of the associative symbolism of rats. Like all legacies, plague too has a legacy and "is wielded as a political or rhetorical weapon in the service of social discrimination or stigmatisation; it is mobilized to critique regimes, dictators or minority groups" (Cooke 2009, 2). Like all plagues, COVID-19 has also engendered massive cases of stigmatization, so much so that the World Health Organization (2020b) issued "A Guide to Preventing and Addressing Social Stigma Associated with COVID-19". Banksy's rats recall the older plagues and their histories, and in a contemporary context where rumours of a plague epidemic following COVID-19 surfaced in the public discourse, and news reports (from Britain in particular) of homeowners being harassed by rats during the lockdown (BBC News 2020b).

Yet, even as they partake of the legacy of the plague-rats and their stigmatizing symbolism, so to speak, Banksy is, I argue, highlighting a divided legacy:

> Rats have therefore come to represent the return of the archaic in the futuristic; fundamen-tally ambivalent, they symbolize both atavism and modernity, citification and savagery, capital and poverty, superstition and science, disease and cure. (Ellmann 2004, 61)

This divided legacy where the rat "can be deployed to represent both sickness, through the diseases they carry, and curative breakthroughs in medical knowledge because of the experiments and scientific discoveries they facilitate" (Cooke 2009, 121) is Banksy's heteroclite, intervening in a history of rat-representation and associated stigma that extended beyond the species to certain ethnic groups.

Evacuating the painting of all human presence – once again iterating a classic apoc-alyptic narrative of the "end-of-humanity" – Banksy leaves the space to the rats. Instantiating the loss of human control over spaces, he signals the return of the repressed, so to speak, in the form of nature (animals). Banksy brings *into* the human dwelling a "postnatural wilderness [ … ] dangerous areas where humans are excluded. [ … ] human exclusion from these areas that makes them wilderness reserves" (Raglon 2009, 64). As a heteroclitic presence and symbol, the playful rats signal, implicitly, how a virus has caused the humans to retreat behind doors, and even within their homes they are besieged by other life forms. While it may be a stretch to claim that Banksy's painting encodes an ecological message, it does imply, I suggest, the loss of human dominion and hegemony.

While it may not be strictly resonant with the Banksy work, it is germane to note that the postnatural wilderness made its appearance felt in Indian cities and suburbs too. One report said:

> In Uttarakhand, an elephant was reported to come down unusually near Hari ki Pauri in Haridwar. A leopard was sighted in Almora. In Karnataka, elephants, spotted deer and sambar deer had transgressed into towns, while in Maharashtra, people spotted scores of civet cats, mongooses and porcupines in communities. (Balasubramanian 2020, n.p.)

The disruption of ecosystems that have rendered numerous species of animals habitat-less in India was reversed in the pandemic, where the animals began entering human spaces. In a much larger sense, the pandemic's inversion of spatialized distribution of life is a decolonial and decolonizing moment, if there ever was one, and it would bear some reflection.

Taken together, COVID-19 art intervenes through its parodic, kitschy quality, in the discourses around the pandemic. As we have seen, constantly referencing both a history and a contemporary "scene", Banksy and other artists – although the former dominates this article – offer us tangential and adjunct sites and sights of a hellish year.

## Notes

1. Numerous song-parodies also appeared during the pandemic. Jon Stratton (2021) has argued that we should not see them as parodies at all, but "they are better understood in the tradition of folk songs, broadly understood, where new lyrics would be created, and sometimes sold, to be sung to already existing well-known tunes" (413).
2. The parody of Banksy's *The Girl with the Pierced Eardrum* can be viewed on the BBC News (2020a) item.
3. In a specifically Indian context of the pandemic, the heliotrope was *not* just a trope, of course, as thousands of migrant labourers walked from the metros back to their home towns and villages in the scorching heat of the March–April sun in 2020 when the nation went into a lockdown. It generated a form of extreme mobility that extended, as argued elsewhere, a carceral condition of the urban poor, with little or no provisions, shelter, or support (see Nayar 2020).
4. Notification of the March 23, 2021 sale of Banksy's *Game Changer*, along with an image of the artwork, can be viewed on the website of the Auction House Christie's (https://www.christies.com/en/lot/lot-6309459).
5. Critiques of this state discourse have argued that these representations are often a substitute for real material recognition and facilities for the nursing and public health community, and even "undermine the professionalism of the nursing workforce, and [this] reinforces the perception that nursing is an innately feminine, nurturing role" (Stokes-Parish et al. 2020, 462). I am grateful to the *Journal of Postcolonial Writing* reviewer for pointing out such critiques.
6. The stereotyping of the woman as carer should not, however, escape comment. Banksy's reiteration of this gendered role, despite his clear attempt to redefine the superhero genre, is troubling for this reason.

7. One only has to search for "nurses – heroes" in Shutterstock to see some of these (https://www.shutterstock.com/image-vector/not-all-heroes-wear-capes-some-1705644040).
8. Images of Banksy's "Sneezing Woman" artwork (*Aachoo!!*) and the process of its removal can be viewed in the BBC News item from March 13, 2021, "Bristol Banksy: Sneezing Woman Artwork to be Auctioned" (https://www.bbc.com/news/uk-england-bristol-56387254).
9. Images from Banksy's *My Wife Hates It When I Work from Home* can be viewed in the BBC News item from April 16, 2021, "Coronavirus: Banksy Makes 'Bathroom' Lockdown Art" (https://www.bbc.com/news/uk-england-bristol-52306748).

## Acknowledgments

This article originated in a small way in an essay "The Languages of Covid-19's Cultural Imaginary", that appeared in *eSocial Sciences*. I am grateful to Padma Prakash for her comments on that essay. It was subsequently delivered as a plenary at the Memory Studies Workshop, Humanities and Social Sciences, April 2021 – much gratitude to Avishek Parui and Merin Raj for inviting me to speak.

## Disclosure statement

No potential conflict of interest was reported by the author.

## Funding

This work was supported by the Institution of Eminence Project, University of Hyderabad.

## References

Akerkar, Supriya. 2020. "Affirming Radical Equality in the Context of COVID-19: Human Rights of Older People and People with Disabilities." *Journal of Human Rights Practice* 12 (2): 276–283. Doi:10.1093/jhuman/huaa032.

Balasubramanian, D. 2020. "Wild Animals in Urban Clusters." *The Hindu*, June 20. Accessed 19 May 2021. https://www.thehindu.com/sci-tech/science/wild-animals-in-urban-clusters/article31877606.ece

Banksy. 2014. "Girl with a Pierced Eardrum." *Mural on a Bristol Wall*. Accessed 7 March 2022. https://www.bbc.com/news/uk-england-bristol-52382500

Banksy. 2020a. "*Game Changer* (Alternatively Titled "Painting for Saints"). Initially Located South Hampton General Hospital." *Oil on canvas 35 7/8 x 35 7/8in. (91 x 91cm.).* Accessed 7 March 2022. https://www.christies.com/en/lot/lot-6309459

Banksy. 2020b. "My Wife Hates It When I Work from Home." Dimensions and location not specified. Accessed 7 March 2022. https://www.bbc.com/news/uk-england-bristol-52306748

Banksy. 2020c. "Sneezing Woman." Dimensions not specified. Accessed 7 March 2022. https://www.bbc.com/news/uk-england-bristol-56387254

BBC News. 2020a. "Coronavirus: Banksy's *Girl with a Pierced Eardrum* Given Face Mask." Accessed 22 April 2020. https://www.bbc.com/news/uk-england-bristol-52382500

BBC News. 2020b. "Coronavirus: People 'Harassed by Rats' during Lockdown." Accessed 27 February 2021. https://www.bbc.com/news/av/uk-england-hampshire-52939812

Brown, Jeffrey A. 2016. "The Superhero Film Parody and Hegemonic Masculinity." *Quarterly Review of Film and Video* 33 (2): 131–150. Doi:10.1080/10509208.2015.1094361.

Bruner, Raisa. 2020. "How People Imitating Masterful Paintings Launched a Sweeping Trend from Italy to Iceland." *Time*, April 10. Accessed 7 March 2022. https://time.com/5817117/coronavirus-art-history/

Bull, Martin. 2015. *This Is Not a Photo Opportunity: The Street Art of Banksy*. Oakland, CA: PM Press.

Cavarero, Adriana. 2011. *Horrorism: Naming Contemporary Violence*. Translated by William McCuaig. New York: Columbia University Press.

Cooke, Jennifer. 2009. *Legacies of Plague in Literature, Theory and Film*. London: Palgrave Macmillan.

DeFalco, Amelia. 2010. *Uncanny Subjects: Aging in Contemporary Narrative*. Columbus, OH: Ohio State University Press.

DeGrazia, Margreta, Maureen Quilligan, and Peter Stallybrass. 1996. "Introduction." In *Subject and Object in Renaissance Culture*, edited by Margreta DeGrazia, Maureen Quilligan, and Peter Stallybrass, 1–15. Cambridge: Cambridge University Press.

DeLoughrey, Elizabeth. 2011. "Heliotropes: Solar Ecologies and Pacific Radiations." In *Postcolonial Ecologies: Literatures of the Environment*, edited by Elizabeth DeLoughrey and George B. Handley, 235–253. New York: Oxford University Press.

Dentith, Simon. 2000. *Parody*. London and New York: Routledge.

Derrida, Jacques. 1982. *Margins of Philosophy*. Translated by Alan Bass. Brighton: Harvester Press.

Diedrich, Lisa. 2007. *Treatments: Language, Politics, and the Culture of Illness*. Minneapolis, MN: University of Minnesota Press.

Eco, Umberto, and Natalie Chilton. 1972. "The Amazing Adventures of Superman." *Diacritics* 2 (1): 14–22. Translated by Natalie Chilton. Doi:10.2307/464920.

Ellmann, Maud. 2004. "Writing like a Rat." *Critical Quarterly* 46 (4): 59–76. Doi:10.1111/j.0011-1562.2004.00597.x.

Erni, John Nyuget, and Ted Striphas. 2021. "Introduction: COVID-19, the Multiplier." *Cultural Studies* 35 (2–3): 211–317. Doi:10.1080/09502386.2021.1903957.

Ferber, Michael. 2007. *A Dictionary of Literary Symbols*. 2nd ed. Cambridge: Cambridge University Press.

Gilman, Ernest B. 2009. *Plague Writing in Early Modern England*. Chicago: University of Chicago Press.

Grilli, Chiara. 2020a. "E. Hopper, *Morning Sun*." *Twitter*, April 20. Accessed 18 January 2021. [@quarantinart]. https://twitter.com/quarantinart/status/1246043050691964930

Grilli, Chiara. 2020b. "Quarantinart." *Twitter*, March–May 31–13. Accessed 9 February 2022. [@quarantinart]. https://twitter.com/quarantinart?ref_src=twsrc%5Etfw%7Ctwcamp%5Etweetembed%7Ctwterm%5E1246043050691964930%7Ctwgr%5E%7Ctwcon%5Es1_&ref_url=https%3A%2F%2Ftime.com%2F5817117%2Fcoronavirus-art-history%2F

Hariman, Robert. 2008. "Political Parody and Public Culture." *Quarterly Journal of Speech* 94 (3): 247–272. Doi:10.1080/00335630802210369.

Hoskins, Janet. 2006. "Agency, Biography and Objects." In *Handbook of Material Culture*, edited by Christopher Tilley, Webb Keane, and Susanne Kuchler, 74–84. London: Sage.

Instagram. 2020. "Covid-19 Art Museum." Accessed 26 September 2021. https://www.instagram.com/Covid-19artmuseum/?hl=en

Kenny, Kate. 2009. "'The Performative Surprise': Parody, Documentary and Critique." *Culture and Organization* 15 (2): 221–235. Doi:10.1080/14759550902925385.

Kumar, Sangeet. 2012. "Transgressing Boundaries as the Hybrid Global: Parody and Postcoloniality on Indian Television." *Popular Communication* 10 (1–2): 80–93. Doi:10.1080/15405702.2012.638577.

Marshall, Louise. 1994. "Manipulating the Sacred: Image and Plague in Renaissance Italy." *Renaissance Quarterly* 47 (3): 485–532. Doi:10.2307/2863019.

Nayar, Pramod K. 2020. "The Long Walk." *Journal of Extreme Anthropology* 4 (1): E1–E6. Doi:10.5617/jea.7856.

Oliver, Kelly. 2001. "The Look of Love." *Hypatia* 16 (3): 56–78. Doi:10.1111/j.1527-2001.2001.tb00924.x.

Raglon, Rebecca. 2009. "The Post Natural Wilderness and Its Writers." *Journal of Eco-Criticism* 1 (1): 60–66.

Reynolds, Richard. 1994. *Super Heroes: A Modern Mythology*. Jackson, MS: University of Mississippi Press.

Rogaski, Ruth. 2004. *Hygienic Modernity, Meaning of Health and Disease in Treaty-Port China*. Berkeley, CA: University of California Press.

Rush, Jeffrey. 1990. "Who's N on the Joke: Parody as Hybridized Narrative Discourse." *Quarterly Review of Film and Video* 12 (1–2): 5–12. Doi:10.1080/10509209009361334.

Seitz, David. 2011. "Mocking Discourse: Parody as Pedagogy." *Pedagogy: Critical Approaches to Teaching Literature, Language, Composition, and Culture* 11 (2): 371–394. Doi:10.1215/15314200-1218103.

Silva, Kumarini. 2021. "Covid-19 and the Mundane Practices of Privilege." *Cultural Studies* 35 (2–3): 237–247. Doi:10.1080/09502386.2021.1898034.

Smicker, Josh. 2021. "COVID-19 and 'Crisis as Ordinary': Pathological Whiteness, Popular Pessimism, and Pre-apocalyptic Cultural Studies." *Cultural Studies* 35 (2–3): 291–305. Doi:10.1080/09502386.2021.1898038.

Stokes-Parish, Jessica, Rosalind Elliott, Kaye Rolls, and Debbie Massey. 2020. "Angels and Heroes: The Unintended Consequence of the Hero Narrative." *Journal of Nursing Scholarship* 52 (5): 462–466. Doi:10.1111/jnu.12591.

Stratton, Jon. 2021. "Parodies for a Pandemic: Coronavirus Songs, Creativity and Lockdown." *Cultural Studies* 35 (2–3): 412–431. Doi:10.1080/09502386.2021.1898035.

Vasseleu, Cathryn. 2002. *Textures of Light: Vision and Touch in Irigaray, Levinas and Merleau-Ponty*. 2nd ed. London and New York: Routledge.

World Health Organization. 2020a. "WHO X Create2030 COVID-19 Arts Festival." Accessed 26 September 2021. https://www.who.int/news-room/events/detail/2020/07/26/default-calendar/who-x-create2030-Covid-19-arts-festival

World Health Organization. 2020b. "A Guide to Preventing and Addressing Social Stigma Associated with COVID-19." Accessed 26 September 2021. https://www.who.int/publications/m/item/a-guide-to-preventing-and-addressing-social-stigma-associated-with-covid-19

Ziegler, Philip. 1991. *The Black Death*. Gloucestershire: Alan Sutton Publishing.

# Afterword – COVID-19 and the other virus

Om Prakash Dwivedi and Aleks Wansbrough

On May 5, 2023, Tedros Adhanom Ghebreyesus, World Health Organization Director-General, announced the end of COVID-19 as a global health emergency. This pandemic, according to a United Nations report, resulted in 14.9 million deaths across the world. While celebrating the end of the pandemic, Ghebreyesus also alerted the world about the deep scars it has left on the world. "These scars must serve as a permanent reminder of the potential for new viruses to emerge, with devastating consequences", he said (United Nations 2023).

Bruno Latour (2020) contended that COVID–19 itself could be a dress-rehearsal for the calamities of climate change, where "the health crisis prepares, induces, incites us to prepare for climate change." For Latour, climate change is "the one in which the reorientation of living conditions is going to be posed as a challenge to all of us, as will all the details of daily existence that we will have to learn to sort out carefully." Indeed, the origins of COVID intimate this ecological dimension. If one believes that COVID originated from a wet market, COVID can be seen as a sign of how humans exploit nature to their own detriment. If one believes that COVID originated in a lab, then it suggests humans should not attempt to dominate over nature. To quote Latour again, "What allows the two crises to occur in succession", referring to COVID-19 and climate change, "is the sudden and painful realization that the classical definition of society – humans among themselves – makes no sense. The state of society depends at every moment on the associations between many actors, most of whom do not have human forms" (Latour 2020). In both cases, a revenge of nature narrative surfaces. The world's actors may be nonhuman agencies, agencies that spring from the world itself. During this time, Timothy Morton and Dominic Boyer (2021) released a book on hyposubjects. Indeed, they open the book with the claim that Morton's celebrated book "*Hyperobjects* is now in a way irrelevant—everyone knows, everyone intuitively feels (which is much more important) what a hyperobject is. Coronavirus is everywhere. You can't see it. It operates on all kinds of different scales" (11). The hyposubject "is companion of the hyperobjective era" (14), and contrasts with the hypersubjects who in Morton and Boyer's words is "the type of subjects you are invited to vote for in elections, the experts who tell you how things are [...] They wield reason and technology, whether cynically or sincerely, as instruments for getting things done. They command and control, they seek transcendence" (14). Although Morton and Boyer conceive of hyposubjects as progressive and almost modest, the word seems also to suggest a sense of powerlessness even if Morton and Boyer attempt to evade that conclusion. Indeed, Morton and Boyer assert "The kombucha is a hyposubject and mosquitoes are hyposubjects and somehow, ecology, politicswise, is all about shrinking down with all the other hyposubjects" (33). There is a sense of powerlessness in a condition of hyperobjects. Human actions become reactions: reactions to COVID and COVID-related policies. Streets were uncannily empty of people and cars amid lockdowns. Humanity seemed to be on the retreat, ceding spaces. While Omicron appeared to signal a post-COVID, or rather a post-lockdown condition, where the virus had mutated to become less lethal, the world did not seem to return to normal. Rather than having vanquished, human agency assumed monstrous proportions amid geopolitical turmoil.

With the defeat of Trump in the United States, Bolsonaro in Brazil, and the return of Lula in Brazil and MAS in Bolivia, there was hope for respite. A Biden Presidency promised restoration. January 6th could have seemed the last shakeup before a period of normality but then there were the horrors of Afghanistan amid the US withdrawal and its subsequent brutal sanctions on the benighted country. Russia's horrific invasion of Ukraine also gestured to a menacing quality to human agency, as did October 7 and its aftermath. As we write this, children are dying in unprecedented number in Gaza. Indeed, the conditions in Gaza make disease more deadly and prevalent. As the World Health Organisation reports (2023), "[p]rior to the escalation of hostilities, respiratory diseases were the sixth most common cause of death in the Gaza Strip. In 2022, almost 82,000 cases of COVID-19 were reported in the Gaza strip, resulting in over 400 deaths." Chillingly, Giora Eiland penned an article, published on November 19, 2023, entitled "Let's Not be Intimidated by the World." Eiland is a former Major General in the Israeli Defence Forces and a former member of the Israeli National Security Council as well as a senior research associate at the Institute for National Security Studies. In the article, Eiland asks "who are the 'poor' women of Gaza?" before answering that "[t]hey are all the mothers, sisters, or wives of Hamas murderers." Eiland then opines that "the way to win the war faster and at a lower cost for us requires a system collapse on the other side and not the mere killing of more Hamas fighters." He continues:

> The international community warns us of a humanitarian disaster in Gaza and of severe epidemics. We must not shy away from this, as difficult as that may be. After all, severe epidemics in the south of the Gaza Strip will bring victory closer and reduce casualties among IDF soldiers. And no, this is not about cruelty for cruelty's sake since we don't support the suffering of the other side as an end but as a means. (Eiland 2023)

COVID and other sicknesses are monstrously reframed by Eiland and his supporters as weapons of war, as "means" to an end. Finance Minister Bezalel Smotrich tweeted that he agreed with every word of Eiland's article (Ofir 2023). Whatever Eiland or Smotrich may say to the contrary, it is cruelty, and however horrific the atrocities of October 7, there can be no justification for effacing the distinction between civilians and combatants.

Such violence speaks of, and to, a violent world. One may, for instance, also consider the violence of the Johnson government in the United Kingdom. The Chief scientific adviser Patrick Vallance recorded that Boris Johnson had expressed the sentiment "let it rip" in relation to the COVID-19 virus. Johnson allegedly said, "Yes, there will be more casualties but so be it – they've had a good innings," and "most people who die have reached their time anyway" (Walker 2023). Indeed, Vallance recorded that Johnson relayed that many of his party "thinks the whole thing is pathetic and Covid is just nature's way of dealing with old people – and I am not entirely sure I disagree with them" (Johnston 2023). The violence did not just come from a eugenic disregard for the elderly. Active measures to prevent the spread also had a strong dystopic quality. One may recall the exodus of migrant workers on foot in Global South countries back to their homes, sometimes walking hundreds of miles. Such scenes have not faded from the world. In 2023, Pakistan's government ordered the expulsion of undocumented people, which includes 1.7 million Afghans (International Rescue Committee 2023). Meanwhile, Global North countries have no reason to feel superior, given the horrors of Trump's border policies or Australia's offshore detention centres or the United Kingdom's Windrush scandal. Indeed, for those around the world who had hoped that the Biden leadership would restore US power and bring a more stable hand to international relations, sadly, if anything, things have gotten far worse. Rather than moving beyond Trump, all the problems seem to have resurfaced. At the time of writing this, Trump continues to lead the polls. Irrespective of what the election result will be, the tendencies of the COVID period persist. Conspiracies continue to proliferate online. A politics of paranoia and a spirit of partisanship has not dissipated. There is still no consensus about lockdowns and whether governments overreacted and implemented measures that were too harsh or whether governments did not act swiftly enough. Perhaps both can be true. This century already looks as though we may be witnessing new expansions of biopolitical, psychopolitical, and necropolitical configurations. Concerns for bodies, controls on migration, tracking and surveillance all speak to the biopolitical, the political control exerted over bodies. But the differential exposures to death also underscore what Mbembe formulates in terms of the necropolitical and necropower, the power to inflict death, with Mbembe (2003) noting that contemporary "[w]ars of the globalization era therefore aim to force the enemy into submission regardless of the immediate consequences, side effects, and 'collateral damage' of the military actions" (31). Amid these sometimes more overt forms of power, lurks also more subtle metric manipulations as what we see and hear is now algorithmically tailored. Byung-Chul Han describes interactive digital technologies in terms of psychopolitics, whereby individuals are manipulated and controlled while also being complicit in their own control and manipulation as the data they feed into the machine enables more complete control. Choice thereby becomes a crucial tool of subjugation, and of course during the pandemic we witnessed a rise in internet conspiracy theories and the breakdown of consensus. Expressed slightly differently, Seán Cubitt captures this apocalyptic quality in his contribution to the volume, evocatively stating that "St John's Apocalypse calls them famine, pestilence, war, and death. The horses of the contemporary apocalypse carry plague, eco-catastrophe, migration, and neo-populism on their backs."

This book then, this collection of articles from a special issue of the *Journal of Postcolonial Writing*, written during the pandemic captures themes that are still with us. The articles, now chapters, consider misogyny and domestic violence, surveillance, the apocalypses that Indigenous peoples have already survived, and ecology. The fact that these contributions reproduced here still speak to our current condition after the supposed end of COVID-19 is then no accident. The purpose of the special issue was to consider the significance and meaning of the pandemic, not as an isolated subject but to think about the pandemic from multiple vantage points. Yet, nevertheless it remains sad that the insights in these articles/now chapters remain so relevant. We are left to consider the question as to whether there can there be a post-pandemic world? And, how do we conceptualize the pandemic – as a biological disorder or a socio-political disorder? If anything, this post-pandemic age signifies that it is the same iteration of broken social structures. Indeed, we can think of two viruses, the one serving the other as we know that the virus is more lethal for some than others, given the differential outcomes based on race, class, and disability. Memorably,

Mark Twain considered different forms of violence in *A Connecticut Yankee in King Arthur's Court* (1889), arguing that,

> [t]here were two "Reigns of Terror," if we would but remember it and consider it; the one wrought murder in hot passion, the other in heartless cold blood; the one lasted mere months, the other had lasted a thousand years; the one inflicted death upon ten thousand persons, the other upon a hundred millions; but our shudders are all for the "horrors" of the minor Terror, the momentary Terror, so to speak; whereas, what is the horror of swift death by the axe, compared with lifelong death from hunger, cold, insult, cruelty, and heart-break? What is swift death by lightning compared with death by slow fire at the stake? A city cemetery could contain the coffins filled by that brief Terror which we have all been so diligently taught to shiver at and mourn over; but all France could hardly contain the coffins filled by that older and real Terror—that unspeakably bitter and awful Terror which none of us has been taught to see in its vastness or pity as it deserves.

In contrast with Twain's two terrors, namely that of feudal inequality and the Jacobins, our two terrors: COVID-19 and the global or world system itself which enabled the deadliness of the former. This second virus is political and economic, infecting global society and even the mind. For it is this virus, this other terror, that also provided cover for the cruel deaths of COVID-19. It is rapacious and predatory; it expropriates humans and more-than-humans equally, albeit in different ways, and enjoys complete impunity from any law. It is cannibalistic in the sense that it feeds off the rest to energize and immune itself, thus exacerbating vulnerability, but often in more accentuating ways in the Global South. That is to underscore the point that the rules of this virus are still the same, deciding who will die and live, underscoring a unity of the terrors. Evidently, those coerced into the non-liveable zone by the virus happen to be "the poor, the racialized poor, seniors in care, the disabled, the migrant worker, the essential worker, the globalized poor [who] are already constituted and doomed" (Ogbogu 2023).

What one witnesses in the post-pandemic era is eventually a ruptured temporal coherency. Seen from the acute level of vulnerability that all forms of life have been subjected to due to the capitalist virus, one can argue that there wasn't any "post". Breathing has become undemocratized as environmental degradation continues to proliferate and living is a matter of choice but not necessarily one's own as the decision is mostly already decided by the state–capital nexus. "Social infrastructures require the state's intervention to check and control the meteoric and sterling rise of capitalist power, as they promote a commitment to protect and nourish the dilapidated living bodies – both humans and more-than-humans, including natural resources" (Dwivedi, 2023) The absence of dependency networks is what one gets to witness even if one is to believe in the grand narrative of this "post." The status of being, of existing, is always already in a battle against oppressive forces in a non-autonomous social world, which also suggests its captive future, which is written, controlled, and decided by the expansionist greed of the virus in the neoliberal world. The "post" therefore, also demands a clarion call for new forms of collective solidarity, that create spaces for global opposition that have been punctured by neoliberal capitalism. Nevertheless, it would be naïve to see capitalism as "a homogeneous logic that can be observed from a distance or a discrete and graspable object,… [rather it is] a heterogeneous regime deployed through multiple practices, forms of knowledge, techniques, and temporalities that have in turn become embodied, created spaces, and infiltrated different forms of life" (Quintana, 2022). Perhaps, what is needed is for different forms of life and different spaces to interpenetrate and overcome the system. One may think of Amartya Sen's (2020) argument that rather than a top-down approach to COVID, we should have opted for increased 'participatory governance' and engagement that holds true for our entire political and economic system. Indeed, Sen argued against the idea of COVID-19 being tackled as one might a war, since war invokes the necessity for strong, concentrated leadership. Such an aim is surely reconcilable with Achille Mbembe's (2022) emphasis on habitability as a way to think about climate change.

However, this volume too affords the opportunity to think through the legacies of the pandemic and their interrelations with other ongoing crises. Often by drawing on fiction, narratives, films, and works of literary production, we gain discern truths about our world. For instance, this volume thereby affirms the cliché that apocalypse also means revelation or uncovering. It forces us to confront what Slavoj Žižek (2006) called the unknown knowns, which denote "the disavowed beliefs, suppositions, and obscene practices we pretend not to know about, although they form the background of our public values" (137). But our post and pre-apocalyptic conditions would be thoroughly dystopian if there is no reckoning with the current disorder and no revelation about our condition. This volume certainly provides an attempt to reckon with global responses to the pandemic and thus an opportunity to think and rethink our condition.

## References


Dwivedi, Om Prakash. 2023. "Precarity and Resilience in Kavery Nambisan's *The Story That Must Not be Told.*" *ASIATIC* 17 (2): 31–42.

Eiland, Giora. 2023. "Let's Not be Intimidated by the World," originally published in *Yedioth Ahronoth*, November 19, 2023. Reproduced: https://mondoweiss.net/2023/11/influential-israeli-national-security-leader-makes-the-case-for-genocide-in-gaza/ Accessed March 1, 2024.

Johnston, Finlay. 2023. "Boris Johnson said Covid was 'nature's way of dealing with old people.'" *Open Democracy*, October 31, 2023. www.opendemocracy.net/en/boris-johnson-covid-natures-way-dealing-with-old-people-patrick-vallance-inquiry/. Accessed March 1, 2024.

International Rescue Committee. 2023. "1.7 million Afghans face deportation from Pakistan." International Rescue Committee website, November 8, 2023. www.rescue.org/article/17-million-afghans-face-deportation-pakistan#:~:text=Pakistan%20has%20recently%20announced%20that,1.7%20million%20lives%20at%20risk. Accessed March 1, 2024.

Latour, Bruno. 2020. "Is this a Dress Rehearsal?". *Critical Inquiry.* https://critinq.wordpress.com/2020/03/26/is-this-a-dress-rehearsal/. Accessed March 10, 2024.

Mbembe Achille. 2022. "Climate, Sustainability & Inequality Seminar: Notes on Planetary Habitability by Prof Achille Mbembe." Wits University Official YouTube channel, November 22, 2022. www.youtube.com/watch?v=d1AKvMN5ock Accessed February 20, 2023. Accessed February 20, 2023.

Mbembe Achille. 2003. "Necropolitics." *Public Culture* 15 (1): 11–40.

Morton, Timothy and Boyer, Dominic. 2021. *Hyposubjects: On Becoming Human.* London: Open Humanities Press.

Ogbogu, Ubaka. 2023. "Pandemic Necropolitics: Vulnerability, Resilience, and the Crisis of Marginalization in the Liberal Democratic State." In Stefania Achella & Chantal Marazia, ed., Vulnerabilities: Rethinking Medicine Rights and Humanities in Post-pandemic. London & New York: Springer Nature. 195–208.

Ofir, Jonathan. 2023. "Influential Israeli national security leader makes the case for genocide in Gaza." *Mondoweiss*, November 20, 2023. Accessed March 1, 2024.

Quintana, Laura. 2022. "," *Critical Times* 5 (1): 50–75.

Sen, Amartya. 2020. "Amartya Sen writes: Overcoming a pandemic may look like fighting a war, but the real need is far from that." *The Indian Express*, April 8, 2020. https://indianexpress.com/article/opinion/columns/coronavirus-india-lockdown-amartya-sAlternatives%20in%20the%20Midst%20of%20Ruination:%20Capialism,%20Heterogeneity,%20Fracturesen-economy-migrants-6352132/. Accessed March 10, 2024.

United Nations. 2023. "WHO chief declares end to COVID-19 as a global health emergency." *UN News*, May 5, 2023. https://news.un.org/en/story/2023/05/1136367. Accessed March 8, 2024.

World Health Organisation. 2023. "Risk of disease spread soars in Gaza as health facilities, water and sanitation systems disrupted," WHO Media Centre, November 8, 2023. www.emro.who.int/media/news/risk-of-disease-spread-soars-in-gaza-as-health-facilities-water-and-sanitation-systems-disrupted.html. Accessed December 20, 2023.

Walker, Peter. 2023. "Patrick Vallance contradicts Rishi Sunak's evidence to Covid inquiry." *The Guardian*, November 21, 2023. www.theguardian.com/uk-news/2023/nov/20/patrick-vallance-contradicts-rishi-sunak-evidence-to-covid-enquiry. Accessed March 1, 2024.

Žižek, Slavoj. 2006. "Philosophy, the 'unknown knowns,' and the public use of reason." *Topoi* 25: 137–142.

# Index

Note: Endnotes are indicated by the page number followed by 'n' and the endnote number e.g., 20n1 refers to endnote 1 on page 20.

# Taylor & Francis eBooks

www.taylorfrancis.com

A single destination for eBooks from Taylor & Francis with increased functionality and an improved user experience to meet the needs of our customers.

90,000+ eBooks of award-winning academic content in Humanities, Social Science, Science, Technology, Engineering, and Medical written by a global network of editors and authors.

## TAYLOR & FRANCIS EBOOKS OFFERS:

A streamlined experience for our library customers

A single point of discovery for all of our eBook content

Improved search and discovery of content at both book and chapter level

## REQUEST A FREE TRIAL
support@taylorfrancis.com

For Product Safety Concerns and Information please contact our EU
representative  GPSR@taylorandfrancis.com
Taylor & Francis Verlag GmbH, Kaufingerstraße 24, 80331 München, Germany